BEFORE CHE

To Alan & Audrey

w/ th love!

ISBN 978-1-880977-49-1

Distributed worldwide by Ingram Content Group

Library of Congress Cataloging-in-Publication Data

Names: Rutkoff, Peter M., 1942- author.
Title: Before Che : a novel / Peter Rutkoff.
Description: [Gambier, OH] : XOXOX Press, [2019] | Summary: "Set in
early 1950s Cuba, this novel explores the earliest days of what became
the M-26-7 movement -- the Cuban Revolution. Ultimately, the socialist
regime initiated by Fidel Castro governed Cuba from 1959 to 2008 and
remains in power to this day. This novel evokes the earliest days of revolutionary struggle before Che's arrival in 1955"-- Provided by publisher.
Identifiers: LCCN 2019030185 | ISBN 9781880977491 (paperback)
Subjects: LCSH: Cuba--History--Revolution, 1959--Fiction. | GSAFD:
    Historical fiction.
Classification: LCC PS3618.U78 B44 2018 | DDC 813/.6--dc23
LC record available at https://lccn.loc.gov/2019030185

BEFORE CHE

a novel

Peter Rutkoff

XOXOX
PRESS

Gambier, Ohio
2019

For my DE

Arthur Hays Sulzberger
New York Times Building
229 W. 42ⁿᵈ St
New York, NY

Dear Arthur,

Since you ask. Yes. I've been here for almost six months. That is why I'm able to write as completely, as authoritatively, as I have about this Castro story.

And yes. I know that you think he's a dangerous man. Especially now that Che has joined us in the hills. But I've spent many days in Señor Castro's company these last few months, and I can assure you that he's exactly what he seems — an articulate, even charismatic, young man who is genuinely radical. After all, given the ruthless repression dished out by the Batista regime to anyone who dares oppose it, we must not startle that Castro's home-grown radicalism has such a popular bite.

But please listen to me carefully. Like our friends the Republicans in Spain twenty years ago, he can no more go about the business of revolution without sidling up to the Communist party than the Loyalists could in 1936. As you know so well, shaking hands with a Communist no more makes you a Red than shaking hands with an Israeli makes you a Zionist.

In fact, Castro has been here in these hills alone since the Amnesty of 1955. He remains in hiding from the world, but not from the thousands of peasants living in the impenetrable vastness of these mountains who provide food and shelter for his movement. They emerge silently every evening and appear at his bohío carrying live chickens, sprays of root vegetables, and their unique sugar-beet "rum." They keep the Movement alive.

If no one in New York, or no one on the Upper East Side at any rate, has heard of the 26th July Movement, they soon will. The story I tell you replaces the crackle of rumors that continue to excite your readers and your city. When this astonishing man finally appears in Havana, when as he claims "the time is ripe," no government source on this island will dare report it.

You tell Pudge not to worry. Under their banners that read 26-7 this motley army of revolutionaries armed with discarded American firearms — and a single rusty machine gun that Che found on the beach last week — will protect me.

The Movement's story is much older than their failed attempt to overthrow Batista in 1953. As you will see, it began in Spain in 1936. That is when I first met the extraordinary men and women I introduce to you in these pages. Their's is a history that will remain in shadows, but perhaps it may answer many of your questions.

My sojourn in this eyrie, a self-enforced exile I have shared with Fidel, has allowed me the time to compose these pages. When he bursts onto the world stage, as he surely will, you will want to know how it began. Rightly so, our confreres will credit the magnetic Che with the qualities that transformed this band of rebels into a revolutionary army. But they will not know what it was like before Che.

That is why, Arthur, I write this piece for you.

Herb

Sierra Maestra, Cuba
December 29, 1957

PART ONE
SO IT BEGINS

CHAPTER ONE
HAVANA

I

"He sent you?"

She doesn't know if she's spoken in English or Spanish. Oliver looks almost the same, despite the decade that has passed.

"Matthews. Yes. He didn't think you would remember him. The Florida Hotel."

Anna smiled at the memory, the warmth reaching her eyes.

"He told me to find you, someone I could trust. Someone to bring us all together."

"Of course I remember him."

He shook the ash off his cigarette. A thin blackened strand fell down onto his lapel. His cats' eyes, gray and sad, darted behind her, searching.

"There's no one here," she looked even more intently at his face. "It's good to see you. Where have you been all these years?"

The wrinkles running from his eyes to his mustache deepened. He tugged at the brim of his worn beret, pulling it down almost over his eyes.

"Chicago mostly. They always know where we are."

"SIM must know too, then." Less a question than a statement. "I thought they lost track of me." She reached for his sleeve and drew him further into the dark apartment, then switched to English. "I don't think I even want to know how you found me. It's enough that you are here."

8

The apartment faced the courtyard, its green walls dull and sickly, its windows open to the gray light of early evening. A fan turned overhead, scattering the ash from his lapel into the air.

She held out her arms to embrace him. "Tell me."

He looked down at her, and she smelt the tobacco and the strong scent of his shaving cream. A gold tooth gleamed in the middle of his smile, giving him the same jolly-sinister look she remembered. Only his eyes suggested anything had changed.

She led him into the front room and pointed to the worn settee.

"I'll make some coffee. Still two sugars?" The gas stove jutted out from the white tiled wall that defined the kitchen. A worn porcelain sink and a half-sized refrigerator occupied the remaining space. Watching as he stared out the louvered window, then down at the shadows cast across the speckled linoleum floor, she realized how happy she was to see him.

"Oliver," she teased his name in the French style, like the stuffy British actor they once mocked, "Ollie." She handed him the coffee, sweet and dark, oil glinting on the surface. "Let's talk."

He looked over at her and smiled tightly, the gold tooth hidden behind his lower lip. "I need some veterans. Anna, I need them. And soon."

"Who else have you contacted?" She remembered all their names. She would never forget how he looked that last time in Barcelona as they marched away from the War. How any of them had looked. "I've kept track of them, you know," she hesitated, "since I returned home."

She smoothed the black skirt that reached down to her ankles and flicked a lock of graying hair from her face. The small table in the corner, plastic-mahogany, shook ever so slightly as the freight lorries rumbled down Calzada de Infanta toward Malecón, and the sea. She worried that he might still remember, as she remembered their frightful confrontation, when she cried and called him a "premature fascist" during those last days in Spain.

"I'm still in the Party, you know," she glanced down at his shoes, the left a size smaller than the right. "Does it hurt?"

He pulled up the cuff of his cotton cord trousers. The wood below his knee had turned red-black, and the skin bulged where his shin plugged into the prosthesis. "Only hurts when I laugh." He grimaced. "I never really believed in all that party stuff anyway. What about you, Anna? When did you come back?" He winced, pulling his pant leg down.

She finds it impossible to believe him.

"In '45. After my mother died. When Franco closed the border and we couldn't go back into le Pays, I moved to Havana." She rolled her v into a b.

"And since?" He sipped his coffee through a sugar cube between his teeth, Russian-style.

"Just living. Translation, mostly. Not that anyone needs a Basque-Cuban translator. English and French, mostly. You always said my family background would come in handy." She grinned and turned around, her skirt floating above the floor, her arms high over her head as she looked up toward the ceiling. "You were wrong."

"Olé!" he clapped his tan-brown hands together, face brightening for the first time since he arrived. Then he stood.

"Now we need to talk. The coup to take down Batista is set for next month."

Oliver explains that orders are to organize a cell of old comrades. People with experience in hit-and-run operations. Oliver is to be the conduit, Anna the organizer.

Until further notice her apartment on 25th and O would serve as a safe-house and procurement station. There would be others scattered across the city, but that was not for her to worry about.

"So it begins again," Anna said with a combination of pride and sadness. "We will be successful this time." She reached out and held Ollie, feeling the hard shell of his chest, the soft murmurs of his heart against her breast.

"Better to die on one's feet — "

"Than to live on one's knees," she finished. The words hang heavy in the humid air. She thought but did not say, *"NO PASARÁN."*

He released her hands, kissed her on both cheeks, leaving her face warm and damp, and disappeared out the door. Anna could hear his halting steps, heavy-light, heavy-light, down the darkened stairway. She tipped the louvers with her fingers, scanning the street below. She spotted Ollie's head as he bent down to peer into the passenger seat of a robin egg blue Buick Roadmaster. He spoke for a moment with a dark suited man slouched in the front seat, his features masked by the metal visor across the top of the windshield. The man in the dark suit turned his head toward Oliver, gave a thumbs up sign, and motioned the driver to pull away from the curb. As Oliver made his way up the steep hill toward the University of Havana, Anna watched as the man tossed the stub of a cigar out onto the empty street where it glowed red in the darkening night air.

Two weeks later there was a knock at the door. When Anna opened the door she found an envelope made of brown wrapping paper bound by a rubber band. Inside was $5,000 in US twenties. She fanned the bills out on the unfinished wood table, then divided them into four stacks and placed each pile on a separate corner. The last she kept for herself.

The government radio station interrupted its "Salsa Tonight" program hosted by Desidario Arnez Y Garcia — *"El Famoso."* Anna tilted her head toward the brown cloth speaker enclosure and twirled the dial of the old Philco. The static moderated and a deep voice intoned:

> *The Batista government announced today the establishment of new laws that will protect the Cuban citizenry from the cancer of communist influence and penetration. President Batista wishes all the citizens of Cuba peace and prosperity.*

She closed her eyes and took a steadying breath. Now, she thought. Now the Orthodoxos will start plotting with the exiles in Miami, the Auténticos pissing in their pants, and the Communists writing Marxist-Leninist tracts signed by Khrushchev's laundress. And that, she mused, will leave the door wide open. She had made her connections the day Oliver left — inviting the old crowd to "just a friendly dinner party." She hoped they understood.

By mid-day they arrived, sitting on folding chairs around the money like poker players ready to ante-up. The apartment felt hot and stuffy, ripe with the odor of olive oil and fish. Outside the sun baked the roof and hammered the concrete of the sidewalks below.

Oliver was already talking to Rena, his gaze never leaving her face. Enrique and Cipriano argued as if no time had passed since there last meeting — although they couldn't agree when that had been. They each spoke several languages, but only shared English and Spanish. Even Cipriano, the terrible scar still visible on his left forearm, found that the Greek of his Cypriot boyhood had eroded into British English laced with American profanity.

"You bloody well know how the motherfucker sounded when he proposed that treaty with the US," he proclaimed when told of Franco's discussions with Dulles, banging the table with his fist at the word motherfucker. And he repeated it for emphasis. Enrique stared into Cipriano's black eyes and squinted. "You know how this goes," he snorted, "there's always payback." The words hinted at reproach and hovered over the table. The others straightened.

"Not that again," Oliver spoke evenly, his hands raised, placating. "Can't you leave that where it belongs? In the ground. Dead and gone. It's ancient history."

Anna glanced around the room and wondered if they could ever recapture the camaraderie they had shared in the past.

"Time for business. Follow me. Five minute intervals."

∎

The crowd began to surge. Men and women huddled in small groups at every corner of the university's inner courtyard, their heads bobbing animatedly. Some were clad in the coats and ties and dresses they wore to class, others in the cotton trousers of farmers, their feet wedged into sandals made of scraps of old automobile tires. Each cluster carried banners and flags, each denounced the new government, each spat on the image of Batista, and each jostled for dominance. Student socialists, communists, democrats, followers of Prío and Chibás, and even Grau — they withheld none of their anger at American support of the new regime. Batista had become nothing more than a tool of Gringo Imperialism.

The police were not difficult to spot. Their guayaberas too white and too stiff, their sunglasses sinister and shiny, they stood with arms crossed, some leaning nonchalantly against the pillars that ringed the courtyard. Anna spotted at least eight, all with flowing mustaches and new huaraches. She didn't bother wondering if they were armed, but whether they were willing to fire.

Four massive buildings framed the inner courtyard, each fronted by Corinthian columns a meter wide and three stories high. The names of great and learned Europeans — Pasteur, Cervantes, Lorca, and Kant — were neatly chiseled into the cornices of the structures, whose monumental scale paid tribute to the Empire of Spain. The University of Havana had inducted generations of Cuban students into the mysteries of the educated middle-class elite. Now as political neophytes they stood and screamed, ready to fight for freedom and against oppression. These children of landowners and industrialists, of government officials and learned professionals, massed in the capital from across Cuba. They aspired not to return to their provincial homes in Guantanamo, or Santiago, or Trinidad, but rather to take their rightful place as leaders of a new society. They paid homage to the true father of Cuban independence, José Martí, the poet-politician who lead the revolution of the 1880s, and shouted slogans that mixed anti-Batista vitriol in equal doses with the usual cries of "Yankee go home!"

In one corner of the courtyard, next to the Faculty of Law, a wooden folding table was covered with the banner of the PSP — the Socialist-Popular Party, last week's communists now with a new name. Someone had drawn a black silhouette of Lenin's head in the space between Socialist and Popular. Anna scoffed at the foolishness. Batista outlawed the Communist Party, so they changed their name. Besides, the traditions of the University of Havana excluded military and police from the grounds, so what were they worried about? She caught sight of a pair of SIM lingering in the shadows, their expressions unreadable. Perhaps, she mused, they were right to be cautious.

Twenty meters away, the table of the Cuban People's Party, the Ortodoxos, self-proclaimed populists but actually moderates, guarded the Faculty of Letters. A warm wind wrapped itself around the pillars and open doorways of the courtyard, darting under tables and into the tangles of Anna's long hair, pinned loosely by ivory combs. She held her skirt to her knees, waiting for the breeze to pass. It made her sad to see the student movement fractured into so many shards. Only unity, she had lectured Oliver as they marched down the streets of Barcelona in 1938, only unity will win.

Oliver arrived silently. His face covered with stubble, his old cord pants tied at the waist by a frayed rope, sporting his old Basque beret. "No one who digs Dizzy," he once proclaimed, "would be caught dead without one of these toppers." His arm grazed hers above the elbow, and she felt the surface of his skin, gentle as if a butterfly had fallen from the sky. They stood next to each other without speaking. Anna glanced across the crowd, her eyes searching the faces of the men and women, mostly in their twenties — as young now as they had been then.

"Look," she jabbed her elbow into his ribs, "over there."

He followed her eyes beyond the grand arch that yielded to the darkened inner hallway that led to the President's office. Rena, cast in shadow, her eyes banded in darkness, leaned against the wall — her arms were crossed and her boot pressed against the white stucco wall behind her, her leg bent at the knee. Rena's black cape, which Anna recognized from the hospital in Brunete, hung from her shoulders. Anna knew that if she were to examine it closely she would detect the stitching of Rena's nurses' military rank. She remembered the fire in Rena's eyes when she recounted how she had carefully cut off the badge in protest, angry that the Commissars had decided to abolish the democratic equality that was the hallmark of the International Brigades. Now only the cape remained. "They will never comprehend the difference between rank and identity," Rena had told her. "Dumb fuckers."

The students wandered from table to table as the sun set behind the buildings. She could see down to the sea where waves beat against the rocks along the Malecon, the spray flashing like diamonds in the air. There, the Hotel Nacional de Cuba towered over the sea, and gold-braided livery men and black Lincoln Continentals scattered along the avenue. A scene in miniature, as if someone had hand carved a set and was moving the pieces invisibly. A world away, like a dream.

Oliver leaned over, the cigar on his breath sour and pungent. "Where are the others?"

Anna checked the courtyard. Cipriano towered over Enrique, exactly a head taller. Except for their height they might have been twins. Olive skin, dark curly hair, long noses, deep brown eyes, and wispy beards that gave them the look of escaped convicts. Any film company would cast them in roles as Italians, Jews, Spaniards, Greeks, or Mexicans. Hardly anyone recognized them as Cypriot and Cuban. When Enrique arrived in Spain in October of 1936, the first volunteer he encountered was Cipriano. He told Anna later that it felt like looking into a mirror. They laughed upon discovering that the militia General, a Hungarian Jew, couldn't tell them apart. Later the Americans could do no better. That Enrique was much shorter made no difference to the Jewish intellectuals from New York or the Polish bricklayers from Chicago. For most of the war they were referred to as one person. Cipriano's name was apparently too difficult to comprehend and so they both became Enrique. As Oliver once tried to explain, "See. Playing baseball, in the States, everyone who ain't pure white, could be Italian, don't matter, gets the same name. Meatball or Gomez. That's how it is here. Who ever heard of Cyprus? You might as well be Cuban. You dig, Enrique?" He looked right at Cipriano. "You dig?"

Across the courtyard Enrique smiled and adjusted his shoulders, hunching them up towards his ears. The gesture pulled the gray, double-breasted wool jacket into furrows, the blue pinstripes curving into the V of the lapels, like a back road between Bilbao and Guernica. No matter that the jacket and his gray-green French army fatigues had nothing to do with each other. Enrique wore them as his own uniform, an unchanging, permanent part of his identity. That jacket was as much a part of him as the twitch in his jaw when he got so angry that he couldn't control himself. "Fight fear with fear," had been his motto in Spain. Enrique locked eyes with Anna. He whispered to Cipriano. The Cypriot blinked as if to clear his focus.

Cipriano moved away from Enrique, shouldering his way in and out of the crowd. Anna tracked the movement of his curls as he wove his way slowly toward the arch that pointed down toward the sea, away from the masses of students already in motion, like a covey of birds flapping their wings even before they spotted danger. Cipriano halted and jammed his hands into his dark trousers. Always a size too large, he wore them with a worn cotton shirt that covered his chest like a gauze bandage. As the students in the courtyard murmured, growing louder by the moment, Cipriano stood completely still, his face into the wind, as if to fathom some invisible and silent motion. His eyes deepened. They always betrayed him just by narrowing. Even from across the courtyard Anna imagined their color darkening from blue to black.

"The Bell!" someone cried. "The Bell is gone!"

As if an invisible hand had set them in motion, hundreds of

students turned, first to one another, then toward the political tables. Murmurs became cries, cries became shouts. "The Bell!" they demanded. "Return the bell!" Within seconds smaller groups of students swarmed the tables, crying the name of their party, chanting as if to drown out the others, "Ortodoxos demand the bell!" and "down with Batista!" The SIM, their brows furrowed, moved to block the entry to the Rector's office. Arms folded across their chests, a phalanx of white shirted, mustachioed, no-longer-secret police glared out at the milling students.

"P! S! P!" the onetime communists chanted. "PSP! PSP! PSP!" They lifted the banner with Lenin's portrait, wrapping themselves in the party's green and yellow flag, and marched on the Ortodoxo table across the courtyard. But the Ortodoxo students had already formed a defense, ten deep, around their own leaders. Like boxers they stood sideways, fists balled, glaring out from behind their shoulders. Some screamed at the charging young PSP students, "Go back to Russia!" And the PSP faithful bellowed back, "Give back the Bell you sons of whores!"

The charging PSP militants surged closer, anger distorting their faces, the tendons in their necks bulging with outrage. As they approached the outer PPC defense they slowed and a young man with a Cuban flag bandana raised his fist. His eyes smoked and spittle sprayed from his mouth, tiny droplets falling to the ground harmlessly.

"Return the Bell!" he screamed. His demand found a hundred echoes behind him. "It is the sacred Bell of Demajagua, the one Céspedes rang in the revolution of our nation."

A voice shouted back, "You stupid bourgeois lackeys! It is the bell of your own slavery!" And the Ortodoxo students stiffened their resolve, digging their heels into invisible dirt, straightening their backs as if they had discovered their moral backbone. Anna craned her neck to look over their heads. Rena remained standing under the arch, arms crossed, under the arch, the human tableau frozen before her.

A tall handsome man elbowed his way into the epicenter of the political storm. He braced his palms on the table, long fingers graceful and smooth. In a single motion he straightened his arms and hoisted himself onto the tabletop. Anna frowned. He seemed familiar, but she didn't recognize him. He wore a new brown wool suit, his white shirt open at the neck, his clean-shaven face long and intense. He towered over both groups of students.

Their response was instantaneous. Brandishing iron pipes over their heads, each side menaced the other. The man on the table reached his hand inside his suit-jacket. A large handgun, dwarfed by his massive palm, thrust into the heavy evening air. The students surrounding the table reached into their belts but not before the gun fired, its muzzle flash bright against the sky.

Everyone stopped.

The man cupped his hands to his mouth and drew the crowd to him, less by his words than by the charisma of his presence. Eyes as bright as the flash of his pistol, his face long and expressive, eyebrows arched and dancing he spoke, about the Bell, the symbol of Cuban independence, hidden, until 1948. The orator removed his jacket, slinging it casually over his shoulders. He urged them to reclaim the moment of historical inevitability, the prelude to a new era of independence. Students from both camps found themselves cheering, some fired their guns into the air, others clapped rhythmically.

"The Bell had been at the University," he reminded them, "since 1948, but only as a guest. NO, he shouted, not as a guest, as a prisoner!"

The students surrounding the table on which he stood surged and raised their right fists, punching them into the air again and again, calling out "Martí! Martí! Martí!"

"Yes!" he shouted back, "Martí! The father of Cuban independence is here with us. But the Bell cannot breathe the air of freedom as long as it remains in the custody of the University and of the State!"

The orator had become his rhetoric. He had been speaking for nearly an hour. It was unlike anything Anna had witnessed since the days of Dolores Ibárruri, *La Pasionaria,* who sang to the masses of workers and peasants in Spain. Anna could feel the vibrations of the students' response. Together they and the speaker had become one.

"Now is the time for unity not for inner struggle," the man proclaimed. "The Bell stands for freedom and it has been taken to remind us all that our freedom has been stolen. It will be returned," he promised, "when the real cause of its theft has been removed. When Batista leaves, I promise you, I vow to you, that the Bell of Demajagua will return. But," and he paused, letting the silence speak to the students who stood below him in rapture, "not a moment before."

With a tilt of her head Ann signaled her team to leave. One by one they filed out of the courtyard, away from the University and down the broad avenue toward the sea. She turned and looked back at the University, mounted high on its own Acropolis, monumental and massive. The students had already begun to scatter, leaving the courtyard in small groups, arms linked, singing *"Guantanamera,"* the song of independence. The handbills announcing the mass meeting lay scattered on the walkways, some fluttering in the wind.

She walked, the night stars bright above, their light overwhelming the yellow street lamps of the city that had already dimmed for the daily hour of "patriotic savings" the government enforced sporadically. The evening reminded her where she had seen the man before. A cigar glowing red in the street below her apartment window. She would have to ask Oliver who he was.

I

SANTIAGO, CUBA 10 JULY 1953

It took three days to drive from Havana to Santiago, encountering SIM barricades every fifty kilometers. They approached each roadblock carefully. The secret police waited in dark sedans peeking out from behind the red and black barriers. Enrique would slow the black and white Mercury to a crawl, searching for cover. Often he positioned the car behind a rickety and refitted yellow school bus loaded down with peasants, cardboard suitcases, and the occasional crate of chickens. It took the green-uniformed police, operating under the surveillance of the agents in the dark cars, at least a half-hour to check the bus for hidden contraband. They always waved the Merc past after that.

They drove with the windows down, hot air blowing through the car, their eyes closed, passing warm bottles of beer between them. Enrique and Anna sat in front, the others in back. Oliver took off his wood prosthesis, resting it on the rear-window shelf. It allowed him, he grinned, gold tooth flashing, "a bit more leg room." Enrique and Anna took turns driving, Enrique in the mornings and Anna at night. Come mid-day they would park under a breadfruit tree and sleep. Some sprawled in the car and others wedged themselves between the tree's enormous roots. The roots, like the trunk of an elephant, were tube-shaped and remained cool and moist even in the heat of the day.

Their last day on the road, with the Sierra Maestra range looming magisterially between them and the sea, they stopped. Enrique stretched his arms wide, bent his head back, and screamed at the top of his lungs. The cry pierced the late afternoon air, heavy with mid-summer humidity, and then, without echo, without effect, disappeared. Enrique grinned and looked around. "Madre Dios," he shouted, followed by an even louder "Motherfucker!" He bent down to pick something up in his hand. "Mira!" he called, "look what I found!" and held out his palm.

Cipriano moved effortlessly, reaching out out and scooping the beans from Enrique's hand. "Edó?" he said in Greek, "Here, see what our friend has discovered. Black gold."

He tossed the green-gold pods, one at a time, to each of his companions.

"We should take an oath," Cipriano hardly moved his mouth. "An oath to all that is in the past and that remains for us to discover in the future." His face flushed. He didn't like making speeches.

"Let us eat one cacao. One for each of our memories, one for each of the moments that have brought us here."

Anna cracked the fruit on her knee, removed one of the seeds and lifted it to her lips, "Teruel."

Then Oliver, "Brunete."

"Aragon," said Rena.

"The Ebro," Enrique answered.

Then as one, standing in the shade beneath a grove of cacao trees, they tossed their heads back, chomped their teeth into the hard skin of the beans, and let the flavor seep into their mouths.

∎

They arrived in Santiago at dusk. The road sloped gently, following the contour of the hills, then fell steeply down to sea level. The mountains to the west seemed to grow as the car descended into the basin of the city and the harbor. An ever-expanding river of people flowed down the street — workers returning from work and peasants driving donkey carts burdened with bundles of brush, second-hand clothes, and an occasional goat tethered from its neck to the axle. They filled the roadway, leaving a single lane open for the cars and ancient trucks still driving in both directions. The closer to the city they drove, the denser the human traffic and the slower the journey. In the blackening darkness Enrique leaned forward over the wheel, gripping it with both hands, and peered through the windshield.

It was impossible to really see. Impossible to actually tell who was walking where. "Like Carnival" Enrique snorted. "They just live in the streets here." He held his breath. "And it stinks."

Anna leaned out the passenger window, elbow propped on the door. She had never been to Santiago before. All that time in Spain and France, then back to Havana. "It smells like — " she took in a deep breath of air " — like plantains, plantains frying everywhere."

The car had entered the city, driving down a broad boulevard clogged with open backed trucks and brimming with men and women returning to the barrios after a day of work in the fields. To their right a concrete structure, lights blazing from atop its walls, dominated a manicured park that extended hundreds of meters along the roadside. "Slow," Anna urged Enrique. "I want to see the people."

The Santiago baseball stadium pulsed with the rhythms of a conga band, and the people poured in and out of the park's entry ramps, wide ribbons of sidewalk that led down to the field. Enrique glided the car, feathering the gas, keeping pace with the walking aficionados.

"Who plays tonight?" Anna called.

A boy, barely fourteen, his jeans rolled to his knees, shouted back, *"Cienfuegos!* El Tiante is pitching." The boy wrinkled his nose. "They are too good. We don't have a chance."

Anna laughed, poking Enrique with her left hand. "Let's go."

Enrique turned onto the Paseo de Martí, a wide avenue that emptied into the smaller Avenida 40 whose tram tracks caught their tires and shimmied the car down the steep incline. Enrique took his hands off the wheel and laughed.

"Look! It has a mind of its own." He turned, winking at Rena who sat with her hands covering her eyes, fingers spread just enough for a peek. "Don't worry," he added, "I can still drive with my feet." With that he snapped in the clutch, nudged the wheel with his knees and the car popped out of the tram tracks and back onto the cobblestone pavement. Rena let out a sigh and nestled into the crook of Oliver's arm. She closed her eyes and reached out to hold his hand. At her touch Oliver smiled, buoyed by the memory of another time and another place.

It was hard to see at first, but the moon offered enough light to burnish the Moncada barracks with an orange-yellow glow. They slowed and then stopped.

"So," whispered Anna, "This is where they hold the prisoners." She swept her arm as if to embrace the entire building. Enrique rolled down the window and muttered "SIM" as he spat a glob of tobacco juice on the dark sidewalk.

The yellow stucco exterior made the barracks appear smaller than its four square blocks. Waist-high concrete walls interspersed with meter-high iron spikes surrounded the fortress. Four concrete kiosks guarded each corner and a central command center controlled a white crossing barrier that barred all street traffic from the grounds. They could not see the soldiers in each corner guardhouse, but sensed their presence. The night offered sufficient light to illuminate the barrack walls, but not the walkways and verandas that defined the inner courtyard.

"*Vámanos*," Enrique said to no one in particular. "We still have far to travel."

It took another hour, driving slowly through dense urban neighborhoods, around several parks and squares, and past the

Cathedral on Parque Céspedes, to arrive at the sea. The road cut between two looming mountain ranges, their peaks steep and dark against the barely moonlit sky. At the mouth of the Bahia de Santiago, just beneath the imposing costal fortress of El Morro the road came to a T.

"To Pailo Castro" announced Cipriano. "Meaning exactly what," asked Anna, her face twitched. "What made you say that?"

Cipriano half smiled, "Just fooling. It means 'old castle' in Greek. You know. My native language. In case you have forgotten, I speak one of the world's oldest."

Anna returned his smile. "For a moment I thought you said something else."

Cipriano cupped his hand to take a long pull from the cigarillo he had lit moments earlier. Anna relaxed and peered out the windshield. They rode in silence for ten kilometers.

"To the left," Anna directed. "Take the road to the left."

Enrique swung the wheel and pressed down on the accelerator, spraying gravel off to the side. The car slid onto a narrow road and shot off toward the sea.

They could hear the waters of the Caribbean lapping at the shore and the outlines of trees and shrubs passed behind them like a movie set on skates. The road ended at a pebbled beach that extended along a graceful crescent cove. Flowering bitter bush trees grew close to the water's edge, and even at night they could spot small grape-like clusters that the peasants boiled into a thick purple syrup to treat malaria.

∎

At dawn, all but Oliver stripped off their clothes and ran into the sea. The mountains rose steeply behind them, a dense green backdrop dotted with pine and palm trees that concealed hand-dug stone roads. Small peasant shacks called bohío lay hidden in these hills. Illegally built, the cabins were made of lath and roofed with the raffia of palm, resembling small circus wagons without wheels, and camouflaged by the overgrown jungle. At the cove's edge an outcropping of gray boulders stepped down into the blue waters. Despite his leg, Oliver clambered to the top of the breakwater and sat with his back to the hills. At his feet the waves crashed against the rocks, sending crescendos of spray up into the sky.

Anna and Rena swam together, side-by-side, the salt coating their faces, stiffening their hair. Closer to shore Enrique and Cipriano were content to float, arms back behind their heads, looking up into the brightening sky. None could tell how much time had gone by, each lost in the moment of reverie. Gulls cried and fluttered wildly before touching down on the pebbled shore. A black dot descended slowly down the switchbacks from the mountain to the sea.

Oliver felt the car's vibration. He craned his neck, shielding his eyes from the sun. He cupped his hands and whistled, a loud piercing sound that melted into the horizon. The car gathered speed and careened faster down the mountain, blinking its headlights. The driver was bent over the steering wheel, his fists tight. A moment later the green Chevrolet sedan screeched to a halt in the grove of trees where the Mercury was parked. A short man in a white linen suit and a stunning woman dressed to the nines sauntered over to Oliver.

"He wants you to find a place. Rent it for a month."

The woman handed Oliver a roll of bills and the man tipped the brim of his hat. Then they were off, driving back up into the Sierra Maestra range.

Anna and Oliver huddled together, heads bowed. Anna read from a small notebook while Ollie nodded along in agreement. The others sprawled under dawn's canopy, too exhausted to dream.

A rooster's crow alerted them to the day ahead. No one needed a watch to tell the time — already past five. Anna stretched her arms, yawned, and glanced again at her notebook. Her whole political life, the past four months, lay in its pages. Directions to meetings, exchange rates of pesos and dollars, initials indicating the brands of weapons, addresses for a seamstress and tailor, bank account numbers. Oliver had asked if she worried about the notebook falling into the wrong hands. Never occurred to her, she told him, and showed him the cover. She had neatly written "Basque Recipes" in black ink and decorated the rest of the page with drawings of the Basque flag, a crossed knife and fork, and a swirling design that suggested a smoked ham.

On one of the unfolded pages she had written "Siboney." When she spoke the word Oliver nodded and extracted a roll of bills from his front trouser pocket. He knew exactly how much they intended for him to spend and had paper-clipped a mark on the roll so that he could thumb to the precise amount and still keep the money concealed. One of the lieutenants, Abel Santamaría, had shown him this trick at their last meeting in Havana. He didn't bother to tell him that the Commissars in Spain had taught him the trick long ago. Nor did he tell him how he would find the rest of the money they required. Because he didn't know.

He touched Anna's hand lightly. "In an hour we'll be on our way. I think I spotted a perfect place just off the side of the road last night. It was concealed, to be sure, by the obscurity of evening, but you'll see *cara mia."*

Anna looked up at him. His hair had gray flecks and his eyelids drooped just a bit. Ollie had always cut quite the figure, trim mustache, shiny bronze skin, long aquiline nose, the rakish gold tooth, and those Asturian cord pants. She found it remarkable that he had recovered from the shrapnel that had destroyed his leg. But he seemed worn, even hesitant. She wondered if he and Rena had ever become lovers.

"You have more blarney than a room full of Irish priests," she grinned up at him.

He laughed, "And you have more Chutzpah."

■

Enrique gunned the motor, bringing the Merc to life. Cipriano sat in front this time, and Oliver wedged himself between the two women in the rear. In daylight the region seemed as wild as it had been mysterious at night. They traveled back towards Santiago Bay, heading into the majestic and lush Sierra Maestra range. Dozens of bohío were scattered, half-hidden, along the hillsides.

"Who lives in them?" Cipriano asked.

"Squatters, *me amigo,"* Enrique replied. "They say this whole range belongs to some *gato gordo,* a capitalist fat cat who stole the property from the sugar combine forty years ago. Some old Spaniard, a '98 veteran who got rich because Batista protected him the first time around back in '45."

"You said squatters."

"Yes. Now. The guy, someone named Ángel Castro y Argiz, lives in Santiago and allows the poor to live here free of charge. Not all his neighbors agree. Not the old *aristos* of American Nickel. Not Batista."

Anna and Oliver exchanged glances, and Anna put her finger to her lips.

The car slowed around a curve just as the road narrowed. The branches of the trees on either side formed a natural arbor.

"There," Oliver pointed ahead and off to the right at a small wood farmhouse painted white, twenty meters off the road. "Stop. We'll find out how much they want to rent the joint."

This time Enrique and Cipriano exchanged glances, but they too remained silent.

■

Five minutes later Anna and Oliver returned to the car. "We got it. Twenty dollars for the month. Told them we were going to raise chickens for an agricultural experiment." She laughed at the outrageousness of the explanation. "We can start moving our gear in right away." They explored the outside of the farmhouse for five minutes and then began unloading.

They had wrapped the guns in blankets. Hardly fool-proof concealment. But someone in Havana had guaranteed their safe passage to Santiago. Just a matter of the right money in the right hands. Something about working with the remnants of the Ortodoxos who still wanted to get rid of Batista. Inside the farmhouse, they lined their arsenal on the red-tiled floor. The farmhouse reminded Anna of a place where her grandmother slaughtered chickens in a tiny village outside Guernica, deep in the foothills of the Pyrenees.

"Not much to brag about," Enrique muttered. He bent over the display of ten Enfields and Springfields that dwarfed the two Mausers and an old Colt .45.

Anna reminded him that he'd have more soon. "First, we need to find money to buy more arms, ammo, and some field gear. Come up with a plan as early as this evening," she said, "once the others arrive. Meanwhile, let's start thinking about the assault."

Enrique stood, the guns mute at his feet, and spoke from his heart.

"What assault? Isn't it about time you told us what's happening? Sure, we trust you. We trust Oliver. We have shared too much in the past. When I got your telegram I was driving a cab in New York. You know I came right away. Nothing could keep me away. But now it is time to tell us what we are doing here."

Anna looked at Oliver, then back at Enrique. "I told you from the beginning — you'll know what you need to know when you need to know it. Too much information is dangerous. You know the protocols."

The others moved across the room. They seemed to know what was coming. They had all seen it before, in Spain. Enrique didn't look very large, and his squat torso and large head, black hair and deep blue eyes, made him resemble a wrestler. Clad in his habitual gray double-breasted jacket however, he looked like an American gangster. Just another mec leaning over one of the tables in Havana, Anna thought. Then, out of nowhere, his mouth began to twitch. Then his eyebrows, black and bushy, moved up and down, his eyes turning hard. He balled his fists and held them rigidly at his side, and exploded.

"Don't be telling me about protocols! I remember the day when someone else told us about protocols. You remember them too, don't you Cipriano?"

Cipriano recoiled.

"When they started telling us to follow orders, remember? The Commissars, those assholes, those Soviet puppets, called us politically 'immature' and stripped away our militia insignia."

Enrique stared at Anna, as if to peer into her memory. His mouth twitched and his eyes bulged. "And you, who no one ever really trusted, you convinced us to go along with the new rules! You even called them 'protocols.' Said it was the right way! You remember, Anna, you used the word 'protocols' then. You use it now, and why should I trust you any more now than I did then?"

The others stood, mouths open. Shocked. Enrique's temper had been legendary. But it was one thing to see him level the enemy with his wrath, another to be on the receiving end.

And then like a spring thunderstorm, his anger subsided. Enrique hung his head and looked down at the arsenal at his feet.

"Sometimes I get overwhelmed. You know I don't mean it."

"No, you are right," Anna played some music into her voice. "We have not told you all there is to know." She put her arms around Enrique's shoulders and motioned for Cipriano and Rena to join them. It took barely ten minutes to outline most, but not all, of the plans hatched in Havana that spring. By the time she finished Enrique's chest puffed out and a smile graced his face. "Maybe we'll have to call you Colonel," Anna grinned.

"Let's get to work," announced Oliver. "We have a few hours to transform the farm. It must look almost deserted. The others will be here by late afternoon."

"Easier said than done," remarked Cipriano.

Oliver nodded and then stared out into the distance, lost in memory. "Anyone remember the hedgerows?" he asked.

It took about three beats for Enrique to answer. France, July of '44. I remember sure as it was yesterday. Earthworks that could stop a tank. Farmers used them as walls for their fields and the Bosch hid behind them with machine guns."

Cipriano laughed, something he loved to do, especially with a beer in one hand and a cigar in the other. "A homemade Cuban hedgerow. I like it."

∎

They found what they needed behind the house. Wood poles, shovels, chain-link fencing materials. As Enrique and Cipriano dug, Anna and Rena looped the fencing to the posts, creating a mesh barrier between the farmhouse and the road. In less than an hour they had erected a shield two meters high and ten meters long. Another hour and they had woven saplings, branches, and leaves over and through the fencing. Not only would the false hedgerow make it impossible to see the farmhouse from the road, but it would conceal the cars once they arrived.

At dusk, three battered Chevrolets glided silently into the alley between the house and hedgerow. Young men in their twenties, mostly recruited from Havana, piled into the farmhouse, each carrying a small bag with a change of clothes and little else. Enrique greeted them, using his best General Líster voice, one he acquired, as he called it, *"al frente,* at the front."* It would be easy enough to mock their soft hands and their educations. But that would not persuade them to follow his credo, one that had guided him for twenty-years.

"Welcome. This is the most important challenge of our time. The most important thing for free men," he paused and looked at their faces, looked hard because he wanted them to really understand, "is to protect the freedom of others."

"Compañeros," he called them. "Companions, you are here to learn how to become guerillas. Not soldiers, not professionals with no ideals. We shall become liberators who live in the forest and strike like lightning. You will learn to bring surprise and havoc to the world, to confuse and destabilize the idiot army and secret police of Batista. My job is to show you how to do this without getting your *cajones* shot-off."

They laughed. They always did. Standing in front of Enrique, these sons of the Cuban middle class, nary a negro face among them, embraced his rough humor. Of course, they had heard of him. Who had not? The only surviving Cuban volunteer from the Abraham Lincoln Battalion in Spain, Enrique was a decorated veteran of the

French resistance, and a clandestine member of the Ahora Tiempo group of independent anarcho-syndicalists aligned with the more infamous Cuban SIA, the *Solidaridad Internacional Antifascista*. No matter. First Franco, then Petain, then Batista, had all tried to hunt him down. Here he was, still kicking.

"Yes, gringos," he told them as the sun filled the farmyard with light, its heat tracing dark wet stains down their backs, "we will learn to infiltrate, to hide, to move silently. And above all we will learn to adapt. You may notice that we seem to have a shortage of weapons. Do not let that small shortcoming become a cancer in your minds. We will make guns from the trees, carve knives from the branches. In short, my *compañeros*, we will improvise."

The volunteers shifted from side to side, unsure of what to make of this man who called himself Colonel Enrique Perez. They had expected to become members of a rebel army, to become citizen soldiers. Now he was telling them how to melt out of sight, how to forage from the land, how to look like anyone and no one. Truth be told, and he didn't tell them, Anna had once been his teacher.

"Here," he grabbed a vine that circled the trunk of the tree growing out back of the farmhouse. "Take this." He twisted the end of the vine, cracking it open. "What can you do with this? Does anyone know?" Enrique put the vine to his lips and sucked the liquid from inside. "It is just water, you know, and it may save your life. Line up," he commanded. "Tell me how you are going to leave this yard, all fenced in, without making a sound. Can someone do that for me please?"

Enrique dropped to the ground and, lying prone, crossed his forearms under his chest, hunched his back, and crawled forward silently on his elbows. They followed him one at a time until they reached the back door of the farmhouse. Enrique turned and surveyed them, lying like lizards in the dust. "I once crawled like this for an hour," he told them. "Past Franco's patrols and into France." He let the memory settle. "Can any of you speak English?" he asked, switching to the language. They all nodded. "That's what you get with a bunch of over-educated university radicals," he laughed. "Now, who knows what a *trogon* is?"

One raised his hand and announced that the trogon was a tropical bird with a distinctive red, green, and blue coloring, whose normal habitation was the middle reaches of the Sierra Maestra mountains. "Very good," Enrique acknowledged, "very good. Now, who can tell me what the trogon sounds like? Enrique tugged his beret down over his eyes, spread his feet apart and placed his hands at his chest. He smiled broadly and declared, "Gentlemen, I give you the human trogon." And then he opened his mouth and sang, just a single note at first, *"Trocooo,"* then two and three more, altering the pitch ever so slightly. "Do it," he commanded. "Sing!"

They obeyed, these young men with dirt and sweat caked on their faces, they sang too.

"You see," he said, "this is all you need. One note for 'over here,' another for 'careful' and a third for 'someone is coming.' Drink from the vine, crawl like a lizard, sing like a trogon, this will keep you alive."

Enrique took a step back and surveyed the collection of not-quite-men. Even after their briefing, Anna and Oliver had only shared with him that he needed to get a group of untrained volunteers ready in two weeks for a "clandestine operation." You know, they had first told him in Havana, like the old days. That phrase made him shiver. Old days, Spanish Civil War days, days spent freezing and days spent broiling, days of death and days of anger. But, they had called him, asked him to trust them, and then instructed him to find Cipriano.

Not as hard as it had first appeared. His comrade, some called them 'partners in crime,' had been living in Miami running a Greek restaurant in North Beach. The Cypriot no longer had a last name, but they had known each other since 1936. And like Enrique, the Cypriot came running when a friend called.

Nearby, Cipriano stood talking to Anna and Rena. The evening dusk deepened the shadows on their faces. Cipriano called out, "Not bad for the first day. When are you going to give them something difficult to accomplish?"

"When the guns and clothing arrive," Enrique replied.

"When we get the money," added Anna.

"Alright, you can get up," Enrique addressed the recruits. "There's about fifteen of you. Form three small columns; that's how you'll live and train for the next two weeks, till the others arrive."

He slouched back against the wall of the farmhouse.

"All right, *amigos,* you are on your own now. Make a small fire for each column, cook some food, dig a fox-hole and see what you can do with this."

Enrique reached into a canvas bag and tossed a smaller brown paper bag in their direction. The contents jingled like tin bells. Then he found a large roll of black electrical tape and rolled it toward them.

"I'll be back later." He stiffened his back and strode away into the night singing *"Trocooo, trocooo, trocooo."*

∎

Enrique found his comrades waiting inside the farmhouse. They greeted him with applause.

"Least I could do after the blow up. I'm sick over that, my friends, sick. Please forgive me. It won't happen again." He looked around at their faces. "Until it does. But, I guarantee next time it won't be aimed at you."

"We understand." Hard to tell if Oliver intended the sarcasm. "We all have our quirks."

"Ok. What's up now. What's next. I get 'em ready to play guerrillas, but I still don't know the objective, still don't know *nada.*"

"We're all in the same boat," Anna replied, gesturing at Oliver. "Only he really knows and he won't tell me either. Only instruction he gave me was to get "the team" ready. To find you, all of you, and get the operation moving."

"That's about it, comrades," Oliver stood up, twisting his prosthetic leg in the way they had all come to understand meant that he still lived in constant pain.

Rena spoke softly. "Do you need a massage? Some times it eases the pain."

Oliver reached his hand down to rub against the place below his knee where the stub fit into the rubber suctioned connection of the apparatus. "I'm alright. Just the quotidian discomfort."

"Listen to him," Cipriano laughed. "Quotidian. Quite the word."

"It's French," added Anna. "In case you don't recognize the root." She looked at Cipriano.

"It's never good enough," Cipriano replied with a touch of sadness in his voice, "that I only speak Greek, Turkish, Spanish, and the ugly tongue you call English."

∎

They ate right out of the cans that night. Garbanzos, black beans, and red peppers, washed down with warm beer. Each of the three columns received identical rations and Enrique showed them how to use machetes to split open the cans. "I'll be back after dinner to check on you. Don't forget. Improvise."

Rena ducked inside to see about cabinets to store medical supplies and Enrique led the others to the "Battalion" camped behind the farmhouse. As they turned the corner into the field behind the farmhouse he spotted the flames. From each corner sparks crackled up into the night sky. The blazes illuminated the field, marking its boundaries. When they moved, their shadows danced with them, lengthening and shortening with each stride. Near the rear-most bonfire Enrique could make out a cluster of men, some with hands on their hips, one waving his arm in encouragement.

"What are they doing?" Cipriano came up to Enrique in the dark, placing his hands on the Cuban's broad shoulders. "What kind of game is this?"

"Ah, my comrade in arms, my old friend." Enrique dug his elbow into Cipriano's ribs. "It is baseball, the national game of Cuba, one we have liberated from the gringos."

Cipriano held Enrique at arm's length, studying him as if inspecting a side of meat. "Baseball. This is," he searched for a word, "non-sense. Makes no sense. There is only one game of real skill."

"I know you love football," Enrique put his hands on Cipriano's forearm, as if to force them off his neck. "But, this sport is for men. The other, for boys."

"Now you make me angry, as you say, piss me off." Cipriano started to twitch the muscles in his face and hold his breath.

Enrique looked wide-eyed. Then stopped and began to laugh.

Cipriano let his own hands fall to his side. "See," he laughed. "Football. For men."

"Baseball," Enrique grinned back. "Our game."

The players' voices became clearer as the two comrades walked silently toward them.

"Come on," a man with the windmill arm called, "come on, you can do it!" As he cried his encouragement another sprinted past him, launching himself feet first toward a marker.

"Go, you go!" shouted someone from the knot of men gathered next to the fire as the runner extended his legs gracefully in front of him, and raised his hands over his head into a Y. His whole body skimmed the ground and his feet hooked onto a small canvas bag on the grass. Above him another man hunched over, his knees bent, his arms extended palms down, parallel to the ground.

"OUT!" someone called. "He is O-U-T. See here. The ball touched him on the knee first."

Another replied, "What do you mean out? You can't see! Never touched him."

A third called from out in the field, "Let's look at the ball!"

"What can that tell us?"

"If he made the tag, the ball will show it."

They huddled together, the runner, the man who tagged him, and several others. Enrique stood behind their shoulders, watching.

"See here," one said, holding up a sphere of black electrical tape, round, pockmarked, lumpy, and the size of an apple. "Look. Here is where the bat hit the *bola*," and he pointed to a depression in the tape.

The other men passed the black taped ball around, each exclaiming, each noting another imperfection.

"What about this," asked the man who had caught the bola. He placed his fore-finger on a spot the size of a coin, a round indent where the tape had worn away and the jagged edge of a bottle cap jutted out. "Look," he continued, "if he made the tag, then the cap will have scratched the runner."

The others nodded and moved to inspect the runner's trousers.

"Here," said the first man, the catcher, "look." He pushed the pant leg up over the man's right ankle to reveal a narrow red set of pin-prick marks just below his calf. "See? I made the tag."

By this time all the men on the field had gathered around the dispute. Hands reached for the ball, heads peered, tongues wagged, each voiced his own opinion loudly, insistently.

"SAFE!" A voice boomed. "He was as SAFE as a eunuch's virgin!"

Enrique, ready to applaud the recruits for their initiative in making a baseball from bottle caps and electrical tape, looked around. Who had spoken? Behind him the others — Rena, Oliver, and Anna — had strolled across the field to see about the commotion.

"Who the hell are you?" one of the players shouted back at the unofficial empire. "Who asked you?"

Anna opened her mouth in recognition. Tall, long nose, dressed in fatigues, a pistol in his belt.

Oliver stood next to her and called out, "Comrades, Compañeros! It is time to introduce you to the man who has brought us together. I am proud to present Cuba's next president — Fidel Castro."

Fidel leaned into the group and plucked the taped ball, the *fifa*, out of their midst. He tossed it softly up and down in his hands, the light from the fires flickering across his broad brow. "Did you know," he said, sounding like a law professor, "Did you know that baseball was brought to Cuba by our patron Saint, José Martí?" With that, Martí, the father of Cuban independence, had been spontaneously anointed the founder of Cuban baseball.

That improbable evening was the revolution's Opening Day.

He had been clean-shaven at the University. Youthful, even graceful. Now he looked weary, his beard a scruffy, wiry nest. Standing, with the fires burning in the corners of the field behind the farm, standing at the center of fifty young men, he took command. The young men squatted or sat at his feet, and in the summer night, with only the flames for light, he spoke.

From the darkness Anna watched as Castro held forth, like a great actor commanding the stage. He transformed himself as he spoke, bringing another person to life with his words.

Castro spoke of his dreams. Of a Cuba that could be remade in the image and memory of the great José Martí.

"Exactly sixty years ago, José Martí founded the Cuban Revolutionary Party. He was forty-two years old. I am twenty-six. We will follow in his footsteps. And this time we will not fail. Let me tell you why."

The men sat mesmerized, staring up at this giant of a man who waved his arms as he talked.

"Martí was a great poet, this you know. And he understood the Cuban people. Spain, imperial and decaying, held us prisoner to its own decline. Without Cuba, without the slaves who landed not far from here, brought by exiles from Haiti, Spain would have been nothing. A million Africans slaved *right here* in these fields to grow sugar and tobacco. This country, our country, provided the labor and the wealth that supported the Spanish empire, allowed it to live beyond its time. And Martí — a frail poet — he dreamed of real independence.

"But he dreamed of more than just independence from a corrupt and despotic empire. He desired a just society, a society where African-Cubans and Spanish-Cubans would be united, a society that lived under a constitution guaranteeing freedom and fostering democracy. This was Martí's dream. Just as we do today, Martí planned for a revolutionary war of independence. You see, my young comrades, Martí understood this above all else: Cuba could not just be free of imperial control, it had to rid itself of the entire legacy of imperialism — of exploitation and racism and oppression and economic inequality. So, it was never a matter of just replacing the king's men with someone else's men. No. It was a matter of change, of allowing the bottom to rise to the top."

Castro paused. He spread his arms out from his shoulders wide as if to embrace them.

"I'll tell you his plan. It was simple. Martí lived in New York as a young man. Did you know that? He studied American History and he knew about one man named John Brown. This Brown tried to start his own revolution, he believed that the spilling of evil blood would be redemptive and that the people would rise to follow him. Listen, this is what Martí hoped for too. Rise up, he urged his followers in 1895, rise up and the people will follow us. He and his general, a black man named Maceo, gathered a small army, like you! I want you to remember this, like you. They came from Havana and some even came from Haiti, and they organized right in these mountains, where they believed they were safe. The peasants hid them, and fed them, and stole food from the plantations for them. They planned for six weeks. We only have two. And I'll tell you exactly why we only have two.

"This is where you must pay attention." He looked out acrosss them, meeting each man's eyes in the darkness. "Martí failed. Not because he had poor ideals. His ideals are our ideals. Not because he lacked courage. His courage will be our courage. He failed because someone betrayed him. I tell you this. NO ONE WILL BETRAY US."

Castro fell silent. Anna could hear the fires cracking and hissing.

The way he wove passion and history and rhetoric was magic. It reminded her of Spain, back when words mattered and roused them all to action — even heroism.

"We must not allow anyone to betray us. We must have trust but we must also have discipline. You will stay here, learn to fight as Martí and our brothers learned to fight, learn to work together, to live as one. For it is here that before we make a revolution we must make ourselves revolutionaries.

"This is the beginning of the great adventure of our lives. We will create a free, independent, and equal Cuba. It will be our duty and our honor. We must learn the two lessons of Martí. The first is that there is no independence without revolution. In 1898 we thought we were free. But the United States only replaced Spain as our imperial master. They will not do this again. We will restore the Constitution of 1940 that Sergeant Batista, who calls himself a general, has desecrated. And then we must tame the beast of exploitation, of Yankee domination of our precious freedom.

"But to do this — and I need you to listen carefully to me — to do this we must preserve our secrecy. When we are ready to act I will tell you how and when and where. But not before. If you know nothing then you will be incapable of betrayal. For even more than Batista and his *"gangsterismo,"* and more than Eisenhower and Nixon and their "CIA-ismo," and more than the SIM, our real enemy lies within. If we are pure we will prevail. *Viva la revolución!!!"*

The men stood, wrapped their arms around each other, and chanted back to him, over and over, *"Viva la revolución, Viva la revolución..."* until they could cry no longer.

A lone voice broke out in song. And the others joined him.

Yo soy un hombre sincero
De donde crece lapalma
Yantes de morir yo quiero echar mis versos del alma
Guantanamera, yeha Guantanamera,
Guantanamera, yeha Guantanamera.

Castro regarded them, eyes gleaming. Anna could see a necklace of red and black beads, the necklace of Santería, of Elegua, at his throat. A white dove, wings fluttering, settled on his shoulder. The men grew silent, awed.

The fires had burned low. Each charred pit a hearth filled with ash. Inside the farmhouse Anna assigned rooms, busied herself with finding linens, and then made coffee. It was well after midnight when she had called them all together.

Enrique and Cipriano spoke at the same time. "That man. With the beard. He was at the University."

Oliver waved his hand. "Yes. That is Fidel Castro. Lawyer, political organizer; he is the one who called us together."

"How?" Rena looked puzzled. Anna understood.

"You understand, now, Arthur. Sure, it was a fluke. A twisted coincidence, if you will. A son of Jewish immigrants I somehow wound up at the center of world events. In fact, these accidents of history enabled me to connect all these people. Don't forget I first met them before in Spain, first in Madrid drinking daiquiris while the bombs fell, and then at the fated Brunete battle, where Mussolini unleashed his monstrous tanks and planes. I was, you might recall, already writing for The Times. That's where I encountered Ollie, Cipriano, Anna, Rena and Enrique. What a team! True anti-fascist heroes, if you need a name for what they stood for. And in 1953 when Castro desperately needed help his people contacted me "you must be our conduit" they told me. You see they needed military professionals who combined activist ideology and field experience. I hoped that Ollie's team could still fulfill that assignment. As I said this was before Che. Castro trusted my reputation and my judgment. He still does. And, even though the Moncado adventure failed, Fidel invited me — now listen! This is important — me and The New York Times, up to these mountains to demonstrate to the world that he is real, that his story will triumph, and that Batista exists as only as the fraudulent puppet of American imperialism. And once again I am, no, we are, his instrument."

"From someone he trusts," Anna replied. "Matthews. We met him in Madrid in '36. Don't you remember? He says he can't forget us. He was covering the Civil War. Now he writes about Cuba. Matthews contacted Oliver and Oliver called on me that spring. And, I found you. All of you."

"Okay. So some guy named Castro wants us for something. And from the looks of things you and Oliver have agreed," Cipriano stood with his back to the stove in the kitchen where they had convened.

"And from the looks of things he wants to get rid of Batista and replace him with…?" Enrique prompted.

"Himself." Cipriano laughed. "He's a revolutionary. He's going to lead a revolution. Right?"

"But who is he? I mean, is he a communist? A nationalist? A dreamer? A politician?" Enrique looked at Anna, eyes gleaming.

Oliver answered. "A little of each."

I

CHICAGO, 14 JULY 1933

Hot as blazes, hot as it could be. Oliver Law wiped the sweat from his brow, ducking into an empty storefront. He could almost smell Lake Michigan in the distance, but when he looked up his own salty sweat about blinded him. How could a guy from Chicago, who once worked in the steel mills and who had gone through boot camp in Alabama, be so uncomfortable in the heat? As Sergeant Weathers had said, "*rhe-fucking-torical!* That is some *rhefuckingtorical* question, Law. Keep it to yourself."

Up ahead Soldier's Field flew the grand red and gold banners of the Fair. Century of Progress my ass, Oliver thought, as he continued down the Midway, past the ice-cream vendors and cotton candy machines spinning sugar into pink birds' nests. He jingled the loose change in his pocket and thought about the new "Chicago" hot dogs all the newspapers were yakking about. Supposedly, it came covered with white onions, pickle relish, and tomatoes. Created special for the Fair to entice the crowds with the Windy City's newest nifty invention.

Oliver wiped the sweat again. Lucky to have a day pass. Major Apgar had decided to give that Sunday off for "good behavior." And, because the "regular" army, meaning the white army, had been granted leave on the Fourth of July it stood to reason that the Negro "fellas" — as Apgar loved to call them — would get a pass too, weeks later.

Easy enough to walk over from the Armory on Cottage Grove and take the bus up Michigan Avenue to 12th. Later he'd stop by home and kiss mama, make sure they had the rent check, and take everyone

46

out to eat at Chickie's Chicken Shack over on Indiana. Just be back at the Armory by zero-six hundred hours, sharp.

Oliver sauntered over to the entry to Soldier Field. *Negro Day at the Fair* the sign read, *Admission 50 Cents*. At the turnstile he stretched his long fingers into the back pocket of his summer Khaki trousers and produced his US Army identity card. The geezer at the gate brought the card to his nose, then extended his arm as far away from his face as it could reach, crushed his expression into a squinting sneer, and said, "That'll be fitty cent."

Oliver looked politely, into the man's rheumy eyes. "Says here," he brandished the hand-bill he'd picked up on Michigan Avenue, "says here service men free on Sundays."

The man's nose reddened and began to drip. He wiped it with his sleeve. "Don't say nothing here about Nigra soldiers."

Ollie spat on the ground between them. The old man looked Oliver up and down three times then mumbled, "Go ahead. You're in."

Every time it happened Oliver bristled, and it happened all the time. But, he held his contempt, froze his face, and smiled. "Thanks, mister, don't mind if I do." Oliver stiffened himself into a salute and marched, eyes forward, past the ticket booth, down the ramp, and into the sunlight of Soldier Field.

He blinked. Hardly anyone on the stroll. The place was almost deserted save a handful of Negro men and women sauntering arm-in-arm along the cinder track that surrounded the football gridiron. They dressed for summer, the women draped in loose-fitting cotton dresses in pastel colors, the men sporting white shirts, open at the collar, straw hats set jauntily on their heads. Along the sidelines red letters on a banner called out a greeting: "COKE WELCOMES YOU TO NEGRO DAY AT THE CENTURY OF PROGRESS."

In one corner two thatched huts perched on the burnt-out summer grass. Smoke curled from the opening in the roof of the one closest, and several figures were seated on the ground outside. As he walked closer he could see two adults and a small child huddled around a second small fire whose smoke puffed into the chalky blue sky.

The family had suspended an iron pot over the fire. They less sat than squatted, these black people, their skin almost blue, yellowed ivory bones pierced through their upper lips. Something bubbled to the surface of the pot, and the woman, bare to the waist, leaned over to stir the mixture. Oliver looked away, first in modesty, then in embarrassment. He couldn't quite fathom who these people were — actors perhaps — and why they were camped out on the ten-yard line.

The man stood, his latticed loin-cloth a spectrum of color, his long woolly hair covered with shells. He touched the woman's elbow and pointed at Oliver. Both of them broke into grins that wrinkled their broad noses. The woman held out a spoon, offering Oliver a taste in a language he had never heard before. It wasn't Spanish or Tagalong, which he learned in the Philippines, or the French that the nuns had tried to teach him at St. Philips. But her meaning was clear and she raised the spoon even closer to his lips.

Then the small boy handed him a printed card, like a beggar on the 'El.

Welcome to the African Village, the card read. *We are your ancestors and we offer you food as greeting and welcome. We come from Dahomey and speak Fon. The food is very good, we call it 'red-red.' Don't be afraid to try some.* At the bottom of the card there was one last line, *Please feel welcome to leave some change for us in the basket.* The boy disclosed his other hand, one that had waited patiently behind his back, revealing a small coiled grass basket.

"I don't know any Dahomey," Oliver scanned the family, "And I don't know any Fon." But they just stared blankly back at him. And then he knew, for sure. They were simply on exhibit, like the zoo or the Field Museum. Showing the Century of Progress Negro Day fairgoers just how far they had all come.

"Progress," he said out loud. Then he shook his head and walked to the entrance, tossing his ticket at the gate-keeper's feet in disgust. "You can keep this." Oliver Law, Sergeant in the 10th Cavalry, still called Buffalo Soldiers, trained as a machine gunner and decorated with a *Croix de Guerre* for his service at the Second Battle of the Marne, lowered his gaze. A tear slid down his cheek.

∎

Sunday, two in the afternoon. Oliver had time on his hands. Why not walk back to the Armory? First over to State, then south down to Washington Park. Why not indeed. Nothing better to do.

He walked for a half hour, strolling through the South Side, past countless boarded up store-fronts interspersed with bars and chicken joints. On every corner men and women sat glum-faced and hungry. The Blue Eagle of the NRA stared back at them from posters plastered to brick walls, declaring the government's plan to help The People. Judging from their empty stares, the people hadn't heard the message yet.

Law clenched his fists as he thought of the African family on display at the fair. It echoed alongside the memory of his own parents who fled a life of sharecropping in Mississippi. In 1917 they had urged him to enlist. "Army the only way out for a black boy," his father had lectured. "Only way you can leave all this." He waved his arm around the one room kitchenette they had found in the neighborhood called the "Bucket of Blood," on LaSalle.

Oliver jay-walked across State just above 47th Street. West side of the street would have more shade. The Regal, around the corner, showing "Body and Soul" by someone named Micheaux. The marquee proudly proclaimed: "Climate Cool. SAT ONLY: See the movie and enjoy the Smooth Sepia Sound of Duke Ellington all for ONE PRICE." He took a step toward the lobby before remembering that it was Sunday. Oliver continued down State, hands in his pockets, lost in thought.

"Brother!" A strong voice called out. Oliver turned. For the first time all afternoon the voice did not belong to someone who looked down and out. Not at all. The speaker held out his hand and offered Oliver a handbill. "Take one. No charge." The man was neither tall nor short, but his shoulders were wide and his chest thick. He wore dark trousers and a light white shirt, buttoned at the neck. Oliver took him for a steel worker. A Chicago guy for certain, from his black booted foot to the gray newsboy hat pushed back on his head. His pale blue eyes and dark flowing mustache finished his look. "Mike." he smiled, "Mike Klonsky. I'm with the Party. You seen one of these yet, brother?"

The handbill bore the stamp of the International Brotherhood of Smelters and Rollers. The logo showed a worker, hammer raised above his head, ready to smash the mass of greedy, well-turned out capitalists (they all wore top-hats, Oliver noted) cowering at his feet. "DEFENCE OF THE WORKERS: THE MOMENT IS NOW." The announcement called all good Chicagoans to a mass meeting at 95th and Halsted, just outside the new library. "Black and white together," the handbill proclaimed, "we can fight and win."

"Thanks, man. I'm in the military," Oliver folded the handbill neatly, creasing the lines of the fold between the pad of his thumb and the second joint of his first finger. "Thanks, anyway." He slid the paper into the back pocket of his pants just behind his wallet. He took a step away, paused, and glanced back. "Never seen this before, 'black and white together'. That new for you boys?"

The man peered up from under the bill of his newsboy cap and smiled. "Just show up and you'll see how new."

∎

Two hours later, Oliver Law presented his pass to the sentry. The MP nodded at him and growled. "CO wants to see you in his office. Now."

Weathers sat at his desk, a fat cigar clenched in his jaws. The smoke curled in the sunlight that angled down from the window and onto the blotter covering his desk. He only had one eyebrow, the other interrupted by a scar that ran from the corner of his left eye to his chin.

"Sergeant Weathers?"

"You are a fucking day late and a dollar short, soldier."

"Sir?"

"You heard me. You are late!" He peered at the roster before him, running his forefinger down a list of names, like the names on a slave ship manifest. "Law. Day pass. August 14. See that August 14. Today is, and has been all day, August 15. You are a day late. And you are so far down this shit list I don't think you'll ever get off."

"I don't understand."

"Don't understand… what!"

"Don't understand, sir!" He stared at Weathers. Found less a scowl than a sneer. "I had a weekend pass. Due back tonight."

"The fuck you are. Says right here in black and white that you were due back yesterday. And I don't allow no one to make a monkey of me. Understand?"

There it was again. The familiar can't win for trying if you are Negro in America whipsaw. Kiss the man's ass and he owns you. Tell him to fuck off and he kills you. Oliver looked his CO in the eye. This had been coming.

51

"Permission to speak directly, sir?"

"Denied."

"I got nothing to say, then, sir."

Weathers took the cigar out of his mouth. He allowed the spittle to drip down onto his fingers and then shook the ash onto his desktop. Blinking, he leaned over, puffed up his cheeks and blew the grey-blue mound onto Oliver's trousers.

"And clean up your pants, Law."

Oliver weighed the risks. Face a court-martial for smashing Weathers in his face or endure three miserable months of peeling potatoes and a dishonorable discharge. Looking Weathers up and down, from the black bristles that sprouted from his ears to the scuff-marks on the cuffs of his pants, Oliver Law realized he had no choice at all. He balled his fists, screwed up his courage, and smiled.

"Sir. You have every reason to discipline me. I expect to terminate my enlistment this fall and ask only that you treat me fairly during the interim." He felt quite pleased with his use of the word 'interim,' certain that Weathers had never heard a soldier, much less a Negro one, use a word like that. He saluted, turned on a dime, and walked out the door.

"Took 'em three months to kick my ass out of the Army," Oliver Law surveyed the men standing before him. "But not before I learned the only lesson I want you to internalize." Two of the faces stared blankly up at Law. "Learn, baby. Learn," Law grinned. He stood there on Halsted, more than two years after his discharge, his green fatigues faded, his-ankle high black boots creased and soft and clumped with dirt. He looked the men up and down, and spoke evenly. "And now I understand you fellas want to fight. Is that right?"

The twenty or so young men nodded. Some were black, some white, but all wore the tattered long-sleeved shirt, white with no collar, of the Apprentice Steel Workers Union. They didn't begin screaming in unison and Law felt good about that. The picket signs stood stacked in the corner of the union hall and he could hear the police sirens outside winding tighter and tighter, louder and louder. They liked to do that, the cops, when they got ready to bust a strike. Someone must have told them that making noise would put a scare into the men.

"What if they offer to settle?" one of the men asked, picking at a scab on his chin.

"Just a scam," a voice from the back sneered. "They'll try anything to get at us."

"Divide and conquer," another agreed. "They'll offer the colored guys a deal, then change it at the last minute."

Oliver scrutinized the workers. Some stood with hands stuffed into their pockets, others shuffled their feet, glancing around. The sirens were louder now. "Only thing for it is a vote." Just like the Committee told him. Go for the vote when the rank and file get antsy. It builds solidarity.

It took ten minutes, but when the speeches finished and the ballots lay crumpled at the base of the table, Local 11 of the Steel Workers Union Organizing Committee had agreed to walk out the next morning following the company picnic. Nice touch, Oliver thought. Assemble peaceably, then walk out.

"We'll meet at eleven," Law announced, "just at the front gate. Don't forget — bring lunch baskets and a few baseball bats." He winked.

■

First thing Oliver saw, even before he slammed the door of his '28 Model T, first thing, was the line of blue.

Blue police hats, brims shiny, blue police jackets their gold buttons up and down in two neat rows, and off in the distance the deeper dirty blue of Lake Michigan.

The chain-link fence around the J and L plant, nicknamed Francis after the founder's daughter, gleamed in the early morning sunlight. Beautiful day for a picnic. That had been the idea. Bring out all the workers and their families for a picnic on the steel mill's manicured grounds. Who would ever dream of disrupting all the kids and wives on a holiday?

They had discussed this for a month. How to take over the plant. Some had argued for a strike. Others urged caution. The compromise, transforming the company Memorial Day picnic into a sit-in, seemed a final stroke of genius. That way, when everyone came into work on Monday, they'd be sitting pretty. But the staggered lines of men in blue, their black billy-clubs at the ready, chest-high, told Oliver all he needed to know. Some fink had already blown the whistle.

The police stood, backs against the fence, shaking their clubs forward and back, forward and back.

Hard to even see their eyes beneath the brims of their caps. Behind them, a man in a light blue summer suit sported a white straw skimmer. He stood with his face turned away from the sun, casting his features in shadow. He held a megaphone at his side and watched.

Oliver watched too.

Watched as a dozen old jalopies chugged up to the field that stretched from the plant entrance to the road; watched as families clambered out or down from running boards and rumble-seats; watched as women in plaid skirts carried straw picnic baskets on the crooks of their arms and shooed their children in front of them with their free hand; watched as the men turned their cars around and, sputtering blue exhaust, parked away from the grounds; watched as the workers and their families stared at the blue-clad police while children pointed, some clinging to the skirts and sleeves of their mothers and fathers; watched as the blue line moved toward the picnickers, black batons beating the air.

The newspapers would call it a police action to prevent violence. Oliver Law knew differently. As soon as the police started walking toward them Oliver waved his right arm, motioning the women and children behind the workers. They didn't move fast enough, not fast at all considering that none of them, save himself, had served in the military. Instead, the workers and their families all stood shoulder to shoulder. Some of the men grabbed baseball bats from the arms of the boys, others turned and raised their fists, and one woman reached into the straw basket on her arm and pulled out a saw-toothed carving knife intended for the ham that the Union pledged to provide. Oliver did not recognize her, but the woman, sturdy and young with a bandana over her hair and a yellow dress that hung loosely from her shoulders, raised the knife over her head and thrust the blade forward toward the advancing line of police.

That was enough for the cops. Snarling, one drew his revolver.

Oliver's breath caught, hoping he only intended to fire into the air. The cop leveled the barrel at the strikers just as one of the workers raised his bat. The bat and the gun exploded at the same instant. A deep gash split the furrowed brow of the cop. A worker standing behind the line of unionists screamed, grabbing at his chest. Blood spurted from between his fingers as he stared, open-mouthed.

The wounded worker fell to his knees, his hands above his head in a V. The cop, face flushed with anger and fear, raised his club. As he cocked his arm back behind his head, a woman darted between him and the kneeling worker. Oliver couldn't tell if the policeman aborted his swing in mid-arc, or if the woman forced him to change the trajectory of his club. It smashed through her shoulder, sending her sprawling to the ground before continuing toward the worker's neck. The force of the blow knocked him forward onto his chest where he reached out, fingers spread wide in supplication. The woman, her dress covered in dirt and blood, lay prostrate.

The two sides surged forward screaming, pistols and clubs held high. Caught in the center of the fray, the wounded striker, the bleeding police officer, and the disheveled woman could only cover their heads with their arms. The two lines clashed, eyes glaring red into the faces of their adversaries, their breath hot and rancid. Oliver stared at his fallen comrades, then forced himself between the two opposing lines. Shielding a group of men with his arms, he pushed back against his own line of strikers, forcing his comrades away from the police, creating a space between the two groups.

Behind him the blue line stopped. The officers bent over, hands on their knees, chests heaving as they fought for breath.

"This isn't the way!" Oliver shouted back at them. "We only came to picnic. Maybe to picket. This isn't the way!"

"That ain't what they said at the station!" one of the policemen shouted back, standing straight with his arms spread, a mirror of Oliver.

"Yeah? Who told you diff'rent?" one of the men next to Oliver pressed up against the barrier of his arms. "Who told you diff'rent?"

Oliver stiffened. He looked at the officer, his voice never rising, trying to command a sense of calm in the vortex of violence that surrounded them. "Who?"

The policeman tilted his head back over his shoulder, in the direction of the man in the light-blue suit. "Him."

Oliver raised his eyes, tracking back to the chain-link fence, now coated red by the late morning sunlight. "No one there," he whispered, dropping his arms. "We've been had. All of us."

"He said you would all be armed and led by a nigger escaped from some penitentiary down south."

"Only got the nigger part right," Oliver smirked. "Rest is bull-shit. Any of you armed?" he looked back at the workers, "Anyone got a gun?" He shot a glance at the woman still lying face down between the two lines. "Maybe you thought she was packing?"

The policeman just stared blankly ahead. "We had enough today, men. Best call an ambulance, get these people outta here and patched up."

"We can help," Oliver bent over to cover the wounded policeman with the flag of one of the workers.

Only then did he allow the grief and to anger rise slowly in his chest.

∎

Two months later Oliver Law walked into the basement of the South Side Community Arts Center and the offices of the Chicago Communist Party. A young Negro man sat at a desk behind a pile of soft-cover books. Bold red capital letters declared Red Front, smaller print adding A publication of the John Reed Society in smaller print.

"Can I help you?" The man offered his hand. "Name's Wright, Richard Wright."

Oliver shook his hand. "I'm here to volunteer my services to the Republican Government," he grinned as he said it, "to the legally elected and beleaguered government of Spain."

"On behalf of the International Brigades," Wright grinned, "Welcome aboard, Brother."

CHAPTER FOUR
RENA

I

She had been instructed carefully. Take the metro to Saint-Lazare, turn to the left, then a short stroll to the small hotel whose name she couldn't remember.

Rena Thompson hoisted the canvas bag they had given her on Eleventh Street two weeks earlier. She was grateful for the weight it added to her thin woolen coat, although she still felt the chill standing in the fading gray light of evening. Men and women bustled past, taking no notice of a lost American Negro girl. The men carried thin loaves of bread tucked under their arms, the women wore colored scarves draped over their shoulders. Like extras on a movie set. Someone on Eleventh had told her Paris would be just like New York. Now she knew they were full of shit. Just like they had been about a lot of other things.

No matter. Put yourself to the task at hand, she scolded herself. When the hospital in New York told her that she had to live with the other "nigra girls" on 137th Street, or when the surgeon told her that she "didn't have any idea what she was doing" or when the Irish cops tried to arrest her for "disturbing the peace," she had taken the blows and kept her eyes on the prize. That's what they always told her at home — "take the punch and move on up, Rena. You better than them. Don't you forget it."

She looked around again, reading nearby signs. Hotel Gare St. Lazare — that wasn't the one. She headed further down the street. Getting darker. Peering into windows and up at white blinking lights clouded by a mist of near-freezing rain she searched for the name of the hotel she couldn't remember. A police officer on the corner peeked a look at her. She could feel his eyes, but didn't dare meet them.

The suitcase was heavy and awkward and made her feel as if she was wrestling with a puddle of pig iron. She plopped it down and sat on top of it, knees almost to her chin. Dealing with crackers in New York was one thing, but being lost in a city where she couldn't speak a word and where she hadn't the foggiest notion of where she was was another dilemma entirely. She felt like Little Orphan Annie, tossed this way and that by, as her minister put it, "dem vicissitudes of life."

A small Frenchman paused and looked at her. She had to lean forward to hear him. "Madam?" He held his palms up and shrugged his shoulders at the same time, his smile wide and welcoming.

Rena struggled to remember the word for hotel. *"Guerre?"*

The man's eyes smiled. "If you are looking for the War, you have missed it by twenty years. The Gare, on the other hand, is behind you." He spoke in the perfect English of a British movie actor, pointing with a flourish to the station.

"Oh!" Rena cried and laughed in frustration. "I meant hotel but I don't even know which hotel and I don't, as you can tell, speak any French and I'm going" — she took a deep breath and smiled. "Well I don't think I can tell you where I'm going. I need to find the hotel. Can you help me?"

"Pierre Mendes, at your service," he bowed slightly, tipping his hat.

He reminded her of Rumpelstiltskin, this tiny man with a big smile and watery eyes.

"Oh, thank you Mister Pierre. I was told the hotel was near the train station. I was so worried about getting here — my first trip outside the United States — anywhere, actually — and I completely forgot the name."

"Hotel Condorcet," he nodded down the street. "Right over there."

"How in the world…?"

"Let me walk you there. It is almost dark. We want our friends in the Brigades to make it to the border, not just to the hotel."

He hoisted the valise to his shoulder and guided her down *rue St. Lazare*, past the *Lycee Condorcet*, and on to a narrow cobblestone street. "This is *rue du Coq*" he glanced up at her and winked. "Means Rooster. Symbol of France."

He led her across the street, avoiding the broom of an elderly woman sweeping water down a gutter. They crossed diagonally then squeezed between two parked cars, a model she had never heard of before. Ren-alt, she said to herself and grinned. Like her name. She stopped to run a finger along the nameplate on the rear deck of the black car. "A Renault," Pierre said, making the name into something that sounded like wreno. "The auto workers in the CGT, the union, walked out last summer and that's how we got to the Popular Front."

Rena had, of course, read about the Popular Front. It was all over the pages of the Daily Worker. She had been walking down 125th street on a hot, hot day last July and a man had called to her, "Hey, Rena! Check this out!" He had pushed the newspaper into her hands. "There's gonna be a meeting about this stuff, the general strike in France, the fascists in Spain. Time to do something." And she had.

That weekend was the first time she had gone to Eleventh Street. First time she had met anyone who called themselves a communist. When she asked what she could do, they asked what she already did. And when she told them, they had replied, "We'll need nurses. Surgical nurses. Can you do that?" She could, and she told them about her training at Harlem Hospital, about working with the white surgeon who liked to pinch her ass and call her a dumb bitch for not handing him the sponge the same second he demanded it. Six months later and here she was following a tiny Frenchman down a rain-splattered street in Paris to god only knew where.

He pressed a small black button on the brass panel next to the massive wrought-iron door. When the metallic click sounded he pushed his hand through the grates and swung it open easily. "After you, mademoiselle." He propped the door open with his shoulder, dropped her suitcase on the floor and walked over to the desk. The concierge's bell pinged down the hallway, followed a split second later by the appearance of a young woman, who introduced herself as Helene and handed a gigantic skeleton key to Rena. *"Vous-êtes dans le 31."* When Rena looked mystified, Helene smiled pleasantly. "Excuse me. I mean number 31."

The room contained only an iron bed, a pitcher of water, and a rickety wood chair. A small mirror on the back of the door obscured the tiny spy-hole, revealing instead her reflection. A young, slim, light-brown woman with a tight cap of short black hair. She hated her lips. Too broad, too full. But her eyes, bright and almost turquoise, now those were her best feature. Didn't even mind when they called her Betty Boop. Hardly looked any different from the young student who lived at the Nurses Residence on 137th for two years. The cold stream of air that invaded the tiny room, bitter even in October, was no different either. The only difference was that she'd be leaving the next day for Spain.

She wrapped her coat closer to her body. That was just like Harlem too. There she slept fully clothed, like a mummy, arms tight across her chest. The tiny radiator in the corner wheezed, clanked twice, and died.

There was a knock so soft at the door that she had to press her ear against it to tell if someone was actually there. She opened it.

"I thought you might enjoy a sample of some of the local fare." The tall black man sounded so classy. He wore his beret tipped to the side and his corded trousers made him look like a long-lost bohemian, like the men Rena had seen in Greenwich Village. He stepped softly into her room.

"Forgive me. I neglected to introduce myself. I'm Oliver Law. From Chicago. Ollie will do."

"I'm…"

He smiled broadly. "I know who you are, Rena. We've been expecting you. Come on. Let's go eat."

■

Compared to the IRT the Paris metro was clean and quiet. It charmed her to open the door with a small metal latch, to flip up the seats, to look around and see the people with their heads buried in newspapers, paying one another no mind.

An old man, his right hand bandaged and gripping the cross-piece of his crutch, glared at her and she gasped. Oliver pointed at the sign above the seat she had taken, *Réservé à crux qui sort mutilés à la guerre.*

She didn't need to read French to understand. The Great War veteran who had lost his leg, the stubble on his face white and prickly, wanted his seat. Rena shuddered and moved aside.

The men on Eleventh Street had painted a picture of democratic commitment, class solidarity, and racial equality. The Party would see to everything and everyone, and they prized the participation of young Negroes. Nurses were needed at the front, they told her, but the battle was between the forces of freedom and the darkness of fascism. Victory in Spain, they trumpeted, would make for racial harmony at home. It sounded grand.

But no one spoke of the man with one leg, dressed in frayed blue denim, his face a mask of pain and anger. How many more injured would she see before this was over, this battle between the forces of decency and evil? The wiry man with round glasses on Eleventh

Street, his striped shirt rolled to the elbows, he hadn't said anything about casualties. Just handed her a set of papers, a ticket for the boat, and sent her off on what he called "the grand adventure of our generation."

Oliver led her to the escalator, his hand guiding her arm. Moments later they emerged at street level. Rena couldn't believe her eyes. Before them spread a vast open plaza, bigger even than Union Square, surrounded by apartments, cafés, and news kiosks. Busses and cars and bicycles sped past, each intent on arriving at their destination first. And people! Everywhere there were throngs of people sitting on benches, walking in pairs, and standing in small clusters smoking cigarettes. Above the buildings, neon signs in red and white beckoned. Madison Avenue or Times Square? Some of both.

Oliver read her thoughts. "It's called Bastille. Where they stated their Revolution in 1789." Rena thought for a moment, remembering her high-school history class and the prison that the Parisians had stormed.

She looked around. "Where is it?"

"Long gone." Oliver jumped back gracefully to avoid a dark black sedan that leapt halfway up the curb at their feet. Before Rena had time to react he was pulling her away again. "Come on, I've got something to show you."

Place de la Bastille churned with life, with action, with drama. In the darkness, only amplified by the damp of the season, the place burned with light. The illumination on unfinished Liberty marble, drew Parisians to the symbol of the Revolution and the Republic. Half a block to the left, a restaurant, the deep red letters of the *Brasserie Bofinger* dominated the intersection of *rue de la Bastille* and *rue Jean Beausire*.

Rena couldn't keep from staring. What in the world was a Negro girl from Harlem doing here? She stared as women in hats adorned with gold ostrich feathers entered on the arms of men in black coats and top hats, swirling ivory canes in their white-gloved hands.

"Yes. I think we should start at the bottom. It should only take you about thirty minutes in this place to figure out our rationale behind enlisting you in the struggle." With that he brushed past the bowing doorman, livery bristling with gold braid. She could hear her grandmother's Carolina accent warning her as she entered. "Gal. We don't mix with dese folk. You be careful, hear. They likely as not to take you for a ride." Essie's speech and always been muddled with smoke from the corn-cob pipe shoved in her jaw. Rena loved the way the old woman clutched her home-died indigo dress, rubbing her fingers against the material as if to make it soft. No one at Bofinger's wore indigo.

The *maître d* led them to the most magnificent table she had ever seen. Set for six with a marble-top covered with gold-rimmed porcelain dinnerware and sparkling crystal, it made the Cotton Club look like a juke joint. A set of walnut-inlaid mirrors reflected the centerpiece that reached up toward the cut-glass skylight. "It is a hand carved ivory Strasbourg Herron," he announced in perfect English. "Monsieur Law thought you might be particularly impressed." With that he pulled back the damask-covered dining chair and bade them a convivial evening.

Rena took in the room in a glance, like drinking a pint of white lightning in one shot. No one had paid their entrance any attention. Bald heads and white beards, diamond chokers and elegant wraps caught their attention. But two black Americans? Not even a raised brow. They must be right, she reflected. The men on Eleventh Street who told her that the revolution would end racism. "No more segregation, no more lynchings, no more Scottsboro Boys," they had proclaimed. These are all cultural reflections of the substructure of capitalism. Like the state itself, the fiction of racial superiority would fade away in the new society.

She remembered the moment in nursing school when she had taken her tray to the table where the white doctors ate lunch. It was as if they had seen a ghost. One minute they had been slurping spaghetti, the next they were shuffling their plates onto oatmeal-colored melamine trays as fast as they could. By the time Rena looked up, the table had emptied. And it hadn't ended there. No. Next day the hospital administrator had called her on the carpet and informed her that she "belonged" at the Negro nurses' table. That the hospital had gone to untold inconvenience to make the table available, even in the face of opposition from those who wanted to ban Negroes and whites from taking their lunch breaks in the same room. If she really understood, the administrator had explained, she would just "play ball."

Something inside her had flipped. "You mean kiss their lily-white asses?" she had shouted, sitting right down on the red and green floral carpet onto which she had been called. "You don't like this?" She stared right into the man's pasty face, "Well, tough titty." The man had been so flabbergasted that he had sent her from his office, and never mentioned another word about the issue. Next week all the nurses, black and white, picketed the dining room, forcing the dietitian to remove the sign on the table that read, White Only Reserved.

Sitting unremarked in this restaurant that looked like the most expensive brothel in the world, now that offered real evidence of what they had meant on Eleventh Street.

"I know," Oliver looked at her, breaking the spell. "You're thinking that if even these rich folks don't notice us, then perhaps…." His voice trailed off. He looked around and raised his eyebrows.

"They are just too damned busy with their own affairs to pay us any attention. If Franco walked in right now they'd stand, applaud, and give him the Falangist salute faster than you can say Cool Papa Bell."

"How…?" the question hung in the air.

"Because it's what we all first think in an establishment like this.

The reason I brought you here was to put the real enemy on display."

Oliver pushed his chair back slightly and leaned on the table, left arm folded under his chin, his right panning the room.

"There. See the man with the cigarette holder?"

The room felt hollow.

"His name is Joachaim Phelps. His business trades high-interest loans for safety."

Rena closed her hands on the table. Her mother once said that her "high yeller" coloring — freckles and turquoise eyes — would open doors. But, until this day, no door had ever opened easily.

"What in the world kind of business is that?" Rena knew about loan-sharking, who didn't, coming from Harlem. But this sounded far more sinister.

"He's a fixer. Dutch and British. Say you need to get out of someplace. Say you're a newspaper editor in Germany, or Italy, or Spain. Doesn't matter. You know they are watching you, that if you try to leave they will toss you in jail and that," he clapped his palms against each other, as if he were washing his hands, "will be that. Phelps gets you out."

"You said the enemy," Rena leaned closer to Oliver, taking in the way he looked at her and at the room at the same time. He was handsome in a way, darker than she, but not dark, with close cropped hair and a mustache like Billy Ekstine. "What makes him the enemy?"

"Because he trades on misery and politics," Oliver adjusted his leather wristband, glancing down at his watch. "His price is eighty percent of his client's net worth."

Rena gasped.

"And then he turns around and makes that money available, at ten percent interest, to the 'host' country's secret police for 'special projects.'"

"Ten for vig, not so bad," Rena shrugged.

"How in the world do you know about vig?"

Rena looked him in the eye and smiled, "You know where I'm from. Who don't know vig?"

"When I said ten percent," Oliver smiled back at her, "I meant a day."

"Oh my," she paused, her mouth open. "My, oh my."

Oliver took her hand in his own. "Don't worry," he whispered as she stiffened. "I'm not making a pass. I don't want them to think we're talking about them."

Her smile said she understood. Her eyes suggested something else.

"On the other side of the room," he continued, his thumb tracing a circle on the back of her hand, "The woman in black. Low-cut short hair, cameo around her neck. She's from Bulgaria. Rumors say she works with NKVD, the Soviet Secret police. Perhaps for the Austrian kleisto. Of course, that is exactly what she intends for people to think. In fact, she is an agent for the Gestapo, gathering information on German Communists in Paris."

The woman rose from her chair, plucked a black shiny tube of lipstick from her sequined evening bag, and walked toward the stairs that led to the lower level of the restaurant.

"She's pretending to powder her nose," Oliver explained. "She's probably going to make a drop."

"Drop?"

"Leave information for someone else. Tuck it away in the toilet tank, or behind the mirror. Doesn't matter. She works against everything we believe in."

Rena rubbed her left hand on her forehead, and looked down.

"I never knew. It's all so complicated. Makes our life back home seem simple. Either one is a motherfucking racist or they aren't. But — all these hidden identities? Where is the real person?"

Something caught her eye.

"What is that?" she pointed behind Oliver, at the wall behind his head. "What's that!"

He laughed. "It's famous. Couple of years ago there was a scandal here. An official named Stavisky was suspected of selling government secrets. Riled everyone up, especially the local fascists. They came looking for a Socialist deputy who ate lunch here. Shot the place up. Those bullet holes are the souvenir. Missed the gent, made a complete shambles of the place. That's why we bring volunteers like you here. Show you how the real world works. No more idealist stuff about defeating the bad guys."

Rena withdrew her hand. "I get it. The real world of cynical Europeans where nothing is what it seems."

"You're a quick study." Oliver raised his hand and summoned the waiter.

He continued speaking softly as they waited for their dinner. "We know quite a bit about you. Rabble-rousing to get on the girls' basketball team in high school, working for that Negro surgeon in East Harlem, and then your stunt with the dining room."

She grinned, straightening her napkin and tucking it into the top of her green-wool dress. "Here's something I bet you and the boys downtown don't know about me."

"Surprise me."

"I got arrested."

"Disturbing the peace in '34," he winked. "We know that."

"Bet you don't know why."

He stared at her for a moment, then wrinkled his nose in defeat.

"Last year, after I'd been working for Harlem Hospital, and after the to-do with the dining room, I noticed how unsanitary the conditions had become. When the city slashed the hospital budget they cut back the staff and it showed. Only two nurses in the newborn unit when they needed six, shifts that didn't disinfect when they should have, a steep rise in staph and sepsis — I was convinced that the hospital needed changes. So I wrote the Regents a letter telling them what I thought. Nice and polite, even had it typed. They told me to mind my own business, transferred my ass out of the operating room, and put me in the delivery room. I was the only Negro on the staff there. Well, you know I didn't like that and I didn't like how they treated the locals who depended on the hospital for medicine. So, I did what any red-blooded Negro girl with an education would do. I organized! There they were covering the hospital with murals sponsored by the WPA and they couldn't maintain minimum sanitary conditions. Got my dander up. Way up. We marched and marched and then one day ten patients came down with diarrhea, then twelve more, and then another twenty. No one died, but it showed the white directors that we were on the money. They put me back in the operation room, added a new schedule for cleaning, and even integrated the nursing staff."

Oliver placed his coffee cup in the saucer and leaned back. "Quite a tale. That's probably why they allowed you to use the hospital as a warehouse for all those medical supplies we sent to Ethiopia."

"Sure it was. They couldn't help themselves. We really had them that time."

She had a faraway look in her eyes. "You know I'd never been so angry in my life. Taking chances with the health of black children like that. And when I thought that there might be some connection between the way they ran that hospital and the way those Italian fascists treated them Ethiopians, and then the rumors about Negro women in Alabama getting sterilized, when I thought about that I said to myself, 'Rena Thompson, you ain't had all this training for nothing. Do something to make the world better. Don't go letting the bastards take it over no more.' And that's why I found a way to get over here."

By the time her story finished, the restaurant had emptied. Waiters had peeled off their black jackets and cleared the tables, the maître d' had fallen asleep atop a table, and the only sound came from the sliver being sorted in the kitchen.

"Look at this," Rena said, lowering her voice to a whisper. "Hell of a place. I'll never forget the bullet holes."

They returned to the hotel after midnight, catching the last metro and walking through the deserted *Gare St. Lazare,* where their footsteps echoed like pebbles tossed gently against the marble floor. When they emerged on the street they discovered that a film of black ice had coated the sidewalk. Rena clung to Oliver's arm, pressing herself against him, holding on as she struggled to find her balance. The streets were empty and they had to ring the bell at the hotel to rouse the night clerk. At the landing outside her room Oliver took a step back and looked into Rena's eyes. Then he took her hand and kissed it gallantly.

"Goodnight. I will not see you again. Tomorrow you walk first to La Madeline, where you will be shown you how to take the train to the border. It is a long and boring ride, but the passage over the mountains will test you, just as I have tonight."

"Test? Does this mean that I passed?"

"With flying colors. We had to know if you were politically reliable."

"And how did you figure that?"

"When you didn't pull your hand away."

"If you'd really been flirting I'd have kicked your ass." Some part of her knew better.

"I know. It was part of the test."

He bowed and said goodnight again, leaving Rena Thompson to sit by herself in a tiny hotel room in Paris, waiting for the sun to rise on the next step of her journey. She had no doubt that she'd meet Oliver again one day. She only wondered whether he'd try to hold her hand next time.

Following her train trip from Paris to the Republican base in Albacete, south of Barcelona, the head of the Loyalist Medical Service had ordered Rena to report to a "restoration" unit in Madrid the next day.

"But I'm a trained emergency room nurse," Rena protested. Loudly.

"Captain Thompson, I appreciate your experience, but the Republic needs you for something else."

Perhaps this was not the right moment to challenge a petty bureaucrat. Later, she thought. Later.

∎

The Citroën took all night to drive from Albacete. They dropped Rena at the gates of Villa Paz, a dozen kilometers south of Madrid in an area where the fighting had substantially subsided. She walked along a tree-lined road to the Villa, which sat nearly a kilometer back from the gold-tipped wrought-iron gate of the entrance. With her cape draped over her shoulders and a white nurses cap on her head, Rena laughed at herself. Who could've imagined a Negro woman from New York walking down such a clearly royal path?

She cast her gaze over the grounds of the Villa and was surprised to see cows and goats grazing everywhere. Scattered randomly across the property were dozens of make-shift huts. Built of wood and cardboard, the windowless hovels had rusted sheet-metal roofs, clearly scavenged from abandoned automobiles. Ahead of her, near the marble steps that led into the white-washed Villa, a graceful circle of cypress trees surrounded a tiled swimming pool. Rena walked through the trees, curious to identify the contents of the pool. Perhaps this wouldn't be such a difficult assignment after all.

But the pool was empty — save for the odor of animal slurry and, of course, the pigs. Oinking and squealing as they rooted through the gumbo of shit and straw and garbage that lined the bottom. "Jesus fucking Christ" she swore as the lowing of a cow interrupted the static of pig grunts and whines. Behind her a woman dressed in black from head to toe, surely a resident of one of the hovels, was harvesting the dung of a small herd of cows that milled around her. She bent down, picked up the dried shit and placed it in the fold of her skirt.

"They use it for heating." The voice was unmistakably British and male. "The peasants took this place over after Franco attacked. Their way of taking back what was theirs, I guess."

He wore the cap of an officer in the medical corps, but the clothing of a street-cleaner. Blue cotton pants and tunic, dark black boots caked with mud and dung.

"Welcome, nurse Thompson. I'm Dr. Livingston. And yes, you may presume." He smiled. "I'm used to that. I'm the head of this," he swept his hand across the vista of shacks and huts and cattle. He hadn't shaved for several days, and the black stubble of his beard contrasted sharply with his ruddy cheeks. If he's twenty-five, Rena thought, it's a miracle.

"Of course, you must be wondering what in the world you are doing here."

"You got that right, Doctor."

"We are a team, and you are part of our team now."

"Go on. I ain't made up my mind on that yet." She smiled at him.

"Our assignment is clear. The reorganization of the army, in defense of the Republic, calls for an end to these fly-by-night medical units that sometimes go to battle, sometimes go home. We are to clean up this place, and turn it into a training hospital. When we are finished they assure me we'll be transferred to the front where they really need us."

"Sounds important. Even noble," Rena's mind was spinning so she kept her words to a minimum.

"Indeed. It does sound noble. But we have two small issues. Them," he pointed to the peasant huts, "and this." This time to the shovel. "They have only given us hand tools, little money, and nothing else. A real challenge, eh? Rather like the Augean Stables, if I don't say."

She liked his British way of speaking. Sounded like the movies. Charles Laughton, someone like that.

"Augean?"

"Oh, just something from Greek mythology."

Livingston guided Rena into the villa and showed her the nursing quarters — a single room behind the kitchen. Then he asked her if she knew how to cook.

"Do you?" she responded, deadpan.

Livingston startled. Then recovered, looking down.

"Forgive me, Nurse Thompson. I meant no offense." His apology felt sincere.

"None taken." Rena thought for a moment, then added, "for now."

∎

Rena discovered that she was the sole nurse in a team of six doctors — all surgeons — and three orderlies. It took weeks of backbreaking manual labor to clean the Villa. They shoveled shit till their arms ached, scrubbed the floors with a disinfectant so strong it made them feel faint, and even painted the rooms upstairs, the to-be wards, all in white. And they all worked. Even the doctors.

Each night the team sat together for something that passed for dinner. Nominally, the meals were field rations, but occasionally they enjoyed a grey substance that Livingston dubbed Mystery Meat. With the exception of Livingston and Rena the rest of the team came from non-English speaking countries — France, Germany, Greece, and as Livingston remarked, "Australia." Tony the Australian-Italian orderly, laughed with everyone else, "Right you are, mate." Still, they all spoke English with each other; after all as Livingston said, it was the "universal language of medical science."

A month into their assignment they gathered in the maternity ward, a space rumored to have been the official boudoir of the King's last mistress and which until recently, had been occupied by a shepherd family and their six breeding ewes. Livingston sat at the head of a table alongside a stranger.

"Colleagues, I want to introduce General Orlovsky. He's here as our Political Commissar and represents the central Republican command in Albacete."

Orlovsky, a slip of a man with close-cropped hair and a tiny triangle of a beard, was dressed in the green field uniform of the Republican Army.

"We have some important directives that we will augment within the next month. They will take effect in the wake of the Brunete Offensive which will begin later this week."

Tony rolled his eyes, then winked at Rena. This Russian bureaucrat, she thought, he's about to tell us the new rules.

He pulled a piece of paper out from the "secret" pocket of his tunic. Rena noted his manicured fingernails and the delicate translucent skin of his hand. The paper, a single page covered in purple-blue stenography ink, fluttered in Orlovsky's hand. Was he nervous?

He read each of the four directives with a flat voice, devoid of affect, save for his eyebrows that raised slightly at the end of each sentence. Makes him look like Mickey Rooney, she decided.

"One — As of today, the General Headquarters of the Republican Army of Spain has integrated the International

Brigades into its central command structure. Two — As of today, all independent militia units serving in the Republican Army or with the International Brigades will cease to exist and will be integrated into the disciplinary structure of the military chain of command." He paused. "Three — As of today, all women serving in the Republican Army of Spain will assume rear echelon responsibilities." Rena felt her blood begin to boil. "Four — As of today, the Command Structure of the Republican Army of Spain will require the proper appointment of officers and the wearing of appropriate insignia of rank. Officers "elected" previously to command positions will be reassigned according to the protocols of the regular army."

He stopped and took off his pince-nez and wiped it with his perfectly-ironed white handkerchief.

"Any questions?" he asked, in a way that signaled he did not wish to answer any. They stared back at him in silence.

∎

The next morning two Renault supply trucks pulled up to the front of the Villa. With green canvas covers tied down over rear flatbeds, the trucks were large enough for a dozen passengers and stable enough to transport medical equipment. Freezing winter rain had coated the canvas, darkening it. It soaked them as they struggled to load their gear. The drivers left the twin top mounted windshield wipers running while they waited, and Rena couldn't shake the swish-swish sound out of her brain.

It took less than an hour for the team to carry their personal belongings and stow them in the lead truck alongside the strapped crates of medical materials that had already been loaded in Madrid.

"Wait," Rena called out, "hold on a minute. I'll be right back."

She turned and ran down the road that led back to the villa.

When she came to the first shanty, one with two goats grazing and three children playing football, she halted. The door of the hut opened and she reached inside and handed the woman a small roll of bills. *"Para los niños."* She had practiced the phrase the day before. "For the children."

Rena rejoined the staff behind the second truck. Livingston extended a hand to help her climb up, then slid down the wooden bench to make space.

He looked exhausted. Rena reached out and touched his arm, squeezing him gently, and watched as he shut his eyes in grateful answer. She hoped he would allow himself the luxury of sleep on their ride to the front. She doubted there would be time for rest once they arrived in Brunete. As if he could read her thoughts, Livingston leaned his head back against the canvas and opened one eye.

"Anyone ever tell you, Captain Thompson? Anyone ever tell you that you are an angel?"

It felt good to be understood by someone she respected — someone who seemed capable of knowing what made her tick, and caring. Or was he? Politics always managed to creep in. It pissed her off to discover this thought mingling with Livingston's tenderness. She shook her head.

"Orlovsky. What did you think about him?" She tried to keep her voice measured, but couldn't hide a touch of disdain in her tone.

"Oh, I try not to bother with political stuff. Do our jobs, keep quiet, that's what I say."

"You can't mean that. Why are you here if not for the 'political stuff?' You don't fool me for a moment, Doctor Livingston."

"You really nailed him on that one!" Tony sat across from them and laughed. "I nearly split me daks." His thick curly hair fell into his eyes, giving him the appearance of a model for a second-rate Renaissance painter.

Rena stared at him with a question mark in her eyes.

"Oh, you know," he gestured at his trousers. "Me daks."

"Well listen Tony, and you too. And all of you. Here's what I think." In Spain Rena had rarely raised her voice, but that Orlovsky. He really got her goat this time.

"Sure. The stuff Orlovsky said doesn't affect us. Not directly. But the idea that this functionary can traipse down here and inform us that they've reorganized us — the whole International Brigades! Why did we volunteer in the first place? To help save this land, and their fragile new democracy from the bloody fascists. And then what do these Commissars do? They subvert the very thing we came to rescue."

She was shaking. The words just came out. The rest of the team said nothing. The humming and thumping of the tires were the only sound between them and utter silence.

Rena unbuttoned the clasp at her neck and took off her cloak. Still sitting, she bundled the blue wool in her lap, then raised it to her mouth. Her teeth found the round of International Brigades insignia that designated her as a Captain. All medical personal were given this appointment when they arrived. In seconds she had torn the stitches free with her teeth.

"If my comrades at the front are forced to surrender their democratic rank, then so will I."

She turned and threw the round patch out the back of the truck.

"Motherfucker!" she called after it. The men looked down in embarrassment. Only Tony looked up and spoke quietly. "Atta girl, Rena. We're with you."

∎

It had taken months of hard labor, from her arrival in Albacete to the pigpens of Villa Paz for Rena to earn her way. When she finally reported to the field tent at the Brunete front she fell to her knees and thanked the Baptist god her parents had prayed to with all the strength she had left.

With the rain still beating down on them, the nurses barely had time to turn on the electricity and test the generators — four Kohlers with their gold-embossed declaration: "Field Tested by Admiral Byrd." Rena supervised the hanging of white sheets from the walls and the lining of the dirt floor with burlap. "Feels like what my grandma told me about growin' up in the South," she commented to an uncomprehending orderly.

Two surgeons carried in a heavy wood table covered in white oilskin. Then a minute later, another. They would serve as the unit's operating tables, illuminated by several mobile lighting posts. Another two tables, also covered with shiny oilcloth held the Poupinel, a copper sterilizer loaded with instruments: scalpels, artery clamps, scissors, needles, saws, bone chisels, retractors, and probes. At last they wheeled in the makeshift anesthetist cart, a wheelbarrow holding an Ombredanne mask. She rested her hand for a moment on the glass and rubber instrument designed for the delivery of ether. "We squeeze this bladder," her instructor had told her a lifetime ago, pointing to a collapsible sac, "and it feeds the ether in this globe through the black rubber gasket to the patient's inhalation apparatus."

At nightfall the initial wave of wounded arrived, first in trickles, then in a flood. The team amputated sixteen legs, four hands, and performed six emergency colostomies. By daybreak the team had collapsed, exhausted, most sleeping where they had worked, tucked into corners of the operating theater.

Sometime in the early afternoon General Lîster, the Divisional Commander, stopped by and pinned two medals on Livingston's white coat, shook hands with the rest of the team, and left. His adjutant remained behind. While most of the doctors went back to catch a few more precious hours of sleep, he ordered Rena and the other nurses to scour the hillside for any survivors who could be "patched up."

Walking that battlefield, touching maimed bodies to detect what life, if any, remained, calling out for orderlies or the grave details, tested Rena. She choked on the human destruction, the mayhem, and the terrible smell of death. It was one thing to see grainy black and white photographs in the newspapers. Standing amidst the devastation and ruin was something else entirely, something no one could have prepared her for.

The human remains scatted across the battlefield made all the petty politics behind the lines seem insignificant, she ruminated. She worked her way back to the Field Hospital, her thoughts heavy with all she had seen. Perhaps now she could find some time to sleep.

How curious, then, to discover that graceful lion of a man, the man she first met in Paris, talking so matter-of-factly with a newspaper foreign correspondent.

I was conducting a battlefield interview with Law. I don't actually recall meeting Miss Thompson at that juncture, but I came to know her quite well later. She told me that I dressed like a Spanish peasant but looked rather tall and almost elegant. It never occurred to her that she would see either one of us, me or Law, again.

I

PARIS, PERPIGNAN, ALBACETE, 9 November 1936

Yiorgos Georghiou, known as Costas, sauntered down the same gloomy street near *Gare St. Lazare* that Rena had followed weeks before. He was looking for a shop that sold Turkish coffee, the kind that reminded him of home, hot and thick and full of sugar. Instead, on rue Tronchet, behind *L'église de la Madeline,* he found himself standing before a small gold lettered sign that identified the offices of Maurice Thorez and the French Communist Party. Posted on the door, the morning edition of L'Humanite announced *"le decisión lache"* of the French and British governments to decline the Spanish plea for help against Franco's invading army.

"Bullshit" he muttered to himself in English, the language of his schooling. "They are doing the same here as at home. Old divide and conquer routine. Bloody English cowards."

It took him twenty minutes to sign up for the first contingent of volunteers. "Anyone else from Cyprus?" he asked the black American who patiently filled out his paper-work patiently.

Oliver Law glanced up at him and asked, "Cyprus, that's part of Greece, isn't it?" Costas nodded, the truth too hard to explain. The English owned the island, and the Greek and Turkish Cypriots who lived there despised the English for a thousand reasons. He also didn't bother to mention that he belonged to a student communist group with ties in both Greek and Turkish circles. This American would never understand what it meant to be truly oppressed. His friends on Cyprus considered American liberals as stubbornly authoritarian as the

81

British. But, as he reminded himself, this was the time of the Popular Front, and they were all friends. For the moment.

Law raised his eyebrows when Costas told him he had turned eighteen that year, then shrugged and said, "In the name of the Popular Front we welcome you to the International Brigades. You leave in the morning. *Bonne chance.*"

∎

The train reeked of garlic and sausages. Men with wizened faces and white stubbled necks sat in their compartments, singing Basque football songs as they sliced cured meats with large pocket knifes, using their calloused thumbs as carving boards. Bottles of cheap red wine lay scattered on the floor of the SNCF regional train that had departed Paris eighteen hours earlier. The railway workers, the cheminots, had assured Thorez' headquarters in Paris that they would take special care of his passengers.

Costas, who had found his way to Paris from Nicosia by way of Rome and Zurich, wasn't aware that the French communist union, the CGT, considered him part of their precious cargo. All he knew was what the intake officer, the American Oliver Law, had told him. He was to sit quietly until the last stop. When it came time to descend in Perpignan someone would contact him with further instructions. The Falangists, Law reminded him, were already en route to Madrid, where a fifth column awaited them inside the city. The Party was scouring Europe for volunteers. Didn't matter if you were a member. Didn't matter what your affiliation was. What they needed was an emergency defense of the Spanish Republic. Democracy, Law told him, was threatened to within an inch of its life. Hold Madrid and they would hold Spain.

The train's arrival at two a.m. startled Costas. The rhythm of the track and the sway of the car had lulled him in a daydream, one that unfolded lazily. In his reverie he returned to Cyprus, to the market square of his small village, Pyla. In his dream he could taste the sweet crush of mandarines, the tiny oranges brought into town each day by a Turkish farmer. Mehmet, a young man his age, had rigged up his Model T truck with baskets to hold the figs and grapes and sweet peppers that he sold daily. Alongside, of course, the bitter lemons, sweet despite their name, that Cypriots spritzed on everything from salad to souvlaki. Mehmet arrived in the square at ten each morning and by noon had sold all his wares and disappeared beneath the red and white striped awning of the Turkish café. Often Costas would lean out from the patio of the Greek café across the square, its awning blue and white, and wave to Mehmet. Over time they had become friends.

One Saturday, as the September sun broiled the pavement and sent even the goats searching for shade, Costas lingered near the market.

"Do you need some help?" he asked Mehmet, watching as the young man unfolded the canvas cover on the back of his truck.

Mehmet smiled and responded in Greek, "Efcharistó," and then in English, "Would you like to have a coffee?"

"Yes. But where?"

Mehmet nodded across the square at the Turkish café. "Ankara has better coffee."

"My new friend, how would you know?"

"In that case," replied Mehmet, "let us tempt fate and go first to Ankara and then to the Hellenica. Then we will be able to decide which is better."

In the end, they discovered what they both suspected to be true. The coffee in the two cafés tasted identical. It was prepared the same way, passing a long-handled copper pot over heated glass beads, and came from the same beans, and was sweetened with the same sugar.

Even better, Costas discovered that the two young women who waited table at each café, Elena and Fezile, were equally enticing. He couldn't decide which to invite for a walk first.

That evening Mehmet and Costas met again over beer, first at the Turkish taverna, Istanbul, where they drank a glass of Efes, and then at the Greek taverna, Zesto-Zesto for a KEO.

Mehmet wiped his mustache with his wrist, "The KEO is crisper. But the Efes, you know — " he put his fingers to his lips and opened his palm to the sky.

■

Surrounded by hard-packed desert cliffs that towered over the dozen streets that comprised its center, Pyla was, in the words of the local barber, "nowhere and anywhere." Between the British barracks to the south, the tourist beaches to the east, the rugged mountains to the West, and Nicosia to the north, most of the village's residents remained content to farm arid fields during the day and watch local teams play football in the evening.

Tall and rangy, Costas had become a keeper on the communist-sponsored AEL development squad. The white-haired coach, called by one and all Mr. Andreas, kept insisting that he had a future in the sport if he would only apply himself. But while Costas loved football, he rather more enjoyed the company of the girls who came to watch. He knew they found him dashing, and allowed his wavy black hair to grow long enough to flow behind him as he ran across the field. Even Elena from the café couldn't resist running her hands through his hair when she came over to clear his table. The loose neck of her white cotton blouse puckered slightly when she leaned forward to take his cup, encouraging Costas to admire her gifts even more brazenly. She blushed when he grasped her hand and raised his lips toward hers.

"What makes you think you can kiss me?" she laughed, tousling his hair before walking away.

Only when he got home did he discover the piece of paper tucked into the collar of his shirt. "I finish at eleven," she wrote.

∎

A month later Mehmet introduced Costas to some older men in their thirties from both sides of the village, who wanted to meet him. "We are part of a network of patriots from across Cyprus," their leader told him, "workers from the fields and the shops who seek an end to English occupation. Will you join us?"

Costas, who loved a joke and a good bottle of wine, thought about the question. "I don't like anyone telling me what to do or how to live my life. If we send the English home, what then?"

Mehmet smiled at him, "My friend. What then, indeed! We will take over, from village to village, sharing with each other what we need, never imposing control on others."

"You mean, we, Greek and Turkish Cypriots will run our own businesses, make our own rules — "

"Yes. And no one in some distant city, not Ankara, or Athens, or Nicosia, will tell us how to lead our lives. We will decide together, democratically, village by village, and we will do it through class solidarity."

"How do we achieve this?" Costas asked.

∎

A week later Mehmet tapped on Costas' window. Elena buried her head in a pillow as Costas rose, shielding her from his friend's gaze.

A glowing crescent moon hung low over the village as the two young men walked through Pyla, posting their program on every wall and door, careful to avoid waking anyone. The poster called for an end to British military occupation and a restoration of working-class political control. It was signed by the Young Communist Committee for a Free Cyprus.

They had passed easily through the Greek Cypriot section of town, north of the market, and now walked softly down the packed dirt road that led to the Turkish Cypriot neighborhood. The air had cooled, a reprieve from the oppressive heat of late summer. Costas studied the broad profile of Mehmet's face, his bushy eyebrows, dark eyes, and soft chin, his solid frame. Almost a head taller than Mehmet, Costas was long and lean with flowing black hair, a prominent nose, and deep blue eyes, and the contrast startled him. They shared the same Mediterranean skin, a shade somewhere between copper and sand, and walked in the same canvas shoes, blue with cream crepe soles.

"Out for a nice evening stroll, are we?"

The voice cut through the night's peace.

The pair turned and bumped into the uniform of the village's British police official, Lieutenant Phillip Conners, known to all as Phil the Copper.

"You must have forgotten about the curfew. Well, don't worry, I won't pinch you both. Home with you, Costas. Mehmet, you'll be spending the night at the station."

Costas turned to protest, but before he could speak, Phil shoved him back, hard.

"Back off!" he said, his jovial manner gone. "Back the fuck off."

Costas felt his ire rise, felt the anger and resentment.

"I mean it," Phil put his mouth close to Costas' ear, "I don't intend to tell you again."

Costas swore softly to himself in Greek, certain Phil would never understand.

■

The wheels of the car locked and the train shuddered to a halt, rousing Costas. Perpignan.

The other passengers in the compartment reached for their marled cardboard suitcases. They tossed their cigarette butts on the floor, and pulled open the inner door to the compartment. When they had cleared the car he sat back down and squinted. The passengers filed past his window and he watched them leave until the station stood empty, deserted.

A last passenger glanced over at him and tipped his beret. Costas noted the signal and followed the man out of the station and onto an ancient Renault bus idling alongside the tracks. He must have been the last to arrive, for the driver shut the door behind him and engaged the clutch. Costas found an empty bench and sat, staring out the window.

Two hours into their labored climb up the mountain the bus stopped and the passengers stepped down one by one into the frigid night air of the Pyrenees. Not a word was spoken. At last a guide appeared and said only "follow me," first in Spanish, then in French, and then in English.

After minutes of walking the column came to a halt. "Put your papers in your bundles," the guide directed. "Not a word." He led them to a narrow path that veered off the road and up into the blackness of the forest. The cold seeped into Costas from the ground, and he shivered, his breath a steamy vapor. The sky had started to shimmer with a hint of light by the time the column descended and found themselves back on the road. Another bus, engine running, was waiting for them. "Welcome to Spain, Comrades," the guide smiled, his voice a whisper. "The Republic thanks you. *No Pasaran!*"

The bus carried them down the mountain, through the bustle of morning traffic in Barcelona, and then onto a narrow one-lane road that meandered south along the coast. No one spoke a word. Costa tucked his chin into his chest and returned to his dozing memory.

∎

The day after Mehmet's arrest, Costas received a visitor. A British governmental official with a ruddy complexion, shock of sandy hair, and a name like Roeloffs knocked at his door.

"I've news for you, young Georghiou. Your friend Mehmet has confessed to his part in a conspiracy to overthrow Her Majesty's government. He fingered you as the mastermind."

"He's my friend," Costas replied, stunned. "He'd never tell such a lie!"

"Well, you know, sometimes friendship is a slippery thing." The official absentmindedly picked at his perfectly clean fingernails.

"I don't believe you," Costas was at a loss for words.

"We told him we'd go easy on him if he just pointed out where the responsibility lay. He pointed right at you, lad." The official's smirk spread like a stain.

"Don't worry, we'll make you the same offer. Just tell us what Mehmet was responsible for and we'll make sure things go your way at the trial."

"The what?"

"The trial, lad. Be at the Inn of Court by one tomorrow and the affair will be over in a jiffy. Don't worry about finding it. We'll tell the car to take you through the Kyrenia Gate and to the square." It all sounded so polite and friendly.

"The car?"

"Of course. We'll be sending a car for you bright and early. And to show you our appreciation we'll just ask Lieutenant Conners to stand outside your door this evening. It's for your own good, you know.

Messy business, this talk of independence. Can't hardly tell whose on which side."

The official straightened his tie and made to leave. He paused halfway out the door and added, "It's the way things are. Sneaky Turks. Can't expect them to behave otherwise. Although that Elena, she's a pretty one, isn't she?" And with a smirk he was gone.

∎

The government car slowed as it approached the Inns of Court. Then, just as the clock tower struck noon, Costas kicked open the door and bolted forward even before the driver had a chance to slide out from the front seat. In a flash he melted into the crowd that jammed Atatürk Square. He allowed himself a laugh at the thought of Phil the Copper desperately flitting in and out of the maze of shops that led from the square to the covered bazaar.

By teatime Costas had reached the seaport of Kyrenia thirty kilometers to the north. The Five Knuckles, as the locals called these mountains, shadowed the capital city in an unearthly light each evening just as the nighttime call to prayer sang its haunting chant.

A day later he was in Athens, and within a week, Paris. Communist friends who had foreseen this sequence of events had provided him with enough money to leave the island and warned him of exactly what the British would do. "Never fails," they'd told him. "They try to pit us against one another, spread lies, and then pretend to be your friend. That's the way it works." He had hoped they were wrong. Now he realized how naive he had been.

■

The bus picked up speed, careening down the narrow road that connected the Spanish frontier with the costal village of Albacete. Costas sat across the aisle from two recruits speaking in Hungarian or Romanian, he couldn't tell which. The ancient bus bumped and lurched its way along for the next three hours, spewing exhaust in its wake. To the east the sea shimmered in autumnal splendor. Even over the tumult of the ride, Costas could hear the thump-thump of far-off explosions. It was only then that he realized he had volunteered to go to war without the slightest idea of how to fight.

■

"Don't fucking matter if you can't find the trigger," the instructor lectured. "Name's Enrique. Not Captain Enrique, not General Enrique. Just Enrique. That's how we do it in this militia. No officers, no big shots, no bullshit." He spoke English with a native Spanish accent.

Costas had been in the training camp of the International Brigades for twenty-four hours. They had taken over an abandoned race-track on Calle de Libertad, hammered some plywood over the larger openings in the stable walls, and painted the whole complex white. It still reeked of horse manure, the odor ripening in the heat and mixing with the dust that infiltrated everything. Earlier the supply wagon had visited Costas' unit, conveying twenty-five motley communists and distributing uniforms. In his khaki beret, an olive field-jacket that extended to his hips and made him sweat like a pig, dark gray cord pants, and ankle-high leather boots, Costas felt like a cross between a Karagoz caricature and a bewildered school teacher.

Already soaked in sweat, Costas looked at his fellow volunteers and then around at the other units scattered across the track's overgrown infield. Enrique, dressed like them but with a black beret and black leather jacket, swept his hand across the scene of five hundred unarmed men.

"They are from all over. Germans in the Thalmann Battalion, Italians in the Garibaldi Battalion, French in the Andre Marty Battalion," he announced, pointing out each group. "And if we get enough men like you we'll call them Americans." He laughed, reveling in his own un-military bearing. "You know, honorary Americans, amigos. Some are from Cuba, like me, others from Mexico, and a few from the Dominican and Canada. I even met a Jewish guy last week. We lived on the same street back in Miami."

"Sir?" Costas asked.

"Not sir." Enrique frowned. "Remember, we are all comrades here. They will explain how it works this evening at your political education training."

"Then what do I call you?"

"Comrade Enrique. And what do I call you?" Like Mehmet, Enrique was a head shorter than Costas, thick and muscular, with dark hair, blue eyes, and almond skin.

"My name is Yiorgos Georghiou. Friends call me Costas."

"Where are you from, comrade?"

"Cyprus. I am Greek Cypriot."

"Ah!" Enrique grasped him by both shoulders, beaming. "From Cyprus! Another island, wonderful. I think I shall call you Cipriano. That way we will never forget."

"As you wish, Comrade Enrique," he smiled. There was something thrilling about starting over with a new name. Cipriano. He liked the sound of it.

■

They practiced at being soldiers for a week. Someone had dug up three Remington single-action rifles left over from the Great War, and they took turns firing them at bales of straw brought into the racetrack by local peasants. When one of the guns exploded the commander informed them that the rest of their training would be political.

Cipriano leaned over to Enrique. "Who is that guy?" He pointed to a short, stocky man with a shaved head, pug features, and fleshy lips, wearing a black leather jacket and high black boots.

"That's General Kléber. Commander of the IB. Real name's Lazar Stern, a Hungarian Jew. They say he was Trotsky's right hand during the Civil War, then advised Bella Kuhn. Now he's here. Comintern picked him. Hell of a tough *hombre.*"

Kléber paced before them, kicking the sand for emphasis as he told them that without the correct political attitude it made no difference how well they could fire a gun. This was a fight about freedom, about defeating fascism, about extending the alliances of the Popular Front to the battlefield. To win this fight they needed to know what they were fighting for.

"And what do you fight for?" he asked.

"For Spain!" someone shouted.

"Para la república!" another voice cried.

"For the Brigades."

Stern frowned, his scowl a mask.

"What do you think, comrade?" Enrique called.

Kléber pulled himself as straight as possible. He scratched the top of his bald head, squared his shoulders.

"We fight for all of these, men," he paused, glancing at the cadre of female ambulance drivers from Britain standing off to the side, "and ladies. But above all else we fight for The People."

"Then let's bring back Franco's balls!" an American voice shouted.

"'E ain't got no bloody balls," a cockney accent replied.

One of Kléber's adjutants rushed forward to whisper in the General's ear.

"There is news, my friends. Franco's troops have reached the outskirts of Madrid. If the city falls, all is lost. The army of the Republic has asked for our help, and help we will provide. You leave for the front tomorrow. When you return to your quarters your first order of business will be to elect your officers."

The volunteers raised their right fists and shouted in a babble of accents, *"No Pasaran!"*

∎

Cipriano and Enrique sat next to each other as the bus approached Madrid. "You may be the officer," Cipriano had to shout over the racket of the bus heaving and tossing on the rough and shell-pocked road, "but we'll vote again." He grinned. He enjoyed badgering authority. Enrique looked out the window, acting as if he hadn't heard a word. But Cipriano could see his new friend's jaw start to tremble, his fists clenching and relaxing. "Just kidding." Enrique relaxed.

"Here we are," announced the driver, a civilian in blue overalls. "Hasta luego," he shouted as they climbed down the steps, "Good luck."

They lined up along the side of the road, the men from the 11th International Brigade. Each wore a colored scarf identifying the political affiliation of his local militia unit: dark blue for the Socialists, red and black for the Anarchists, red for the Communists. And each carried the gear born of improvisation: wool socks transformed into cartridge sacks, rifle slings fashioned from linen shirts, shovels reimagined as weapons for close combat, torn bed linens in rolls across their backs for sleeping bags.

"What's next?" someone wondered.

"Who the fuck knows!" another replied.

"They forgot to give us maps," a third.

Enrique stepped backward onto the road, watching as the bus rumbled back to Albacete. "Madrid is this way," he pointed to the northwest. "The tram line ends just ahead. Take the number 10 to Grand Vía. We'll assemble there and see what they need." He turned and started walking toward the city, toward the distant sounds of shells falling and the bright flashes of explosions that trembled the earth.

"You coming, Cipriano?" He glanced back over his shoulder, holding out his hand.

Then, the two men, one 9mm pistol between them, headed off to war.

Hard to believe that a great city had been reduced to rubble in less than a week. The posters plastered on the crumbling walls declared Madrid will be the tomb of the Fascists, but to Cipriano and Enrique, the city already tottered on the edge of destruction.

As they walked that first night down the *Gran Vía,* Madrid's answer to *Champs-Elysées* and Fifth Avenue, they were met by empty streets. The city's four-story buildings, some with their sides blown away, others reduced to rubble, formed a grim corridor along the broad cobblestone avenue. Tangles of fallen streetcar wires sparked where they touched the sidewalk, and the blue painted streetlights cast the scene in an unearthly glow.

They ducked through the arcades that arched from street to street, abysmal shelters for the shops whose plate glass windows lay shattered on the sidewalk. The windows of the apartments above framed clusters of women and children, some watching the rag-tag parade pass below, others in such distress that their eyes had dulled into blackness.

The moonless night had reduced the great city to a state of shock. Cipriano could feel it as much as he could see it. The streets were silent apart from the crunching of the glass beneath the boots of the 11th International Brigade, too dead for dreaming. In the distance, hardly five kilometers away according to Enrique, in the University District, all hell had broken loose, and the siren wails of battle echoed relentlessly.

"Havana and Madrid were twins once. I can't bare to see it," Enrique spoke quietly.

"You haven't told me, yet," Cipriano looked up at the sky. "Why did you volunteer?"

"Because the *Juventud Libertaria,* the labor-anarchists, invited me. I joined two years ago, after that asshole Batista corrupted the government, pulled some strings, and pushed President Grau into exile. Communists were the only ones who didn't protest then. So I said, I'll stick with the labor movement, with the tobacco workers, the longshoremen, the sugarcane workers. They said go to Spain, our brothers in Barcelona need us. So here I am. Simple. Democratic control."

The rest of the company followed behind them, marching up Madrid's shattered commercial artery. They passed beneath a banner strung between two apartment buildings. Tied to the wrought iron balconies that graced Madrid's apartment windows the banner read *NO PASARAN.* The two soldiers, unbloodied and untested, raised their left-hands in the close-fisted salute of the anarchist Republic. The others behind them did the same. With the gesture the windows above them opened, and, as if by some silent consensus, the citizens of Madrid began to cheer, *"Viva la República, Viva la República!"*

∎

The guns boomed like a stampede, reverberating louder and louder as they approached Madrid's university district. The fighting lit the night sky, turning it red and yellow. Along the cobblestone streets leading from the Plaza Espana to the University scores of men struggled to dig trenches, hoping to render the avenues impassible to armored cars and tanks. Sandbags filled doorways and wine bottles lined ground floor window-sills, necks stuffed with cotton wicks. Radios on corners played the Republican station full blast: *"BE VIGILANT. BE BRAVE. BEWARE THE FIFTH COLUMN. CITIZENS OF MADRID TODAY WE FIGHT. TOMORROW WE CONQUER."*

■

The day broke red and angry. They had crossed through
the center of Madrid by night, without sleep, and the battle now
raged less than a kilometer away. Messengers appeared from the
International Brigade headquarters to inform Enrique of the situation.
The Nationalist Army had already crossed the Manzanares River into
University City. Hand-to-hand, house-to-house combat had rendered
Franco's German tanks ineffective. General Kléber had ordered the
11th into the University as part of a counter-offensive planned for later
that morning. The order of battle was perfunctory: take weapons from
the dead. The strategic directive was even more brief: kill the enemy.
Viva la República.

Enrique and Cipriano hunched over the map that the messenger
had left them. It was dated 1899, well before the metro had been
built, before the boulevards had been widened. Red arrows pointed
to Nationalist troop placements and gun positions. Enrique yelled in
frustration, tearing the map in tiny pieces.

"This tells us nothing!" He turned to face his company of thirty-
five men, their faces still fresh, many unarmed, boots polished. "Follow
me."

Two Fiat CR32 bombers, their fixed wheels clawing down
from the sky, dove out from behind the early morning clouds,
screaming overhead as they released a dozen black bombs. The
ground shuddered as two apartment buildings less than a hundred
meters ahead imploded in a cloud of debris and dust. The gate to the
University hung open, its iron scrolling twisted into a macabre jumble.
The brick paths from building to building had been pulverized into
piles of rubble by the treads of the Soviet T-26 tanks that had smashed
a path into University City for the International Brigades. Ahead lay the
Faculty of Philosophy, a massive building graced by Corinthian columns

and a portico with inscriptions bearing the great names of European learning: Descartes, Cervantes, Pasteur.

Kléber had established his headquarters in the building. Barbed wire and sand bags encircled the place where the poet Lorca and the cineaste Brunel had studied only ten years earlier.

"How did you know that?" asked Enrique when Cipriano shared the fact. "You never cease to surprise me."

"When you are from Cyprus you have to know about the world. For it never knows about you," replied Cipriano.

Machine gun fire ripped into the ground, kicking up puffs of dust that raced directly toward them.

"Move!" Enrique pushed Cipriano off to the side as the bullets danced to their left. "Take cover," he ordered, sprinting around the side of the building and ducking inside. Cipriano followed, his throat tight, his heart beating high in his chest.

∎

"Where you fellows been, anyway?" The American eyed the company, still clothed as they had been when they left Albacete twenty-four hours earlier. He spoke with an accent that Enrique placed as New York. "I'm Leo Wolfe," he stabbed his bayonet into the base of the crumbling wall next to them. "Been here three days. It's a pisser. We need you. Up there." He pointed to the stairway that led to the second floor. "This fight's building-to-building, floor-to-floor, door-to-door." He surveyed them again. "Any of you ever fire a machine gun?" He exhaled at their blank expressions. "Ok. Don't matter. I'll send someone up when I find 'em. Just take your men upstairs. Kill anything that moves."

Dust and rubble and blood covered the stairwell. Enrique ordered the unit to spread out across the building, two to a window. He and

Cipriano kicked open a door to a classroom. Inside the plaster had cracked, large chunks crumbled on the floor, leaving lathe and brick exposed. They pushed the chairs and desks into a pile in one corner, floor-to-ceiling, then carefully duck-walked over to the waist-high window. Shells had blown out the glass and frame, leaving a jagged opening in the wall. From their knees the two men poked their noses over the sill.

They could see small figures on the tops of nearby buildings, their silhouettes scurrying as they ran hunched over, rifles in one hand. Impossible to tell which side they were on. The Nationalist troops wore standard wool army uniforms and soft-field caps that reminded Enrique of the ice-cream vendors in Havana.

"Look for berets. If they wear berets they belong to us," he called to Cipriano, who knelt off to the side of the window. Enrique stood on the opposite side, gun held at eye level.

"IN THE NAME OF THE MOTHERLAND, THE CHURCH, AND THE NEW HEAD OF STATE, FRANCISCO FRANCO WE WILL RECLAIM THE HISTORIC CAPITAL OF OUR NATION. DO NOT FEAR, WE ARE FIRM IN OUR RESOLVE. WE WILL ENTER THE CITY THROUGH THE DOORS OF THE UNIVERSITY. SURRENDER NOW BEFORE ALL IS LOST."

A stream of bullets shattered the loudspeaker dangling from a tree in the courtyard below. Soldiers wearing the unmistakable green field caps of the military sped across the yard, crouching, firing, running. Their building erupted with a deafening explosion as muzzle fire sputtered from the windows up and down the length of the Faculty of Law.

The Nationalists, trained in North Africa, attacked in greater and greater numbers, firing into the windows as they raced toward the building. Several of Enrique's men fell from the windows, tumbling head first to the ground below. Screams of agony echoed in the courtyard.

A stranger appeared in the doorway of their room. Short and stocky with a red scarf, breathless the soldier called out, "give me a hand."

"I've got a machine gun. Put it there, by the window, and stay low. I'll be back with the ammunition boxes. You have the best field of fire."

Enrique and Cipriano shoved two desks up to the window, then another two behind them, creating a raised platform large enough to support them and the gun. They mounted the weapon far enough out the window to allow the barrel to swivel across an arc of almost 180 degrees. The handles of the brand new Hotchkiss felt smooth and cool. Enrique remembered the day they had first seen the weapon at Albacete. They hadn't used it then.

"Here are the belts. Do you know how to fire this thing?" The stranger returned, clambering onto the table.

"Sure," replied Enrique, not sure at all.

They set the tripod to allow them to pivot the machine gun up and down as well as sideways. The three of them, Enrique in the middle, stretched out on the table, facing the window. Enrique held the trigger handle while Cipriano prepared to clear the expended belts as quickly as the red-scarfed soldier could feed fresh ones into the gun's breach.

"Don't you dare touch the barrel," the newcomer said, taking off a red beret to reveal a nest of dark hair held in place by two ivory combs. "It will take your hand off once it gets hot."

They stared at her.

"Move over." She slid between them. "I'm Anna."

The courtyard filled with more Nationalist soldiers, firing, running for shelter, screaming. Enrique squeezed the trigger. The gun recoiled. He thought about adjusting the sight but muttered "fuck it," and he swept the barrel from side-to-side, firing at anything that moved.

"Just hold your finger steady," Anna instructed. "Like this." She placed her hand over his and pulled their fore-fingers smoothly back on the trigger.

■

They lost all sense of time in the heat and noise of battle. The Hotchkiss glowed dark red as the spent casings chattered like hail on the floor. Anna used both hands to feed the 8mm shells, and Enrique could feel the slight pressure of the length of her body alongside his own. He glanced at her, found her brown eyes staring back at him, then ducked as the whine of a bullet from the courtyard slammed into the wall behind them. Anna covered her head with her arms as the shrapnel of a mortar shell rained down from a strike on the roof. Someone in the next room screamed, "My leg, my leg!" Another called, "Mercy, mother of god!" Then it all stopped.

The three of them peered down into the silence. The courtyard had filled with the bodies of the dead and the wounded. Men poked their guns and then their heads out the windows, searching for targets. The Nationalist thrust had been blunted, stopped in its tracks, the proof right at their feet.

A messenger appeared with a dispatch bag slung over his shoulder and announced that Kléber had ordered the unit to hold their position in preparation for a second wave. Together Enrique, Cipriano, and Anna made the rounds of the building, counting their comrades, tending to the wounded, calling for medics. Enrique watched as Anna wrapped the thigh of a man in the next room with a tourniquet, and saw him turn white with shock as he realized that his left leg and boot remained standing across the room. Two medics came and took him away on a stretcher. They never knew his name.

They moved methodically from room to room. Enrique paled when he realized that of the thirty-five men in their unit only fourteen remained standing. A dozen had died and the others suffered a range of wounds. The 11th no longer existed.

Anna removed her field coat, leather, worn by officers. Enrique remembered the weight of her body against his, then the weight of the legless soldier as they lifted him onto the stretcher. He felt faint. She pulled a bottle of brandy out of her kit and took a long pull.

"Want some?" she pressed the bottle into his hands. "It will help with the shock. I can tell this was your first action. It's always like this. Most first-timers wet their pants. I did."

She was a head shorter than Cipriano, with broad features, piercing dark eyes and black hair. "Now that we've fought together," her eyes danced, "perhaps it's time to introduce ourselves."

Cipriano spat the plaster dust from his mouth and blinked. "I had no idea — "

"That there are women like me in the militias?" She had a slight accent, somewhere between French and Spanish. "I'm Anna Ekudal. And, if you're wondering, I'm Basque. From the Pyrenees, the French side, actually, but Basque is Basque. We fight for the Republic. The Republicans say they will honor our independence. Franco only wants to crush us."

A cheer went up from the courtyard. The trio leaned out the window. The Republican flag, held by two Loyalist fighters, unfurled at the center of the killing field. Someone cried out, "They have pulled back. The University is ours. Madrid is saved!"

Anna and Enrique and Cipriano embraced, then raised their left fists. "Viva la República!" Their shouts joined with the others.

"What should we do now?" Cipriano asked.

"A drink! We have earned a drink," replied Enrique.

"I know just the place," Anna turned. "Follow me. There are some people you should meet."

■

They found a taxi. One of Kléber's staff, a captain from Thorez's French battalion, had commandeered the dented Citroën. "I'm headed down *Gran Vía,*" he popped open the door from the inside, "take you as far as the Hotel." As they clambered in the driver called out, *"Regardez!"* and pointed to the sky. Overhead a dark shadow of a dive-bomber tracked down toward them steeply, engines wailing.

The plane dropped, twisting as it tried to level off. The cockpit opened and the pilot leaned out, two large black sticks in his left hand. He had pushed his goggles up over his leather helmet, and they could just see the bushy mustache that covered his upper lip. The plane flew directly overhead as the pilot dipped his wings slightly, then let the two sticks drop as delicately as if they were baby sparrows. They seemed to float, forever. Then, suddenly, the projectiles slammed into the open hatch of a German tank whose turret had targeted the Citroën.

The armor of the two-man tank shielded them from the concussion. One of the tankers flew into the air, and as the bomber climbed steeply upward and away, the dead man landed on the ground with a dull thud. Anna covered her eyes. The tank split into a hundred pieces. The small cache of ammunition inside burst, cracking and pinging and ripping the tank to shreds. The driver of the Citroën looked down and then grabbed the wheel.

"Lucky. Never would've seen that coming. Must have been one of our planes then, a Katiuska by the looks of it. Soviet."

Ten minutes later he deposited them on the *Gran Vía. "A bientot,"* he waved before accelerating down the boulevard, dodging mounds of upended paving stones, overturned cars, and bent lampposts.

The three veterans picked their way through the rubble strewn along the *Gran Vía.* "Here," Anna pointed down the boulevard toward the Hotel Florida. The two men followed her — just as they had since the moment they met. "I don't know exactly who they are but the Florida is where the foreign press stays in Madrid."

"What's that have to do with us?" Enrique adjusted the bedroll across his back with a quick shrug of his shoulders, then patted the Beretta pistol he had recovered from a dead Nationalist soldier in the courtyard. The dozen clips of ammunition weighed him down, but they made him feel powerful, like there was nothing he couldn't handle. He looked past Anna to Cipriano, "What about you, my friend? Interested in meeting some writers?"

■

Anna held the door to the Hotel Florida open. The glass had cracked into dozens of scattered lines, like parched earth. The Florida had once been grand. Its elegance — gold fixtures, deeply polished wood accents, damask wall covering — was now less frayed than distressed. Lamps that didn't turn on, clocks frozen at random hours, and opulent stuffed furniture without cushions all stood testimony to the siege. Only the bar remained as a reminder of the peaceful days of September. Dark and wood-paneled, it commanded the rear of the lobby. Beyond the lobby's brass and glass-paneled doors two men and a woman sat around an oval table, sipping on tall drinks as if unaware of the fallen hotel around them.

The larger of the men, tall and broad with a short trimmed beard and glasses, noticed them and stood politely. He wore a khaki field jacket, twill riding pants, and well-worn and polished black leather boots. He exuded an air of good-humored joviality and his eyes twinkled as he motioned them to approach. "Fresh from the fighting, are you? Please, sit. Join us for a drink. What can I get you?"

"Just wine," Anna replied as Cipriano and Enrique nodded their assent. "Thank you."

Clearly a war correspondent, he waved to summon a waiter. At his elbow, Enrique spotted a smudged mimeographed newsletter. The masthead read, "Hotel Floridita — Havana, Cuba." He caught the correspondent's eye. "I have had many of their special daiquiris over the years. Have you ever been?" He withheld his customary *"amigo"* for another moment.

"Forgive me," the writer half-bowed, "I have neglected to introduce myself and my colleagues. Ernest Hemingway, and this is Martha Gellhorn," he motioned to the stunning woman to his right. Dressed in black and adorned with the silver-turquoise jewelry of the American southwest, the petit woman nodded her head. "She writes for Colliers in New York, and this is my dear friend from The New York Times, Herbert Matthews."

Gellhorn sat quietly taking notes as Matthews and Hemingway took turns interviewing the three veterans. They were interested in their political affiliations. Enrique answered passionately.

"You know. I am most sympathetic to the anarchists. Of course, here they are called the POUM. They fight all authority, as we did in Cuba, and are fierce to defend their independence. They are the true democrats."

Hemingway listened carefully, all the while reaching his hand under the table caressing Gellhorn's knee, something Enrique couldn't help but admire. Clearly the two of them were already together and Matthews, who spoke such wonderfully good Spanish, was already the third wheel.

"And, you," asked Hemingway as if he needed to deflect Enrique's attention, "tell us, how did you come to this good fight? We are a long way from Cyprus."

The hotel lights flickered to yellow and then went out. Hemingway picked up the packet of cigarettes in front of him. Deftly, with one hand, he wrist-flipped his Zippo lighter open, flicking the wheel and shooting a bright flame onto the wick of the stubby white candle at the center of the table, then closed it with a satisfying click. "Must be five," he said wanly. "It's like clockwork. The Nationalists bomb when the people come home from work, the electricity fails, people duck into the Metro. Then at six the German pilots are ready for some schnapps, the Condor Legion closes up shop, and we return to normal." He paused to consider the faces of the three soldiers sitting with him. "But it will never be normal again, now, will it?" Hemingway asked Cipriano.

Enrique held his hands in front of him, resting lightly on the table. He took a swallow from his glass, replaced it on the white cloth and admired the way the candle light reflected in miniature on the ruby-red wine. He looked at Hemingway.

"In Cuba I joined the young anarchists in 1934. I was eighteen. Born in Havana. My uncle works for Bacardi. He's a watchman in the warehouse, leads the union there too. Spends half the year in Havana and half in Santiago."

"Santiago? What's that like?" the American woman brightened, joining the conversation for the first time. "I've never been."

"The opposite of Havana," Enrique grinned. "Havana is a little like Madrid, very Spanish. The only dark-skinned Cubans you see are those sweeping the streets or cleaning the bars at night. Even looks like Madrid. But in Santiago, everyone is black. Sugar and rum control the city and at Carnival!" He blew out his cheeks. "What a time! Parties and parades in the streets for days."

"My father always said that the Yankees and the aristocrats in Cuba would try to control everything. They took the gift of our independence and made it into something for themselves. The people got nothing. Do you understand? Nothing. It is no different no matter who is in power, the Spanish, the Americans, Grau. No matter."

Gellhorn looked up at him with her eyes that shaded from green to amber. "But why the young anarchists in Cuba?"

"I have seen, in my own country, how easily people with black skin are placed at the bottom. Even by whites who have no more. Maybe even because of this. And when the labor movement tells us that everyone is equal, they mean it. Only ones who stand up for them are in the unions. That's why I am here. I came from New York, I signed their card and they gave me a ticket to France. In Paris a guy named Oliver Law, an American, told me that I could lead a company, train them. Get to our training camp in Albacete, he said, and we'll take care of the rest. He said that I would be in the 'vanguard of the proletariat.'" Enrique drained his glass. The lights came back on for a moment. Everyone blinked. Then the lights dimmed to half-strength, casting the room in a brown-yellow gloom.

"Don't worry," Cipriano jumped in. "He knows the difference between good bullshit and bad. But, my friend also knows that the Party also has answers. If we listen to them, really pay attention, they will take us somewhere. I love the idea of the Popular Front. When I fight fascism, you know, I also fight against racism, and for the people. You'll see."

Enrique couldn't keep still. "Listen," he said, voice on the edge of anger, "when more Cubans come to join the International Brigades they will be the African ones, the ones from Santiago. And they will not come because of your Party. In spite, perhaps, but not because."

Hemingway looked up at the ceiling as Gellhorn ran her index finger around the rim of her wine glass.

He turned his attention back to the others at the table. "So, one of you is a communist and the other an anarchist. What about you, Miss?"

"I am Anna. My parents are Basque. I am just a soldier who fights for the independence of my people. The militia trained me as a machine gunner and loaned me to Kléber's army. I found my new friends only earlier today," she winked at Cipriano and Enrique, "They have learned about war very, very quickly. I was glad to instruct them."

The journalists seemed at a loss for what to say.

"Yes. There are women soldiers in the volunteers. We fight as well as the men. Some say we are more clever too."

"I'll drink to that." Gellhorn emptied the bottle of wine into all their glasses. "What would they do without us?" She raised her eyebrow at Hemingway.

Enrique noticed that Hemingway sat staring out into space again.

The lights came on, then dimmed again, and then stayed on.

As usual it took Hemmy, a name I know he detested, somewhat longer to acknowledge me. I'd like to think I was the real reporter, and he, a *farceur*. I had sat with them for a couple of hours and endured his reaching under the table to stroke Martha's thigh as if she were an amulet.

What a relief to find these three Lincolns *avant la parole*. And what a sight. Covered with plaster dust and sweat. Anna — A vision of incredible strength, her arms and hands as muscular as any man, yet her features as delicate as porcelain. And her companions. Right out of the pages of a pulp western — mustachioed gunslinging *desperados*, armed to the teeth and with hearts as large and as deep as the sea. To them I was just The Thin Man with a pencil mustache and fine features who wore a white shirt tucked into the blue cotton pants and espadrilles of the working classes. I offered my hand, rose from my chair and announced as graciously as possible given the circumstances, in my very best Spanish. "We are honored to meet three volunteers from the International Brigades, please do sit down. We have so many questions." This was how I first met those three. I shall never forget that moment. Never.

"Why did you join, if you don't mind my asking?" My inquiry was genuine and not misplaced, if I must say so, given the role he was to play in Castro's coup. I really wanted to know what Enrique thought. Clearly I already found him a fascinating blend of contradictions: hot tempered and thoughtful, traditional yet a revolutionary.

Henry interrupted, "Do you know this place, Herb?" he asked me, holding up the Floradita mimeograph. "Best bar in Havana, don't you think Enrique?"

I couldn't resist. "Oh yes. And the most expensive," I paused and said pointedly.

"Six p.m.," Herb announced, tucking his notepad into the drawstring of his culottes. "Time to file our stories."

PART TWO
THE BUSINESS OF WAR

General Kléber was not nearly as tall as he might have liked. With his bullet head and thick neck he bore an uncanny resemblance to Erich von Stroheim.

"Velcome, Commander Perez. On behalf of the International Brigades." He paused to belch.

"Here. Please put these on your uniform at your earliest convenience." He handed Enrique the brass badge of a Major in the Army of the Republic. "The Internationals have been reorganized and I am assigning you command of the Second Battalion of the Abraham Lincoln Brigade. You will report to Colonel Oliver Law, an American. I believe you already know him." He rifled through the folder on his desk. "You may include the Cypriot, tEnrique as your aide-de-camp if you wish."

Enrique stood silently, choosing not to acknowledge Kléber's shit-eating grin.

"This must come as a shock." Kléber clasped his hands together, leaning forward. "We are imposing military discipline. We must integrate the new Americans into our operation. The militias are a thing of the past. Our casualties were disastrous in Madrid. The Comintern Central Committee are in full agreement."

"I understand, sir." Enrique's mind raced with a hundred protests. But Spain's freedom was more important than a fight between the remnants of the anarchist militias and the new communist bosses. There would be time for that later. After.

"Don't forget to salute on your way out," Kléber turned back to the reports piled on his desk.

Enrique walked back to the small stucco house where he and Cipriano had been billetted since the Nationalists withdrew from the outskirts of Madrid. He shook his head in wonder. Prime Minister Negrín had always tolerated the independence of the anarchist militias. It was good propaganda and good politics to allow them to choose their own officers, to vote on non-military decisions, even to allow women to fight side-by-side with men. And Russian advisers, some with a direct line to Kléber, were glad to go along. It was, after all, in the spirit of the Popular Front — "no enemies on the left" and all that. Did this about face mean that the Party was taking over? What would that mean for his independence — not to mention his friendship with Cipriano?

∎

"News. I have news you should like, Captain Cipriano." Enrique wiped his sleeve with his right hand. "The militias are over. They have centralized control of the Internationals. Kléber is Commander in Chief. That guy Law is our CO, I am the new Major, and you, my friend, are my executive officer."

Cipriano sat up, rubbing his eyes. "Do you mean this?"

"Every bloody word. I knew you would be surprised."

"I don't know what this means."

"None of us do, so hold on." Enrique held out his hand, "Whatever happens, we remain friends, right?"

Cipriano smiled faintly. Shook his head again, then grasped Enrique's hand. "For an anarchist, you're alright."

Enrique let the moment sink in. The thud of cannon fire echoed in the hills beyond the city, and he reached for his packet of cigarettes. He offered one to Cipriano. "Now."

The Cypriot narrowed his eyes. "What else did Kléber say?"

"How did you know?"

"English Cigarettes. You never share them."

"Kléber's sending us to Barcelona."

"Y-at-E? How come?" Cipriano replied in Greek, taking the cigarette.

"I imagine they'll tell us when we get there.

The sandbags draped over the rubble of Barcelona's grand avenue had melted, turning the city into a Dali painting. Dust hung heavy in the air across the city, choking anyone who braved the streets. Even the scent of the sea, once so ubiquitous to the port and the old districts that housed the workers and seamen, had dissipated. In a city that lived to eat, the war had forced Barcelona to reverse the terms of its existence. The burlap sandbag covers revealed their faded origins and the luxuries of another time. *"Frutas"* from Valencia, *"Riz"* from Cordoba, even *"Garbanzos"* from nearby Zaragoza. Where once workers had stopped to consider the merits of tapas covered with anchovies and salt ham, now children wandered like feral cats. They scavenged for scraps of food, cigarette butts, or cast off random pieces of metal, stuffing their new treasures into rusting tin cans that once held tender fillets of tuna packed in virgin olive oil.

Where *La Rambla* has once been an elegant nightly parade of gaily dressed couples strolling arm-in-arm, *ecru* parasols resting on dainty shoulders, now the avenue witnessed a motley assortment of mendicants and pitchmen. They stared mutely ahead, shuffling around the rubble of the promenade, dressed like harlequins or in rags. Contrary to the conceits of capitalism, war rarely helped the common citizen. In Barcelona it had tossed them headlong into the gutter.

Enrique Perez picked his way down the avenue, past the ritzy hotels and their shattered plate-glass windows and then past the tapas bars and tourist joints devoid of customers. Only the kiosks located at hundred meter intervals along the inner walkway of the avenue showed signs of commerce. They overflowed with dozens of newspapers, each printed by a different faction, union, or militia. He passed past a crippled Gypsy selling black balloons painted with white skeletons, then turned off the avenue, climbing over an embankment of sandbags before ducking down a side street.

The sunlight disappeared behind a bank of dark clouds. A chill enveloped him and shadows darted across the cobblestones. On both sides of the narrow street six-story apartment buildings loomed, windows shuttered, laundry fluttering from narrow wrought iron balconies. He was in an old Jewish ghetto. He turned left on *Carrer del Call* onto the even more ancient *Carrer de L'Ensenyanca,* barely three meters wide. At two o'clock in the afternoon the shops were all closed for siesta. He stared at his reflection in the window of a sombrereria filled with wool fedoras and Basque berets. His long bushy mustache needed trimming, and the lines that mapped his eyes had turned his skin into leather. "But at least my eyes are clear," he whispered to himself. At least.

Ahead, just beyond the banner displaying the red and black letters, CNT, he spotted the oak-paneled doors of Casa Almirall. Kléber assured him that the working class taberna would be a safe meeting place. When they left Albacete the previous day, they agreed to rendezvous at the Almirall. "Be careful with these scarves," the adjunct instructed as he handed them the red and black checked insignia of the anarchist National Confederation of Labor. "If the Communist Party UGT sees you," he told them, "you'll be in deep deep *mierda,* so only wear the scarves when you get to the *taberna."*

Enrique had simply shrugged. Fascists against Republicans, Franco against the Loyalists — these lines he understood. He had even come to embrace the restoration of military discipline mandated by the Soviet Union's advisors. And while he had once understood the equally bitter conflict between anarcho-syndicalist and communist militias, his appreciation for the divisions had all but vanished. The roiling mire of ever-changing political alliances and infighting had twisted his brain to mush.

Enrique reached into the back pocket of his olive twill trousers, held in place by a web-canvas belt, and pulled out the CNT scarf. He felt a chill across his shoulders and froze, the red and black checked scarf dangling from his right hand. Beneath his palm the door was worn smooth by the thousands of thirsty patrons that had preceded him. But that, he mused, was from a time when Barcelona had been a city of celebration, offering a thousand places to drink *cava* and revel till dawn.

As the door creaked open he actually felt the darkness escape from inside. It passed over him, making him vulnerable. A long wooden bar stretching along the right side of the tavern was laden with stacks of serving platters filled with *tapas del día*: smoked ham and fragrant cheeses, red and yellow peppers shimmering in olive oil, wafer-thin slices of *fuet de Vic*, a smoked sausage adored by locals. As Enrique squinted into the darkness, struggling to fix the bartender with his vision, a hand rested on his shoulder.

"Do not move, Amigo. Not one false step."

Enrique jumped, his jaw twitching, temples pounding. He hunched his shoulders, feeling the strain of the buttons of his dark-blue double-breasted jacket against his chest. Fist clenched, he swung around, pivoting to his right. Two arms, lanky and muscled, held him tight.

"Just me." Cipriano grinned down at Enrique, watching as the tension drained from the Cuban's face. "Just me, motherfucker," he jostled his shoulder. "Just me."

A door opened at the rear of the restaurant. A young man, red and black checked scarf casually tied off at his throat, walked toward them. He stopped an arm's length away, looking past them and into the large mirror that hung on the wall behind the bar. He never made eye contact, only grunted, "Follow me."

■

The blood-red *Hispano-Suiza* growled, then revved higher into a rumble. The rear-door swung open as Cipriano and Enrique stepped into the open-roofed car. The car accelerated sharply, tumbling them backward into the luxury of glove-leather polished "smooth as a whore's behind," in Enrique's words.

The driver, decked in another CNT scarf, glanced back at them.

"Drink?" he asked, swinging open a cabinet door attached to the rear of the front seat to reveal a bottle of absinthe and two small, elegant, crystal glasses.

The two men stared at him, dumbstruck.

"We have liberated this wonderful machine from the Director of Public Utilities in Barcelona. Later he will find a note telling him where to recover his grand car. Unless the war drags on, of course." The driver laughed wildly and pressed his foot down on the gas pedal.

The speed of the car and the bite of the green liquor brought tears to their eyes as the car roared down Barcelona's grand avenue, the Diagonal — always known to the locals simply as *La Diagonal* — then back into the tangle of streets that carried them deep into the bowels of the city.

The car lurched to a stop. The driver looked straight ahead, reaching back with his left hand to push the rear door open.

"Guess this is where we get out," Cipriano looked around at the street. The sun had dipped low in the sky, red and yellow rays streaking out from behind the mountains to the north and west. The scents of the sea, of fish and seaweed and oil, permeated the air.

As the car roared away, its exhaust a cluster of bass notes, another arrived — this one a battered piece of tin with skinny tires, a canvas top, and a crank still dangling from the rusted radiator. The wide double chevron told them it was a Citroën, but not like any model they had ever seen before.

"Shall we pick it up and carry it?" Enrique inquired of the driver. The young man had long stringy hair, a sparse beard, and one arm. His right sleeve was pinned up over his elbow. He smiled out at them forlornly.

"Hurry. We don't have much time."

Like a rat in a maze, the car worked its way down one narrow and twisting street after another, darting around elderly women with tattered scarves and street vendors with empty pushcarts. The city at dusk was virtually invisible thanks to the blackout the Provincial government had ordered to protect against Franco's bombers. A half-hour had passed before the car slowed to a rolling stop. Enrique and Cipriano jumped out from the rear seats, the Citroën rising delicately as they exited.

The car sped off, leaving them alone in the middle of the street, disoriented, confused, and exhausted. A banner fluttered from the shutters of a grey stone building before them. Enrique exhaled in exasperation. They were back at the CNT office.

∎

"We needed to be sure," one of the men seated at the table explained. "You passed."

"And now?" Enrique stared at the unshaven, beret-clad man. "Are you fucking sure now?" He felt his anger rising like a fever, felt his hand shaking under the table. "Are you fucking sure now, amigo?" Cipriano's hand rested gently on his shoulder.

"And now you come with us." The man ignored his outburst and stood. He pulled his beret almost level to his eyebrows and walked to the door. With that he raised his clenched left fist in salute to all present. "My brothers."

"When I asked them to send the best they choose you," he led them outside, his shoulders hunched against the rain.

They walked toward the docks, along the same streets they had driven earlier. The cobblestones shone with a dull filament of blue and green oil. Cipriano pulled his jacket close and hitched up his dark brown wool trousers. He glanced at Enrique, looking down at the shorter and stockier man, double-breasted jacket tossed gallantly over his shoulder. Catching his eye, Cipriano raised his eyebrows, questioning. Enrique shrugged slightly and tilted his head to the right. "Who the fuck knows," he muttered.

The seaport in Barcelona might have been any other, from Shanghai to Santiago. Dozens of freighters were tethered to ancient wood piers, their scuppers leaking rust and water, their iron railings orange with age. Men leaned over the rails, thin spirals of cigarette smoke the only sign of life. Railroad tracks ran alongside the piers, separating the ships from a row of ramshackle wood structures — bars, warehouses, whorehouses, rooming houses. What distinguished Barcelona's waterfront was the sandy beach that stretched from the end of the industrial piers several kilometers north along the shore of the Mediterranean, ending only at the single airstrip of the military airport.

Before them a motley array of tramp steamers bobbed at their moorings, running lights shimmering with the motion of tide and wave. Empty, the ships rode clumsily, high above their water lines, awkward and unladen. Expectant.

"Will you tell us now why we're here?" Enrique asked. Their guide's dark features remained passive in the night. "We've come a long way."

The guide unhooked the blanket roll from his left shoulder. "Here," he unfolded the blanket, laying it flat on a nearby table, the ships gently yawing across the empty rail tracks. "Your manifest."

He handed Enrique a sheaf of papers covered with numbers. Dozens and dozens of pages, hundreds of numbers.

"Your assignment is simple. Boxes come off the trains, there," he pointed to the spur that curved out to the foot of the nearest pier. "And as they are loaded onto the ship, you check off the numbers."

The pier was empty. The loading crane a silhouette against the moonlight, its roped cargo net collapsed and tangled on the worn wood slats next to the vacant mooring slip.

Before Enrique had a chance to verbalize the anger in his eyes, Cipriano stepped between the two men.

"You needed the 'best' for this?" he brandished the papers, "This accounting job!" Hardly a question. "Why us? For shit sake, why us?" Cipriano's voice rose higher than he intended.

Enrique shot him a look-who's-talking glance, the lines in his eyes crinkling with amusement. Usually he was the one losing his temper. It was fun to remain calm. He decided to remember this moment.

Cipriano exhaled. The CNT agent started to speak. Then he sighed, jamming his hand into his back pocket.

"Look," he opened his other palm, placating, "Look. This cargo is precious. We need to ensure that every box is loaded. Let me assure you that this is vital to the defense of the Republic and that your skills are exactly what the government requires for this critical task."

Enrique glanced at the empty slip behind them, then gazed down the railroad tracks. "When do we start?"

"Tomorrow night. Be here at one."

They spent the day sleeping in a tiny room, airless room above a nearby tienda, where a collection of cockroaches and spiders shared the musty wood floor with empty tins and mold. The bartender, who doubled as the local militia chief, a mass of a man with red cheeks and a bald head, told them there was not a safer house in Barcelona. At midnight he ushered them down the stairs to a pot of café con leche and a hunk of salchichon, blood sausage drenched in wine. "It is a Catalan specialty," he told them proudly. "Makes a man of you." He winked and wiped his hands on the greasy half-apron that hung below his paunch.

Within the hour they were quayside, the manifests folded in their hands, pencil stubs behind their ears. The listened to the clacking of the freight train as it moved through the night. The engineer guided the locomotive to a gradual stop, minimizing the hiss of the steam breaks that might otherwise disrupt its silent arrival. Men wearing the traditional blues cotton pants of longshoremen emerged from the shadows of the blue-black night. Long metal hooks hung from their shoulders, wood handles flat against their chests.

"You see them?" Cipriano strained his eyes against the dark. "Scared the shit out of me."

Enrique laughed. "No working class in Cyprus, then? Only Party cadres, I'll bet."

Cipriano let the gibe pass. Neither the time or place.

"Wait here," he instructed Enrique.

■

The temporary work lights, borrowed from a local theater company with Loyalist sympathies, cast the whole scene — train, men, docks — in a lurid yellow hue. Shadows stretched at crazy angles, lengthening and contracting each time a worker stepped.

By the time Cipriano returned, the longshoremen had begun to unload the first boxcar, stacking the crates on wood pallets that the cargo net would then hoist to the deck above.

"Get up there," he instructed Enrique, enjoying the role reversal. "Make sure all the crates match the manifest."

Then, for the first time, they both turned to inspect the ship. What they saw astounded them.

"You read it," Enrique looked bewildered, "it's got weird letters like in your Greek newspapers."

Cipriano squinted. "Looks like l, e, i, n, i, e — ahh, it's Russian! That's Cyrillic, see, the first letter, like an upside down U, that's their l. He plucked the pencil from behind his ear, scratched thoughtfully, and put it back. "My friend, this ship is one you will love. Its name is Lenin. Must be a Soviet freighter. So, what I ask you is this — What the fuck are they doing here and what the fuck are we putting on that ship that's so valuable that it requires an army of ants in the dead of the night?"

Enrique smiled. So that's it. This assignment had to do with the new Russian command of the International Brigades. Perhaps the dismantling of the militias. Something was at hand and no one had taken the trouble to explain it. The intentional omission showed the real value of the cargo. He and Cipriano had become the guardians of a cargo whose worth had rendered it invisible.

"Well, what are we waiting for?" he raised an eye at Cipriano, then walked toward the ship. Its gangplank angled down to the pier, the two service cranes already doubled over waiting for the cargo nets. Dozens of stevedores grunted against the dead weight of the crates, calling out to one another, counting in unison before shouting *"heave!"* The commotion stirred the seagulls from their roosts. Perched on top of pilings or drifting lazily in the sea just beyond their berth, the scavengers were disturbed by the lapping of the sea and the murmurs of men moving in ten directions all at once. The harmony of their environment askew, they fluttered about anarchically.

∎

Enrique shifted his weight. The cavernous hold of the freighter had barely begun to fill with cargo. For the last three hours he had dutifully checked the black numbers stenciled on the crates against the ones listed on the manifest. Strange that the numbers were out of order, in no obvious sequence. Every ninety minutes the crew chief, an older man with the red and black checked scarf of the CNT draped around his neck, called for a ten-minute break. The blues walked silently away from the slack cargo net at Enrique's feet and clambered topside for a smoke. He found himself alone, deep in the ship's hold.

Enrique ran his hand against the rough, unfinished, pine lid of the top-most crate. The faint light shimmered and moved with the motion of the ship, catching on the pine slat of the front edge of the crate. Absentmindedly, he reached out and snagged his hand on the raised head of a corner nail. The slat gave way, opening a few millimeters. Glancing about, he pulled the slat higher, wood creaking against the nails at the other end, and peered in.

Gold ingots glimmered in the low light.

He drew closer, running a finger along the imprint of the nearest bar. He felt lightheaded. Men's voices broke his daze, and he quickly he shoved the slat into place, deftly striking the nail level with the flat of his hand.

■

By dawn the blues had unloaded two boxcars. Five more remained. The stevedores hung their baling hooks over their shoulders and melted into the city. Enrique took another glance at the ship, now resting lower in the water, and then searched out Cipriano. The Cypriot was leaning over the railing smoking one of his yellow Gauloises. The Cuban waved, flicked his own cigarette butt into the water, and headed for the gangplank.

"I have a pretty good idea what they are loading," Enrique drew even with Cipriano, his front teeth gleaming.

"So do I," replied Cipriano. "It answers many questions, my friend. But not why they have entrusted us with this mission."

"You first." Enrique's grin stretched from ear to ear.

"Simple. Printing paraphernalia, presses, Linotype machines, lead, all the things a peasant society needs to become literate. It's exactly what we have in abundance and what they desperately need."

"Convincing guess, my idealist friend. Fill the needs of the Party, make the workers strong. All that merde." He spat the last word folding his arms his arms. "But not right."

Cipriano rolled his eyes and gestured for him to continue.

"It hardly explains this secrecy, the middle of the night transfer, the way we kept track of the boxes. Clearly the cargo is something even more valuable than printing presses."

Cipriano lifted his palms to the heavens. "Is this something you know, or are just guessing, like you always do?"

"I know it like I know my mother," Enrique put his hands on Cipriano's shoulders. "I looked inside one of the crates that had tipped over in the hold. You won't fucking believe this. It smelled like a machine shop."

"It sounds too simple. Why do you look away?"

Enrique hesitated. "Because I lie to you. Here's what's really there." He held Cipriano's gaze, trying to impress upon his friend the severity of this secret. "It's gold! All the fucking gold in Spain. The entire reserve of the Republic."

"And you weren't going to tell me? You son of a bitch." Cipriano felt the anger gathering in his throat. "Fuck you, comrade. Fuck you." He pulled away from Enrique's grasp.

Enrique's face started to tremble. "I'm telling you now. Don't be stupid. I was just playing." He watched his friend's anger subside with his words, and felt his own follow.

"I don't understand," Cipriano stared mystified at the ship. It made no sense. "Whose gold? And why send it to Papa Stalin?"

'Think about it. Guns, planes, tanks, ammunition, even the Commissars — they all cost money. The Republic is broke. But Spain's reserves, all that gold, a mountain of it, will pay for the rescue of the Republic. It makes sense — even if we lose we have denied Franco our national wealth."

Cipriano took a breath. "But if we win, the Soviets will be in the driver's seat. And even I know that's dangerous."

'They have no choice, don't you see?" Enrique pressed his palms down heavily on his friend's shoulders, looking directly into Cipriano's eyes.

Cipriano considered this for a moment. "Maybe we have another choice."

"What do you mean?"

"Look, I support the Party. But it is supposed to be the party of the workers. That's why we are here — in solidarity with the working class of Spain. If all the wealth goes to the Soviet Union, what happens to the people?"

"What are you thinking about, you devious Cypriot?"

Cipriano furrowed his brows and reached into Enrique's pocket for a cigarette. He lowered his voice, glancing back up toward the city as the sun crept to the edge of the horizon, hovering over the sea like an orange ball of lava.

∎

They awoke before midnight that evening. The streets of the waterfront hummed with activity. Barcelona's workers ignored the civil war that night, indulging in tapas and wine, cigars and chorizo, to them food and drink seemed more important. A fascist air raid rained bombs into the sea, shooting towers of water high into the night sky. The longshoremen, barkeeps, whores, and pickpockets reacted with mocking distain. Any fear that might have crept into their spirit was rooted out with more bravado, more wine, more cigars and then a kiss.

The neighboring building, a wood structure on a street of stone houses, looked like an ancient quilt, its black and gray and white rough-hewn walls mottled and pitted with age. Behind the row of houses a hill traced a jagged line against the horizon as it climbed back up toward the city. A concrete anti-aircraft bunker huddled low on the hilltop, the muzzles of its battery of British QF 3.7-inch anti-aircraft guns pointed toward the sky. The militia men who lived on the street below took turns defending their city, firing the guns randomly as German bombers flew past.

The longshoremen's union office, bar, and hiring hall remained open. It had been cobbled together out of two tiny shacks and an old pissoir. The indented footprints from its prior life were still visible beneath the counter that raised on hinges to allow the waiters to slide sideways out from behind the bar. The wall behind the bar displayed the insignia of the *Coordinadora Estatal de Trabajadores del Mar.* A black fist striking a bollard like a steel hammer, red sparks flying, spoke to the union's militancy. The red and black CNT scarf that hung below told Enrique and Cipriano all they needed to know. Four blues had already seated themselves at the rear of the room. They waved the strangers over to their table.

"You're the comrades who checked the cargo, aren't you?" one of them, the oldest and clearly the leader, stubbed his cigarette out on the table. "Hernando Echivera," he introduced himself. "I am the union harbormaster here." He looked the part, with a flowing mustache, long black hair, deep-set eyes, and a faded scar that ran from his collar up to his scalp behind his left ear. He spread hands out in front of him on the table and leaned back in his chair. "And you are from Albacete, Kléber's eyes and ears. I see you are not Spanish," he looked at Cipriano. "And you," he smiled at Enrique, "You, it is harder to tell. I say Cuban from the way you soften your t's."

He looked back down at the table, then waved his hand for a waiter. *"Dos para nuestros amigos,"* he spoke softly. "We will have a drink and I will explain why I know about you."

The dark-red *Rioja Baja,* sharp and pungent, filled them with a radiant warmth, easing the inherent mistrust they felt for this Echivera. Enrique leaned back in his chair. "To the working classes." He held his glass high. *"Salud."*

"I know what my men are transferring to the ship. You can't unload dozens of boxcars of ungodly heavy cargo and not figure it out. The Soviet agents must think we are as dumb as the Greeks. No offense," he shot a grin at Cipriano. "Yours is the only country where the Royalists and the fascists, that ape Metaxas, are in bed with each other."

"No offense taken. I'm only Cypriot. My country may be an island with Greeks, but we are no Greek Island."

"What do you propose?" Enrique poured another round.

"The cargo is too precious, don't you think, for us to stand on the shore and wave 'bon voyage.'" Echivera laced his fingers behind his head. "As loyal unionists we ought to keep some of the Reserve in reserve. Rainy day, if you understand my meaning."

Cipriano and Enrique exchanged glances.

"My uncle, Luis Merlo, runs the docks in Santiago. I know he would keep this 'tithe' in trust for us."

"A trust fund for the revolution." Enrique mulled the idea. "No, not just the revolution, but a revolutionary international federation of workers and peasants." He coughed, "This cargo is just too precious to simply deliver it all to the Soviets."

"Yes. Brother." Echivera looked over his shoulder and then returned his gaze to the table. "A trust fund for the Solidaridad Internacional Antifascista."

Enrique couldn't believe his ears. SIA, the Cuban counterpart of the CNT, had recruited him, trained him, and sent him to Spain. Like his Spanish comrades, Enrique detested authority, hierarchy, and men who gave orders. It felt good to be among his people once again. Fuck the fascists and fuck the Party. This was where he lived. *"Viva l'anarchia"* he said to himself. He picked up his glass, swilled the wine in a single gulp, and winked at Cipriano. "Great minds, eh *amigo?* Great minds."

∎

Over the next two days as the blues dutifully unloaded the boxcars, straining under the weight of the cargo, Cipriano and Enrique took turns in the hold. During every break they lingered, removed six gold bars from a crate, and put them into a casket that Echivera had placed in the rear of the hold. Draped with the flag of the Republic, three caskets sat unlocked, the tags of Líster's Eleventh Division dangling from their brass handrails. On each tag Echivera had written *"MUERTO/BRUNETE."* He also inscribed the tags with a red double

XX, the universal designation for degraded remains. No one was likely to open these coffins. Líster himself, the Republic's first hero, had grown up in Cuba, and to Enrique and Echivera the return of three soldiers for burial in Santiago offered a perfect cover.

After the third day, the three draped coffins of Republican heroes killed in action at Brunete were hoisted out of the hold and placed on the dock. Two SIA militia stood sentry. Barely an hour after the Lenin weigh anchor for Odessa, a ship of Cuban registry steamed into the harbor. The Atlantida, a tourist freighter belonging to the Standard Fruit and Steamship Company, slid into the vacated pier just long enough to load the coffins of the Republic's fallen heroes. As befitting the dignity of the three soldiers' remains, the coffins were placed in one of the staterooms reserved for the directors of the line. Just before the ship departed, one of the blues slipped quietly aboard and removed the coffins' tags, replacing them with the red, black, and gold label of Bacardi's Caribbean Warehouse in Santiago. The reverse side of the new tags included the initials BKS, Barcelona-Kingston-Santiago, and the number 701.

Later that day, Hernando Echivera handed Enrique an exact replica of one of the Bacardi tickets. "Our brothers in Santiago will hold this for you. The warehouse pallet number will guide you to their location. No one else has seen or recorded these numbers. They belong to you alone. Be of good speed, my brothers." Echivera kissed them on both cheeks and turned to depart.

"Wait," called Enrique. "We can't let you go without compensation."

"No worry, amigo, no worry." Echivera grinned and revealed another Bacardi label. "We have kept a small token in remembrance."

"Gracias," Enrique smiled. "Perhaps we will not see each other again."

Echevera smiled back. "Perhaps you are right. We go to the front tomorrow. To Brunete."

CHAPTER TWO
TEACHING TACTICS

I

Anna ran her finger down the page. "We have less than two weeks to get ready. Two weeks to make these boys into soldiers. Enrique, I want you to set up a training schedule. You are Cuban, they will respect you. You served with us in Spain, and we respected you."

"But why should we do this?" Enrique spoke slowly.

"For the same reason you came when I called for your help. Because we trust each other. There is much blood and history between us."

"But why here?" Cipriano raised his voice.

"Because Castro is from here, from the hills, from Santiago. He knows the local people and he trusts them. They will help us if we need them." This time Oliver answered, looking around the room.

"But we have something else we must do first, before we begin training."

"Tell us please," Rena leaned in the corner of the kitchen, her sweater hanging loosely from her shoulders, her eyelids half-closed with exhaustion. Anna knew better than to confuse her posture with a lack of spirit.

"We need money. Real money. We need to buy more guns." Anna spoke softly. "Any ideas?"

Cipriano and Enrique looked at each other, then nodded.

"How much?" asked Enrique.

"Enough to arm everyone. I can't tell you specifics, but we must all be armed. By the time we are ready to move, we will number at least a hundred."

"Give us two days," Enrique looked at Cipriano, "right, *amigo?*"

Two days did not prove adequate. The next morning Anna announced, "We need to secure some provisions." She looked directly at Rena and Oliver. "We have two days of food on hand and no money. It will be some time before the Cypriot Brothers get back here. I'd like to be alive when they do."

They sat at the porcelain counter that served as the kitchen table in the *"Bohío de Cuba"* as they had dubbed their disguised farmhouse. Anna was dressed in black, with a sash of red around her waist. Oliver wore his usual gray cord trousers, beret pulled down to his eyebrows. Rena had found a pair of overalls, the bib dangling free from one strap, a wore a pink long-sleeved shirt underneath, and an ancient pair of hiking boots.

"And glean some intelligence," Oliver assumed command, glancing at Rena to gauge her reaction. When she didn't respond he turned to Anna. "I'm not very useful to you out in the field…"

"We know," Rena suddenly came alive. "I was there too."

Anna stepped in. Old patterns, old friends. "Let's think about what we need and how to get it." Always the problem solver.

"We can either appropriate the food we need. Remember how it worked in Spain? Knock on the door, sound official, give a Republican salute, take the pick of the pantry. Or, we can find a sympathetic local farmer who will join the Movement and share the bounty of his efforts willingly."

Oliver stared out the front door, wondering why exactly he had agreed to come on this adventure. He knew the answer, or at least suspected he knew. He never could say no to Anna. But he had wondered why Rena had accepted the call, and whether she would accept the gig too.

"I say we try to make allies." Oliver wasn't at all sure about his voice. He looked for some assent in their eyes. "Drive to the next village. No one knows us there, right?"

The two women remained silent.

"We work together. A *cantina* will be the best place to start. Just engage the locals and see what transpires."

Rena considered him, remembering how he had screamed about his leg in the hospital. "Sure, Oliver. Sounds like a good idea. Anna?"

"I think we need a story, something more definite. Like that we are looking for something. Something that won't raise suspicion, that will open doors."

"Got it," Oliver brightened. "You speak on our behalf. Rena and I will be bereft parents looking for our missing child. We be Americans from the American Nickel Company who have employed you to help us locate our child."

Anna squinted thoughtfully, and then waited a moment. Good for Oliver to watch her considering how to respond, a way to establish authority. "Not quite, my friend. Not quite. That will be our cover story, if anyone asks what we are doing. But, dear Ollie, it doesn't secure us what we are after. We need political friends, sympathizers."

"How do we find that out?" Rena was torn between the wisdom of Anna's strategy and her feelings for Oliver. She looked at him quickly to see if he had flinched at her rebuke.

Oliver did not disappoint, his mouth tightly drawn.

"It's really quite simple." Anna liked the way her voice sounded, liked the way command felt. "We pass by some farms, ones with livestock grazing, and introduce ourselves. From Santiago, on holiday. We've taken a wrong turn and need to get back."

The others nodded in agreement.

They sipped dark Cuban coffee from tiny cups and wandered out on the green-painted veranda. The air smelled fresh, cooled by the night, but they knew the reprieve would not last. Not in the tropics.

"We better shove off before it gets too hot," Oliver moved between Anna and Rena, looking out past the compound into the massive mountain rising behind them. He grabbed the keys to the car, tossing them to Anna. "You drive. We'll provide moral support and sound advice. Right Rena?" He smiled as the two women followed him to the automobile, enjoying the moment of authority.

The Mercury had a white roof and black body and was covered with dust and missing its front left hubcap. The car started easily, the gurgle and then full throat of its exhaust the only sound in the valley. Windows down, the passengers rode silently as Anna guided the car out from behind the hedgerow and onto the hard packed dirt road that led to the foothills of the Sierra Maestra.

"The squatters," Anna called over her shoulder. "They are the ones we need. Let's get up into the hills and see what we can find."

∎

The higher they drove, the slower their progress. The Mercury labored in the hills, pinging like shrapnel. The jungle closed in on them, green and lush, and they soon lost any sense of time or distance. The road narrowed, then vanished, save for two parallel tire tracks. When Rena questioned if they hadn't perhaps gone too far, Oliver pointed out the way the grass on the tracks had been matted down.

"Someone has traversed this road recently," he intoned seriously.

"Yes, boss." Rena shot back. Silently Anna shrugged.

Then she stopped the car. "Here's a place to start." She turned off the ignition.

"I don't see anything. What about you, Rena?" Oliver turned in his seat, his hand on the rear door handle.

"It's not obvious," Anna spoke softly. "But, see, over there?" She pointed to a curl of smoke rising from behind the brush. "Someone is

133

cooking."

"Copacetic," Oliver slid out of the car, holding the door open for Rena. "Copacetic."

The underbrush thickened with each step they wandered down a barely discernible path toward the clearing that Anna had noted. She took the lead, with Oliver and then Rena following. They pushed through the boxwood shrubs, thick evergreens that grew to shoulder height, only the whooshing-scratching sound of the foliage, dry and brittle in the sun marking their progress.

"*Stop!* Who are you? Stop where you are." A young man, a boy really, pointed an ancient hunting rifle directly at Anna. "What do you want?" He wore trousers of light denim and neither shirt nor shoes. A fearsome machete was slung across his back. The blade extended above his head, like a sliver feather. If he felt any fear his eyes did not betray him. Anna stared back at him, relieved by the sureness of his gaze.

"We are looking for help. Are your parents about?"

"What kind of help?" He spoke evenly, without menace, but Anna could see the muscles of his arms tighten under his light brown skin.

"We have lost our way. We were out for a hike in the mountains. It is quite beautiful here, and we thought we thought to escape the city for a day — all that traffic and garbage."

The boy held up his hand. Anna guessed that he was no older than thirteen. His dark eyes and black hair glistened.

"You must think I am *estupido*. No one comes up this way to hike. Only the SIM, and I don't think you are with them." He looked them up and down, his gaze taking in first the two women and then the pant-leg of Oliver's artificial leg. It had caught on the brush, exposing the dark wood that extended up from his old-field boots. "Even though you were once in the army." He smiled, pleased with his deduction.

"Are your parents here?" Anna asked again. "Perhaps they can help us. Tell them that the Sargentino sent us. They will understand."

The boy turned away from the intruders. "Wait here," he instructed, and pushed his way back into the brush. In the space of a breath he had disappeared.

"What now?" asked Rena.

"Evidently, we wait," Oliver liked sounding sure, although Anna could sense his uncertainty.

The three veterans huddled in the hot shade of the Sierra Maestra foothills. They stood mute, waiting, ears straining to hear the boy's return.

"What...?" Oliver began.

Anna cut him off with a glare, pointing in the direction the boy had disappeared, reprimanding him for even thinking of disrupting the silence. When he didn't respond, Anna smiled inwardly. She liked it when he stood his ground. Made him resemble the leader she once knew, before his terrible injury, before the crushing defeat of their Battalion in battle, before the Party sent them packing home.

The boy reappeared.

"Follow me." He turned and led them back into the brush.

The *bohío* stood in a clearing, its brown-gray thatched roof covering white scrap-wood walls and a flamingo pink veranda. An apron of brown sandy soil framed the structure, separating it from the lines of tobacco plants nearby. A handmade rain-barrel stood under the far corner of the roof. The air smelled damp, redolent with the scent of the mariposa that grew wild, their white petals covered by tiny drops of morning dew. The door stood open, a dark shadow across the white front of the house.

A woman in a white cotton dress that reached her bare feet stood in the doorway. Her face, round and leathery, made her look old and young simultaneously, her bright eyes encased in a web of wrinkles. She smiled broadly and managed to keep the half-smoked cigar squarely in her teeth. She motioned the boy inside, then stepped out onto the veranda.

"She wants us to come in," Anna turned to Oliver and Rena, "but I think we should take off our shoes." The woman had spoken in a language that sounded like Spanish, but which even Anna couldn't quite understand. She remembered that some peasants in the East spoke a pidgin sprinkled with native Taino that rendered it nearly impossible for most Cubans to comprehend.

The woman motioned for them to sit on the dirt floor Except for Oliver, whom she pointed to a simple three-legged stool on her right. Oliver raised an eyebrow, and the woman simply pointed to his leg. Oliver tilted his head to one side, astonished, but silently obeyed. The woman puffed heavily on her cigar, and began waving a spray of greens, fanning the smoke into the room. Behind the woman Anna could see a table loaded with a full layer cake, dozens of candles burning at different levels, several bottles of rum, and an entire dead chicken cut into pieces and soaking in its own blood.

Anna was sure that neither Oliver nor Rena had attended a Santería service before. She glanced over at their faces and read only bewilderment in their expressions.

Reaching behind her, the priestess took a large bottle of rum from the altar, uncorked it with her teeth, and held it out for Oliver and Rena to drink.

Rena took a sip of the warm alcohol, then passed the bottle to Oliver. The woman stood behind Anna and together they watched as the pair passed the bottle back and forth. Taking Anna's hands in hers, the woman looked deeply into her eyes and spoke.

Anna brightened and held out her arms to Oliver and Rena.

"She tells us that we are welcome to all the food we need."

"How could she possibly know?" Oliver still held the rum in his hands.

"She found out by touching my spirit. That's what she just told me."

"But they are so poor. How can they have enough?" Rena stood, amazed.

"They have several goats that she will donate to our cause. And one pig that we can have on credit."

"Credit?"

"Yes. After we win, she says we can pay her back."

"But how could she know?" Oliver didn't seem to comprehend what had just occurred. "And why did she allow us entry to her cabin?"

"When I told the boy Sargento he passed it on to his mother and she let us in."

"Why? Pray tell," Oliver let his mouth drop.

"Around here they call Batista Sargentino, the little sergeant. He was a sergeant when he grabbed power the first time. He hates the nickname, it reminds him of his modest origins. People up here detest him because he wants to evict them. I gambled and we won."

∎

They returned to the farmhouse in Siboney at dark. The two goats, still alive, were strapped to the trunk, a rope securing the animals' legs to the lid. Inside the trunk the boy had helped them store the carcass of the pig, its tail curled into a tight ball. On the roof of the car they tied three baskets of vegetables — yucca, malanga, and potatoes. The stews they could make with the roots and goats, flavored with cumin, would feed them for many days.

It took four hours to drive back to the farmhouse. The goats required they go slowly, avoiding bumps. The alarmed braying of their two passengers and the unmistakable odor of dead pig accompanied them all the way back.

PART THREE

CIVIL WAR

CHAPTER ONE
BRUNETE

The cluster of commanders and politicians around Líster had grown restless. Too much time planning, they thought. Too much time waiting. Even more so for Commander Oliver Law. He shifted his weight, took a drag from the cigarette dangling from his lips, and dug his elbow into the ribs of the man beside him. Cipriano's eyes popped open and he wiped a drizzle of drool from the corner of his mouth. Then he smiled sheepishly, and Law could see the life returning to the Cypriot's eyes.

"We have decided to take the war to the Nationalists." Líster's bald head and wire-rimmed glasses gave him the look of a Cossack. "We will attack tomorrow."

∎

The Republican Army had regrouped in the wake of a stunning defeat earlier that year at Jarama, one that cost the Lincoln Battalion more than half of its number in casualties. Soviet advisers had insisted, despite Kléber's opinion, on reforming the International Brigades by merging the tattered remnant of the Lincolns with the remains of the British, Canadian, and Cuban volunteers.

General Líster, Spanish born, Cuban educated, and dedicated member of the Communist Party in both countries, had been given command of the new 11th Division of the Republican Army. Fluent in English, Spanish, French, and German, he spoke all four languages with equal obscenity. And it was he who had called on Law to take command of the Division's Tom Mooney Machine Gun Company.

"I don't give a fuck. You hear me, a fuck, Law. I don't give a goddamned fuck what you do, who you take, how many casualties you suffer." Just follow the tanks down this hill across the valley, and up to the ridge, there, where the enemy has dug in." He pointed a bony finger west toward the opposing heights.

Oliver had served with Líster earlier at Jarama and knew what he was in for.

"Only request, Commander, only request is that I continue to serve with my closest and most trusted comrades."

"Look, you son-of-a-bitch, you do what you need to do. This is it for the Republic. If we fail to relieve Madrid, fail to stop the Nationalists, it is kaput, fini. Can I be any clearer? And another thing. Cut out that comrade crap. Way I hear it we'll all be generals in the Red Army soon."

Oliver saw the gleam in Líster's eye. Not a good idea to press him further when he was in this kind of mood.

"One more conundrum, if I may, Commander."

"That two bit word ain't in my vocabulary. But, if you insist on keeping that mujer machine gunner, don't fucking ask me. Just do it."

As Oliver turned, Líster came up behind him and gripped him by the arms. "You know, my friend, I trust you. The only negro commander," he paused, "on our side." He laughed deeply.

∎

At six the following evening the bombing and shelling began. West, on the far side of the valley the village of Brunette — ancient buildings along stone-filled narrow streets — commanded the heights of the region. The Republican General Staff had identified this objective, twenty-five kilometers from Madrid, as critical to their goals: take the pressure off the capital, hold Franco's forces at bay, and prevent the Nationalists from inserting a military wedge between Barcelona and Madrid. Given enough time, they may be able to consolidate their international position and put more Soviet arms in the field. It might even prevent Franco's deployment of German bombers in the Basque country to the West. Brunete, then, held the key to the future of the Republic.

Líster organized his new XV Division into several independent commands: a tank company, an infantry company, and a machine gun company. Oliver was to serve as the machine gun commander.

"And you only talk to me. Me. Get it?" Líster spoke with authority. He turned to their Comintern operative named Milikov and instructed him in no uncertain terms, "Stay the fuck out of my way." Milikov pulled his black leather jacket tighter and stalked off.

For an hour, just as daylight disappeared, leaving only the hint of a pink sunset, a massive Republican barrage walked across the valley below. It shattered the evening sky with flashes of light, popping erratically, strobing irregularity, one shell on top of another, filling the air with the smell of cordite. Overhead, flight after flight of Tupolov SB-2 fighter-bombers raked the hillside that climbed to Brunete.

Oliver, flanked by Anna and Enrique and Cipriano, watched through field glasses as Nationalist fighter-planes rose to attack the bombers. The Russian pilots were skilled, and during the first hour shot down plane after fascist plane, sending them spiraling to the ground where they crashed in the valley in a series of fireballs that sent black smoke rolling up into the sky.

"Front row seats," Oliver leaned his elbows into the sandbags that surrounded them. Their position, a forward observation post overlooking the valley, had been dug out the night before.

Armed with three new QF 3.7-inch guns the unit's gunners,

ammunition feeders, and a dozen carriers all served under Oliver's command. Anna, Enrique, and Cipriano each fired the guns, but the guns' weight made them awkward for teams of even four to operate effectively. Water-cooled and clumsy, they, nevertheless fired 10-20 rounds per minute. "Body shredders," the British called them, "bloody body shredders."

By evening the brutal Republican offensive had shattered the landscape and shrouded the valley in gun smoke. Down below they could still make out the destruction born of the assault. Olive trees split in half by shell-fire and scrub oak splintered by shrapnel had transformed the agrarian valley into a vale of craters, filled with bones and waste.

Oliver ordered their three guns into position, ready to advance as soon as the General Staff deemed the preparation complete. He shuddered as he recalled the language from WWI, "softening up." He exhorted each team to spring from the dugout and follow in the shadows of three Soviet T-26 tanks down into the valley. The *rat-a-tat* of the machine guns joined the explosive volleys from the tanks. Oliver stood on his toes, trying to gain a better view of the battlefield.

"Look." Ollie pointed toward the valley below. "It's about 1000 meters from our position to the floor. We follow the river, there," and he nodded their right, to the North "and take command to the approach to the hills on the other side. Then tomorrow we go again. It will be tough. Up the opposing hillside. Intel tells us it's steep, dangerous, and the route forces us to enter the dense vegetation planted by some crazy duke, Alba something. Once we get through the groves and vineyards and trees our orders are to storm that ridge, atop what they call the Romulan Heights." He directed Anna's gaze across the valley, up past the village of Brunete nested in the hillside. "Our objective there is Mosquito Ridge, that notch in the heights above the village." He hesitated for a brief moment. "We'll be lucky to make it."

Without warning, a green fountain of fire spewed high into the night sky, casting their position in an eerie light. A Nationalist shell shattered a tank hidden in the trees on the hillside behind them. Oliver could hear the screams of the men as the tank exploded. Suddenly, firing from the heights on either side of the valley, both armies brought to bear all they could muster. Líster had warned against this and only Oliver resisted firing back at the fascist positions across the valley. Red and yellow tracers stretched from one hillside to the other, live strands of barbed wire that whined and ricocheted in a wail of destruction.

"We wait," Oliver announced during a short lull in the firing. "We wait, conserve our ammunition. Keep your heads down, but your attention up."

Anna muttered something that Oliver could not make out. He looked at her. Something about her spoke of courage, perhaps just the way she rested her chin on the sandbags and looked over the battlefield with enormous concentration. She never, not for a single second, showed any sign of fear. He thought to ask her about where she found her courage. But a cascade of fascist bullets and shells forced him down again.

Another shell burst, this time directly overhead, bright enough to illuminate the whole tableau. For an instant, Oliver could discern the clear silhouettes of thousands of men and hundreds of tanks advancing like toy soldiers set in motion, down toward the valley floor.

"That's our signal!" he pointed to the orange starbursts. "Let's move!"

Up and down the line, along the hundreds of meters where the Loyalist troops massed, tanks and then men moved out. At ten minute intervals each of the infantry companies rose, battle flags raised, and set off double-time down the hillside. The plan, Oliver remembered, was to mass enough men and materiel on the approaches to the

Nationalist positions on hills across the valley by daybreak, then to dig in and wait for the next night.

"Now!" Oliver Law called out to his unit. *"Now!"*

He pulled himself up and out of the dugout, boots scrambling to gain a foothold in the dirt. *"Follow me!"* he called, advancing with his pistol drawn toward the three tanks that waited, engines running, to serve as moving shields. Around him shells exploded, sending showers of dirt and slivers of metal that thudded into the earth. Machine gun fire whizzed, tracers glaring, from across the valley. "Everyone out?" he called, checking over his shoulder at his three teams of gunners, loaders, and carriers as they clambered over the sand bag embankments.

The tanks engaged their gears and slowly groaned their way down the hillside. Oliver's unit followed in their tracks, bent over, carbines and ammo boxes on their shoulders, hands free to steady against slips and falls. To his left another unit, a dozen men from the Lincoln Battalion, followed their own tank. A rifle company, they held their carbines in one hand, fingers on the trigger, the leather straps bound tight across their arms, just above the elbow. A Nationalist shell hit the lead tank just behind the turret, setting off the magazine. The burning tank tipped over on its side, a flame bursting skyward. The soldiers behind the wounded tank froze in mid-step. Oliver could see them all now, their figures outlined in the half-light of the orange-yellow glow of evening. Suddenly they ignited in a blaze of sparkling red flames. Still burning, these human torches tried to dive to their stomachs, elbows tucked beneath their chests, some even crawling toward the olive trees.

Further down, below the olive grove, the rest of the column penetrated a vineyard. Oliver and his three teams followed, still behind the armored vehicles. New orders had arrived telling them to take control of the floor of the valley and set up an impenetrable barrier to protect the division before the next surge. They joined more Republican soldiers from another unit, men who had previously survived the slaughter at Jarama, and together they moved through the vineyard like ghostly shadows. These veterans all wore improvised uniforms: gray twill trousers tucked into ankle-high leather boots, cotton shirts in khaki or brown, leather suspenders, Sam Browne belts with pockets loaded down with gear — canteens, knives, collapsible shovels, extra socks, maps, pencils, printed directives from the company commissar that remained folded and unread, and crumbled packets of American, French, and Spanish cigarettes. To Oliver's chagrin, none of them wore a helmet, and all wore the dark blue berets of the CNT and POUM militias. They can't survive this, the thought the burning platoon alive in his mind's eye.

The smell of burning gasoline and cordite assaulted Oliver's nostrils as bullets collided with soldiers around him. Their bodies jerked from the gunfire or they simply fell to their knees, staring down as their intestines spilled out before them in a burst of steam. One soldier, his gun drawn, kept screaming "Advance!" even as the bloody stump of his leg twitched. A moment later he fell silent.

Oliver signaled his team to hit the ground. There was no way to communicate with the tank commanders. Within a minute the tanks had moved a hundred meters ahead, leaving the thirteen members of his unit exposed to the relentless machine gun-fire that sliced through anything in its path.

Oliver holstered his pistol, then crouched and zig-zagged from one member of his unit to the next, speaking softly, comforting those who were unhinged, praising the veterans who had survived this battle.

"You showed uncommon fortitude today," he whispered to Anna who remained prone, her face buried in the ground. "I'm terribly proud to serve with you."

He touched her back lightly. "Stay put. I will inform you when we may proceed."

Anna smiled. "You are a brave man, Señor Law. And I love more the way you use the English language."

Oliver had already moved ahead, running past and through the machine gun fire that peppered down on the Loyalists.

Then, at last, silence.

Broken only by the groans of the wounded, of the men alive but without limbs or eyes or guts. And their whispers as they called out to one another, checking on the living, marking the dead. As he felt his adrenaline subside, Oliver looked across at his unit, counting twelve comrades. He gave them the thumbs up and wiped muddy tears from his eyes.

On the morning of the 27th of July Oliver's unit regrouped at the bottom of the hill. They had almost made it to the valley floor and the trees that followed a long creek as it flowed down from Brunete. Rena pulled her cloak closer to her. The night was warm but she needed the comfort as she moved through the battlefield tending to the wounded. She had been sent to Brunete the day before to train a new group of medics, and as a Captain her authority rested uneasily on her.

Captain Rena Thompson might have had a nice ring to it initially, but not now, she thought, glancing down at the dark circle on her cloak. Party be damned. Harlem Hospital be damned too. She was a medical professional — not an orderly. The scene before her erased any sense of achievement or righteousness. Thousands of bodies spread out before her — dead, wounded, dying. The Nationalists had counter-attacked in the middle of the night and their dead and wounded lay among the Republicans.

The dead and wounded were scattered among burnt hulks of shattered tanks, treads up; charred armored cars on their sides; field guns with barrels peeled open like overripe bananas; wingless fighter planes with crumpled cockpits. The detritus of war as far as the eye could see. Nurses in her group wandered through the littered hillside, offering tin cups of brandy to the living and tagging the toes of the dead. The aid station behind their lines would be operating full blast, and Rena knew she'd be up all night working in the primitive operating room they had constructed earlier in the day. To her left she saw a man rise from his prone position, extend his hand for a cup, and then drop.

Another man approached and at first she did not recognize him.

His dashing gold tooth, of course, told her who he was. But his eyes were wary and exhausted and his face, smeared with dirt, made him look older, sadder.

He recognized her. "Nurse Thompson, is it? You've come a long way."

"You're one to talk, Commander." She stopped. The time for cleverness had long past. She looked into his eyes, really looked. "Are you alright?"

He sagged inwardly for a moment, then recovered.

"We are all intact. My unit is installed down there," Oliver pointed to their new position tucked into the bend of the creek. "We need to sleep. It starts again tonight, you know."

Rena knew. The command had instructed her to scour the battlefield for walking wounded. "We need to get them back as soon as possible," they had said, "the situation is dire, we will need anyone who can hold a gun."

A man appeared, a specter in the mist. He held a notepad in one hand, scribbling furiously with the other. He caught sight of them and, tucking the pencil behind his ear, offered his hand. "I'm Herbert Matthews. New York Times."

Arthur, to this day I still can't fathom discovering two American Negros on that battlefield in Spain. I knew that the Internationals were just that, but until our encounter I simply had no idea. In retrospect, it was like so much of American twenty years ago. We thought, those of us who were educated, Northern and cosmopolitan, that we were color-blind. In fact, we were, and maybe still are, blind to the color around us. I remember my first question. "May I ask what brings two Negro Americans to a Spanish battlefield?" He held a pencil at the ready just like a newspaperman and wore blues and beret. "What do you think about this place, this battle?" He swept his hand in a grand gesture. "What do you see?

Oliver turned from Rena and surveyed the scene before him. "We dealt them some shit today."

"But, Commander," Matthews looked first at the nurse and then at the soldier, "who are 'they'"?

"The fascists," replied Oliver. "The Nationalists."

Rena considered the journalist thoughtfully. She moved a bit closer to Matthews, peering down at his notepad. "What do you see?"

Matthews waved his hand across the battlefield again. "Look carefully. Not at the soldiers. Look at all the equipment. See those tanks — " he pointed at two burnt hulks, "they are Italian. L6/40's to be precise. Younger and lighter brothers of the British Carden Loyd tankettes. Crew of three, fast and maneuverable. So too are the planes, single engine Fiat CR32s." He paused for emphasis. "This is Mussolini's operation, signed, sealed, and delivered. If you look carefully at the dead you'll see that many of them are Italian. A few months ago the German Condor Legion destroyed Guernica and now the flower of Mussolini's 'volunteer' army is dug in over there." He pointed across the valley, back up the hills toward Brunete.

"And we are both," Oliver looked at Rena, "from the International Brigades. Both American, both Negro, both fighting for democracy, both struggling against fascism and racism wherever it comes from. You asked what we are doing here. That's what."

Rena nodded. It had taken five minutes of conversation with Matthews for her to recall her memory of the charming officer who had guided her through the initiation process in Paris. Now he was a powerful military leader, an unknown hero.

"You have my deep respect, Comrade." She said.

Oliver Law looked back at her and she could feel the power in his gaze.

"You are too generous, Captain. We are all in this struggle for human dignity together. I salute you."

Rena felt the power of his restraint embodied in the richness of his language.

"God's speed, Commander. I look forward to serving with you another day."

As she continued her ministrations on the bloody hillside, she noted that Matthews and Oliver still stood together further down the hill, pad and pencil between them, locked in conversation.

Law and Matthews.

The warrior and the writer.

It took the rest of the morning for the Republican units to regroup. They worked tirelessly to triage the wounded and identify the dead, as if they could not contemplate continuing the battle without first clearing evidence of the slaughter.

Oliver rejoined his unit. They had finished digging into their new position, a semi-circle of sandbags arced around a trench, only half-way down the hill from where they shoved off a day earlier. They positioned their three machine guns to cover 180 degrees of fire. Twenty meters to the rear a second trench had been dug to hold the boxes of ammunition belts.

The Commissars who briefed Oliver and the other commanders earlier that day had praised them for their courageous victory the night before. The commanders had estimated casualties at fifty percent and pleaded with the Commissars for a respite to reorganize.

"We attack tonight," the Commissars responded.

The objective once again were the Nationalist positions on the other hillside. Each of Oliver's three crew chiefs sat by their guns, smoking as they sagged into the burlap sand bags. Overhead a Soviet biplane flew lazily, the pilot leaning out to better gauge the Nationalist displacements. The map they sent down to Law identified the objective for the next evening's attack as a march on the Heights, nicknamed Mosquito Ridge. He was to defend his position first, then advance behind the shock troops, then take Mosquito Ridge and defend it.

Anna seemed lost in thought. The daylight had already faded and despite the heat she curled inside the brown leather jacket she first wore in Madrid a year earlier. She held her beret between her knees, her legs bent into twin V's. Her dark hair, still held in place by her ivory combs, was caked with dirt, and her wide-brown eyes were half-closed in mid-reverie or fatigue, Oliver couldn't tell. He glanced at his watch and slid down beside her.

"We still have a couple of hours," he smiled and popped an Old Gold out of the packet in his chest pocket. "How did you come to be here, Anna? I have often conjectured, but not actually concluded."

She laughed. "I haven't told my story in a long time." She began to speak, her accent lilting, as she told him about her Basque upbringing. About waking up before the sun in a dirt-floored bunkhouse with five other miner families. About her father, stripped to the waist, standing in icy water, shoveling iron ore. How he taught her to read at night by an oil lamp. About children who peed though cracks in the floorboards in the winter, and her mother who died of dysentery at the age of 29, leaving behind two children to join the four who had already died. About a life that was a deep pit without horizon.

No one had to teach her to hate authority, she told Oliver. No wonder that the first Communist Party organizer who appeared found her so receptive to his class analysis. She worked in the mines too, but as an agitator and organizer. Once she was thrown in prison for handing out strike pamphlets. They put her in a holding cell with the early morning round-up of whores.

"By noon, I had them clanging on the bars with tin cups demanding their rights." She laughed at the memory. "The Party relocated me to Barcelona just after the Popular Front elections in 1936. They told me to join the CNT militia, to infiltrate it, and to learn how to shoot."

"So, that is where you learned to use this baby," Oliver patted the barrel of her gun.

"It is also where I learned that the Party didn't give a fig about Basque independence. So I became an anarchist and a machine gunner.

Joined the defense of Madrid. Met those two characters," she nodded at where Cipriano and Enrique slept peacefully next to each other, impervious to their surroundings. "And here I am."

Oliver took a deep breath. The Party had brought him this far. He saw no reason to change his beliefs, but he did appreciate the meaning of Anna's political trajectory.

"It hardly matters now, does it?" she asked. "We are here to save the Republic from the fascists. The revolution will come later." She tucked a strand of black hair back into her beret, her eyes calm.

"I guess I've been an anti-fascist even before I knew what the word meant." Oliver's voice sounded far away to him, as if he were listening to the conversation.

The high shrill of a dozen whistles sounded the attack, jolting the unit to attention. Oliver glanced at his watch, 2000 hours already. The others rose and packed their gear — machine guns and tripods hoisted on their shoulders, carbines grasped in one hand, belts of ammunition draped on the same arm. A walking arsenal, bristling with firepower. Overhead a dozen Soviet fighter planes circled the battlefield, swooping down to disrupt the Nationalist defenses.

Oliver led his company, one at a time, up toward the ridge. He positioned Enrique at one end of the line and Anna at the other — two of his most trained gunners front and ready. On the slope up towards Mosquito Ridge, the earth changed from moist brown loam to hard-packed sand as they moved toward the Romanillas Heights. Nationalist units had already begun to rain fire down on the lead elements of the attack, 200 meters ahead. For the moment, Oliver's group was spared their raking gunfire, and he marched straight ahead, upright, head bare, shoulders back.

The company trudged along deliberately, the weight of their armaments making each step of their advance arduous. Further up the hill the sandy soil now, overgrown with knee-high grasses, gave way to a web of narrow dry gulches that snaked their way towards the river to their right. Oliver divided his unit into three machine gun groups and motioned for them to follow separate gullies running parallel to one another. Fanned out across an arc fifty meters wide, the three machine gun groups worked their way slowly up the hill. Oliver, in the lead, moved the teams up and across the hilly terrain, directing them with hand motions as they worked their way up the Heights closer toward Mosquito Ridge, where they could see the steeple of an ancient church rising above the smoke.

The mid-summer heat had baked the battlefield and even in the early evening the humidity left them drenched in sweat. Up ahead where the battle had already exploded, just at the foot of the Ridge, Republican and Nationalist forces exchanged a furious volley of automatic gunfire. Oliver could hear the hammering of dozens of machine guns, each model — Vickers, Maxim, Hotchkiss, and Browning — with its own distinctive sound and rhythm. Above, a new German M-109 swooped down on the Republican advance, its twin cannons kicking up a double row of deadly lead, dirt, and debris. As it pulled away, the pilot slid the cockpit window open and casually tossed out a bundle of grenades that destroyed the lead Soviet-Republican tank that had arrived at the base of Mosquito Ridge.

"Comrades!" Oliver called out, trying to make himself heard above the din, *"Faster! We must move faster!"* He discarded all the unnecessary equipment he could get his hands on — blanket, mess kit, food tubs, even his gas mask. It hardly made the burden any lighter, but it communicated his point. He could see the others doing the same, as they picked up their pace, sweating mightily, as they approached the notch that marked the entry to the single trail that would take them up to Mosquito Ridge.

One of the ammunition carriers in Cipriano's team stopped and bent down to pry something out of his boot. He straightened, then collapsed as a jagged hole on his forehead spurted blood, covering his face in a deep red mask. Moments later the hillside above them erupted with gunfire coming from a church atop the Ridge. Law's gun crews dove face down into the shallow cover of the gullies, without time or space to set their own weapons. Only Cipriano had the presence of mind to brace the barrel of his machine gun over his left arm, firing with his right. Three belts of ammunition fed into the gun, but without the tripod or priming water the gun began to heat rapidly, glowing red as it burned through the sleeve of his left arm.

In the face of the fusillade Oliver rose and raced over to Cipriano.

"You crazy Greek. I told you to be careful." He kept his voice low and reassuring, helping Cipriano roll onto his side. He tore the man's sleeve, plucked a strip of gauze from his pocket, and bandaged the blistered arm.

"How many times I tell you I'm not Greek," Cipriano whispered.

"Okay. You crazy son of a bitch, does that sound better? You crazy Cypriot son of a bitch, you are going to use up all my medical rations." Several mortar rounds whistled overhead and Oliver kept bandaging. "Time for you to go to the aid station."

Cipriano stared at him as if he were insane. "Put another bandage on it and I'll be good as new."

The third-degree burns had already begun to blister.

Enrique and Anna had moved further up the hill and now the machine gun fire coming from the church steeple at the center of Mosquito Ridge had them pinned down.

Oliver patted Cipriano on the back of his head and took a deep breath. "Alright soldier. Cover me!"

He sprinted forward, his carbine in one hand and a brace of grenades bumping from their perch on his suspenders. The splat splat splat of machine gun fire tracked him as he ran, spitting down at him from the church.

Shells from a Italian 77mm field howitzers, The Bonnie, that weighed 7 kilos. Its burst rate of 200 meters/second made it a weapon of great popularity. It could, the brains at the rear headquarters argued, provide a maximum field of damage at a minimum caliber. It was the standard field artillery piece in the Italian Army. Mussolini only sold 25 of them to Franco's forces. They were all deployed at Brunete.

The gulches disappeared and the terrain changed again, giving way to a miniature forest of Ilex trees. Oliver's map said the land belonged to the Duke of Alba. The forest had filled in along the hillside below Mosquito Ridge, but now the evergreen and wild olive trees stood shattered and splintered, limbs akimbo, branches scattered helter-skelter on the ground. The wild game that inhabited this aristocratic hunting ground, pheasants and rabbits, remained miraculously immune to the destruction around—save a brace of birds machine-gunned in mid-air just at the edge of the wood.

Oliver ran, crouched low, making a bee-line for the other gunners. He found them spaced 20 meters apart, sheltered by a grove of trees whose tops dangled like broken arms and legs, their trunks bullet pocked. The gunners and their support teams were firing at will, and Oliver realized that a mass of Nationalist troops had begun to pour down from the ridge, firing as they advanced. The machine gun in the church continued to chatter, sending its tracers back down the hill. As the dark of night began to fall, Oliver could see other units of the International Brigade disengage and, like figures in a shadow play, melt back into the protection of the trees.

He turned to Cipriano. "We need to withdraw," his voice was flat. "We don't stand a chance."

He raced to the others, pointing them back into the trees, pushing them along. When Anna looked at him imploringly, he smiled and smacked himself in the chest with his right hand. He turned to provide covering fire as they made their way back to the gullies that would lead them down to the river.

■

The downpour began at 0100 hours and likely saved their lives. But, at the time it only made their retreat even more difficult. The sandy earth at the bottom of the hillside turned into a sea of mud. Thousands of International Brigade soldiers from a dozen battalions — Washington, Lincoln, Thalmann, and Garibaldi — were all mired in the muck. The soldiers unlaced their boots and looped them over their necks as they slogged back toward their line and the positions they had left just only hours earlier.

Hours later, with the faint pale light of morning barely tinting the gray sky pink, Oliver finally caught up with his unit. He found them huddled together at the river, soaked to the skin, boots coated with mud. They had all, save one, made it back alive.

They roused themselves at his approach. He could see the anxiety in their faces even as and raised their fists in the Republican salute. They stood fifty meters away in a circle, their guns drawn. Reminded him of a covered-wagon movie he had seen at the Regal on 47th Street back in Chicago. He was relieved tat the sight of them, and smiled at Anna and then at Cipriano and then at Enrique. They waved back, cheering.

The shell landed with a whoooomp, a long bellow of a noise that turned night to day. When it burst, the howitzer shell carved a crater four meters wide in the space between Oliver and his company, ripping three tripod carriers and two ammunition support troops to sheds. In the sandbagged dugout Cipriano, Enrique, and Anna were shielded by the bodies of their comrades, who were dead before they hit the ground.

A jagged piece of shrapnel severed Oliver's leg below the knee, right at the meat of his calf muscle.

■

Rena Thompson waited in the field aid station behind the lines. Someone had passed along word that the offensive had failed. The Republicans' last-ditch effort to push Franco back from Madrid and prevent the division of the Republic into two zones had stalled. Líster's Division, the heart of the offensive, was now in full retreat.

In the morning a panting messenger brought word that the Loyalist line had broken. Coffee cups in one hand and surgical instruments in the other, Rena and the team of surgeons and nurses prepared for the next wave of wounded.

Standing in the open-flapped entry to the Field Hospital, her white surgical coat splattered with blood, Rena waited for the first arrivals.

Three International Brigade soldiers burst into the operating theater carrying a stretcher. The man on the stretcher looked barely alive. His left leg had been severed, and the blanket covering him was soaked in blood.

Rena noted the primitive tourniquet, someone's black and red checked militia scarf, tied off around his thigh.

"I'm going to replace it," she announced, fingers already at work tying a belt two centimeters below the scarf, then pulling it as tight as possible, and only then releasing the scarf.

"Put him over there," she pointed to the operating table. Two orderlies reached their arms under the body of the wounded soldier and shifted him to the table. The man moaned in pain and delirium.

"Get Livingston," Rena commanded, "There is no time to lose. We need to operate NOW!" She stepped aside, knowing that Livingston would enter momentarily. She turned to examine the three comrades who had carried in the wounded soldier. Their faces were caked with grime, their hands slick with blood. One of them was a woman.

"I see you didn't get the Directive," she spoke softly to the woman. "Good for you."

"We've been fighting for three days," Anna replied. "No time for that crap." The way she rolled her "r" made it sound like chrap, deep and guttural.

"Look, I know you must be worried. We'll take good care of your comrade. I'm sure he'll recover. We do this all day long." Rena decided not to use the word amputation. The man's leg was already missing. Normal procedure called for visitors to be escorted from the operating room. But Rena's heart went out to these three anxious soldiers. "Please wait outside. You can even lie down underneath the roof overhang in the back. I'll get you as soon as I know something."

Rena turned back to the wounded man and jabbed a long needle into a vein in his arm. The needle was connected by a length of rubber tubing to a bottle of plasma hanging from a stand behind the table. The soldier fluttered his eyes, trying to regain consciousness. She mopped his brow and began to attach the ether mask. "This will help." She squeezed the leather bladder that pumped the ether into his mouth and nose.

Livingston had already assumed his place at the end of the table and was busy cutting away the remnants of the soldier's pants and cleaning the severed leg with sterile water. Rena knew he would soon begin sawing away the uneven splinters of bone and cutting the leg back to allow the man's skin to form a flap to close over the stump. Once Livingston had tied off all the arteries, he released the tourniquet, throwing it in the corner.

"We can't keep him under indefinitely." Livingston removed a fragment of bone from the end of the man's leg. "Get me that jar," he pointed to the supply shelf. The green container reminded Rena of a Mason jar. It held hundreds of sterilized maggots that Livingston shook out into a clean mesh dressing. He then applied the dressing directly onto the wound, pulled the flaps of leg skin over it, and sewed three large stitches to hold it all in place.

He looked up at Rena. "They'll clean this up in a jiffy. Keeps infections away. Buggers love necrotic tissue, turn their noses up at the healthy stuff. Some bloke during your Civil War figured this out."

She stared at the wound, stunned. None of her training had prepared her for emergency battlefield surgery. This poor man, she thought. And then she recognized him. Oliver Law from Paris, from the battlefield only a few hours earlier.

That evening, as they left the station, Livingston presented Rena with a copy of *All Quiet on the Western Front* to read, "in your spare time, of course."

For the next three days Anna, Cipriano, and Enrique took turns at Oliver's bedside. The battle had settled into a military stalemate, giving Rena more time to care for the wounded. The task was to get men like Oliver well enough to travel to a real hospital in Barcelona. There they would fit him with a prosthesis and ship him home.

"Should take about six months to heal," Rena told him on the fourth day.

She had made sitting with Oliver a fixture of her daily rounds. But only on that fourth day did she understand why Livingston had given her the book. Later that day Livingston removed the maggot therapy, injected the wound with a heavy shot of Novocaine, and stitched the skin tightly over the stump.

Oliver remained awake for the procedure. He had recovered his senses admirably, Rena thought, and had not disintegrated, as many others did, into catatonia or madness.

But when he looked down at Livingston working on his leg he began to sob.

"Doctor, I can see you fixing me. I can hear the needle and thread, I can even smell those damn worms." He sighed deeply. "But I can still FEEL my leg, as if it's still there. What do I do about this cognitive contradiction?" If there was a moment when Rena knew that some part of her loved this crippled hero, it was then. She had never heard anyone speak that way — "cognitive contradiction." Where in the world? He must have seen her gazing at him. He mustered a smile. "I've always been a reader. I knew what to expect. Remarque prepared me for it. Still, I can't believe it." When she reached down and cupped his hand softly in hers, he turned his head away.

Rena never understood what it was that brought his friends to the Field Hospital ward at that moment. It seemed a bit like magic. They had visited daily since they first carried him in. Like family, she thought. Little by little, day by day, they had come to accept her as one of their band. "Your dedication to Oliver is something we all admire," Anna told her. And little by little she came to appreciate them in their own unique ways. Anna's tough clarity, Enrique's warmth and righteousness, and Cipriano's easy-going nature that hid his iron spirit. And, of course, Oliver, who bound them together. At the end of the week when they wheeled him to the hospital bus for the long journey to Barcelona they had become fast friends. None knew if they might ever see one another again.

A blustery wind blew up from the sea, as if following *La Rambla* back to the center of the city. It swirled around the three hundred surviving veterans of the Lincoln and Washington Battalions of the International Brigades, blowing scraps of newspapers against their legs. The volunteers marched along *La Diagonal* for several miles, crossing *Gran Vía*, with *La Sagrada Familia*, Gaudí's cathedral, towering in the distance.

Oliver struggled not to limp, but the rubber sleeve of his wooden prosthesis irritated his stump, making each step painful.

"Maybe we should have availed ourselves of the Metro," his voice was soft and sardonic. He nodded in the direction of the Catalunya station.

"Perhaps if the CNT and POUM workers were not on strike," Anna replied, resisting the urge to put her arm around him.

"Even today?" Oliver looked exhausted.

"Especially today," Anna bit her lip, aware she was entering dangerous waters. "The Negrín government has kicked us out. The anarchists believe this is suicide. The Germans will never match the withdrawal. The war will be over in six months.

"I never trusted the Party and the Commissars once they integrated the army and the militia. I thought the abandonment of the Popular Front ideal, of the position of no enemies on the left, was premature." Anna had been thinking about this for while.

"What in the world do you mean?" Ollie tried to keep up with her even as she slowed to match the hitch in his gait. The crowds had thickened since the start of the parade, with women and children lining the whole length of the Diagonal.

"Viva La Republic!" they cried as the International Brigade units marched in turn past the reviewing stand.

"I mean that it wasn't time for that kind of alliance." She didn't need to look to feel the pain in Ollie's eyes. "Look, the Nazi's took advantage of our liberal conscience, of our tolerance. To them, working with the anarchists was only proof of our weakness."

"I can't concur. It was time for such accommodation. History will demonstrate the sagacity of that opinion."

"Ollie, you are a wonderful man. I will always love you." Where did that come from, she wondered? "

"Anna, if you stop there, I will be a very happy man. Somehow I don't think that is your intent."

She saw a young girl, perhaps ten, standing on the side of the road, a bunch of wildflowers in her hand. Anna watched as the girl drew back her hand and let the flowers float towards them. Is this a sign? she wondered as the bouquet landed just behind them.

"What I think, my dear Ollie, is that your thinking reflects the American milieu of its creation. You are from a new country. We are old, and cynical. You are naïve and your analysis is less developed."

He stopped in the middle of the road. Turned around, picked up the flowers, and handed them to her.

"From your favorite premature anti-fascist," he declared.

Anna knew that she had crossed a line. Did it really matter who was right in this argument that no longer mattered? Why risk alienating his affection over coffee house politics?

She watched his face turn cold, as if a draft had chilled him.

"Let's keep walking," Oliver regained his composure. "Look. The others are just ahead. If we step it up we can join them."

Although he winced with every stride, Oliver led them through the ranks of the other volunteers and veterans of the Lincoln Battalion. He shook hands with Milt Wolff, another tough guy from the States, and then Alvah Bessie, who could throw a grenade like Christy Mathewson and wrote like Ring Lardner. He greeted Irv Klonsky, working class union guy from Sacramento, best hand-to-hand fighter in the Battalion, who was walking with Moe Fishman, a truck driver from Brooklyn who always said he wanted to be a Rabbi.

Anna followed him until they came to Cipriano, his left arm a sea of angry scar tissue, and Enrique, who carried three pistols, a semi-automatic carbine, and a vest filled with grenades.

"We're leaving," Oliver clapped Enrique on the back, "or perhaps you have not yet been informed."

"He's not finished just because our war is over. He's a real mean motherfucker. Right?" Cipriano clapped his friend on the back. Enrique stared straight ahead. Then he looked at Oliver.

"Brother my country, my Cuba, will need me soon. They suffer under the same boots as these poor people," he gestured at the crowds who continued to cheer. "And one day, you mark my words, one day we will finish the job we started here. And I intend to be there when we do."

The parade slowed as they neared the reviewing stand. Rena was just ahead of Oliver and Anna. He reached out for her and she turned, embracing him and then Anna. They stood together, arms around one another's shoulders. Cipriano and Enrique stood immediately behind them.

Someone next to them pulled a newspaper from inside their tunic. "Listen to this," the American volunteer called out to those crowded around him. "The grand farewell to our dear friends from the International Brigades will culminate at noon with a stirring address by our own La Pasionaria."

The tiny woman standing at the base of the reviewing stand wore a white gardenia in her hair. Her black dress, short black hair, and her raised right fist all identified her as Dolores Ibárruri, *La Pasionaria,* the

165

spirit of the International Brigades.

As if on cue, Ibárruri began to speak. She was a tiny woman. But what a voice!

"Mothers! Women! When the years pass by and the wounds of war are stanched; when the memory of the sad and bloody days dissipates in a present of liberty, of peace and of wellbeing; when the rancors have died out and pride in a free country is felt equally by all Spaniards, speak to your children. Tell them of these men of the International Brigades."

"You know," Anna whispered to Ollie, "our fathers worked in the same mine. We are like sisters."

"Is she politically mature?" he whispered back.

She hushed him with a glare.

"We shall not forget you; and, when the olive tree of peace is in flower, entwined with the victory laurels of the Republic of Spain — return! Return to our side for here you will find a homeland — those who have no country or friends, who must live deprived of friendship — all, all will have the affection and gratitude of the Spanish people who today and tomorrow will shout with enthusiasm — Long live the heroes of the International Brigades!"

Rena rubbed a tear from her eye and turned to the others. "I will never forget you, my friends."

And then they went each their separate ways.

PART FOUR
CUBA LIBRE

CHAPTER ONE
LOGISTICS

I

Enrique pushed the Mercury to the limit. In less than twenty minutes they arrived on the outskirts of Santiago, and ten minutes later they drove into *El Tivolí*, the historic *barrio* overlooking the harbor. Enrique coasted up to a narrow alley above *Calle Padre Pico.*

In the harbor, freighters and fishing boats jounced against the piers and loading docks. Beyond them, in deeper water, more freighters, dripping rust, waited to offload their cargo into empty boxcars positioned on the rail sidings connected to each pier. Avenida Jesus Menendez ran parallel to a rail line along the harbor. The great warehouse and distilling operation of Bacardi Rum, a testament to the sugar-cane that made Cuba the wealthiest island in the Caribbean, dominated the boulevard for a kilometer from Calle Heredia to the Railway station.

"You know this place?" Cipriano asked.

"Of course, friend. Like the back of my hand. It is my second city, Santiago. Did I not tell you back in Spain? My uncle Luis worked here. Sometimes I think you are too suspicious."

"Sometimes, I think you are bullshitting me," Cipriano spiced his words with menace.

"Careful what you say, amigo. You remember my famous temper, don't you?" Enrique unleashed his crocodile grin that he knew made Cipriano flinch.

"What do we do next, Major?"

"Gather intelligence," Enrique replied, ignoring the sarcasm. "Or as they say in American movies — 'Let's stake out the joint.'"

Behind them the warehouse door creaked open. A young woman poked her head out and looked around as if trying to spot an intruder or the source of a strange noise. Whatever she was looking for, clearly they were it. She wore a white blouse, open at the neck. She looked like a dancer, dark and mysterious, and music flowed out of the open door behind her. A marimba and trumpet called back and forth over the multiple rhythms of several drums. The music was light and syncopated, and for a moment Enrique forgot the reason they had come to the city.

"Would you like to come in?" The woman smiled enigmatically, her dark eyes darting. "Follow me, I am Sylvie."

Three flights of iron stairs led them to the rooftop. The sun blazed on the pale concrete and dozens of men and women, some playing drums, some dancing, some black, some not, engaged in the entertainment. Men in loose fitting balloon pants, tight at the ankles, commanded the drum orchestra. Their bare chests glistened with sweat, their gaze fixed deeply into the distance. The women all wore white, and Enrique realized that Sylvie was, in fact, one of the dancers. Their long hair braided with cowrie shells, the dancers held their heads off to one side, kept their backs straight, and launched themselves ever so gracefully into the humid air.

"Why don't you wait here?" Enrique whispered to Cipriano.

"Why?"

"Better that way." Hardly an explanation. Sylvie led Enrique to the other end of the rooftop, leaving Cipriano to watch from the corner. They stood next to each other, elbows bent on the thick concrete railing, heads close. Then she reached her arm out and touched Enrique on the shoulder.

Cipriano crossed the rooftop. Sylvie reached over and took his hand too.

"You see, my friends, we are preparing for Carnival. It begins in ten days. The great summer celebration of our region! It is when the African blood in Cuba comes to a boil. For three days we dance and sing and drink. *Santería* emerges then, during the heat of Carnival. If you are lucky you will see it!"

"When does it start?"

"In ten days, on the 25th of July. Did you not know this?" she laughed.

Cipriano looked at the dancers, then at the drum orchestra, "And they will be part of Carnival?"

"Oh, yes. But this is just the rehearsal. Look over there," she pointed to a corrugated metal closet entirely open on one side, "that is what I will wear during the parade."

In the closet stood a wire mannequin clothed in a costume made entirely of white feathers. It was as if a swan had been transformed into a bride, her wedding dress covered with a thousand tiny diamonds that sparkled like stars. The headdress mounted above the costume was equally elaborate and stunning. Plumes of feathers spread outward in a meter-high Mariposa flower. It would require great coordination to both dance to the pulsating music and keep the headdress atop one's head.

■

"Silvie tells me that this is an ideal spot to see the warehouse," Enrique guided Cipriano by the arm to the ledge. "See, down there? This long yellow building follows the street. This is also the Bacardi warehouse."

Cipriano cut him off. "Where's the package?"

"I have the pallet number here," Enrique patted his front pocket. "And the storage receipt too. Remember, the one we filled out at the docks? Echivera, the Syndicalist," he drew the word out for emphasis, "promised they would honor it as long as it took for us to get here. I told you it would work. Addressed the package to my uncle Luis, and he kept it for me all these years. Maybe next time you'll trust me."

"You are a persistent bastard," Enrique said. "I know she is who she says she is." He put his arm around Cipriano. "The daughter of the local anti-fascist leader. She is my cousin and her name is Sylvie Merlo."

Cipriano smiled in a way that made Enrique think he had a secret.

"Remember, her father, Luis, is the guy who runs the CTC, the confederation of all the dockworkers in Santiago. He'll help us load; he'll be our new connection to Barcelona. Like they told us in '37. She's sympathetic to the movement too."

"I understand," Cipriano sounded mistrustful. "Although it seems too much of a coincidence — even if that's the same name Echivera gave us in Barcelona."

"Don't worry so much." Enrique rubbed his hands together. "They are Cuban anarchists, trade-unionists. Many of them were in Spain, like us. They came back here. They wait for the Revolution. They don't know about the gold. Not even Luis. There! That should reassure you."

Cipriano shrugged. "Okay, then. We need to convince them that that Castro is on their side. Then Sylvie can unlock the door." He watched as Enrique glanced across the rooftop searching for her. She sat with her back to the wall, smoking.

"She will take us to them tonight." Enrique trembled a bit, shaking his head as if trying to shake free from a thought. "She already told me."

∎

Like Barcelona, Santiago came alive after the sun went down. Unlike Barcelona, Santiago was not at war. But in both cities everyone loved to spend evenings drinking gaily, singing love songs while they sat at shaded café tables.

Enrique reached into his pocket and felt the edge of the tag he had carried with him since Barcelona. He didn't need to look at it to remember the pallet number. He kept it close like a talisman, a reminder of the ideals he had spent his life fighting for. *"La guerre est fini,"* his French friends had said to him. He did not agree.

Enrique turned to Cipriano.

"It is almost dark," he wrapped an arm around his friend, "time to get moving. Sylvie will meet us at the warehouse at 2100 hours."

"Yes, Major." Cipriano executed a perfect IB salute, fist raised to shoulder height. Enrique did not smile.

"Did you remember the truck? We can't very well haul the cargo away in the front seat of the sedan, can we?" Enrique's voice rose higher in pitch and Cipriano tried to avoid eye contact.

"You never talked to me about a truck," Cipriano replied gently, modulating his voice softly. "It's a good idea."

"Idiot. We talked about it just before we left. With Anna." Enrique inhaled sharply. "Don't you remember anything? Its what everyone can't stand about you. You always forget everything and then can't be macho enough to admit it." Enrique's face went red and his jaw began to quiver.

"Maybe we should talk about this later," Cipriano looked away. "When you are less agitated."

"Just like you. Coward. You want to duck out when it gets tough. Just like always." Enrique clenched and unclenched his fists.

"How about we see if Sylvie wants to drive with us?" Cipriano desperately tried to change the subject. "She's really a lovely young woman."

"You keep your hands, your eyes — your fucking eyes — you keep them off her! Here you go again, you self-righteous son of a bitch." Enrique's eyes burned. "I'm not letting you off so easy. You make enough mistakes for the whole army." He paused to consider what he had just said. Sweat pearled below his lower lip. "The Cuban army, I mean. The Cuban army."

Cipriano fought back a smile. Then he stiffened, raised his shoulders, and wrapped his right hand around the massive scar on his left arm. The gesture only intensified Enrique's anger.

"You know, since I first met you, seventeen years ago, since then, you have fucked up endlessly. You should hear what people say. People you admire. They think you are a mess. No one trusts you. That's why I'm here. Anna doesn't trust you to do this on your own."

Now, only truly now, did Enrique see the effect his words had on his friend. Enrique's rage had a way of planting seeds of doubt deep within Cipriano.

"What do you mean, no one trusts me?"

"Like I said, that's why we have to work together."

The absurdity of Enrique's claim finally broke Cipriano. He paused, clenched his fists as if to smash Enrique in the mouth, reconsidered, and walked away. But Enrique knew that hurt and mistrust now ate away at Cipriano's spirit.

"I'll meet you down the hill at 2030 hours," Cipriano called back over his shoulder. "I'll bring a fucking truck."

∎

The dark green Ford flat-bed had been parked on the Square. Like all drivers in Santiago, the owner had left the keys under the driver's seat. Thirty seconds later Cipriano pumped the clutch as he thrust the floor-mounted shift into first.

The episode with Enrique had left him exhausted. He decided to put it out of his mind. Instead, he concentrated on driving through the city's streets, headlamps dimmed. Santiago was still, the streets empty save the shadows shimmering in the last light. The streets descended steeply the closer he got to the harbor. Then, quite suddenly, as the car crested an intersection and jumped forward, he found himself staring at the last rays of sunset dancing off the sea, bathing the ships at anchor in a yellow glow. A beautiful moment, one he might never again experience.

Below, separated from the harbor by double freight tracks, the Bacardi warehouse dwarfed everything around it. Bright yellow, its jumble of peaked roofs covered in black tarpaper, the warehouse gleamed with its own importance in the last light of day. The rail station, directly across *Aveninda Jesus Menendez,* was deserted. Two Brazilian freighters bobbed at their moorings. Across the bay rose the hills, dark and foreboding, a faint outline against the horizon.

He pulled the truck behind the train station and into a parking lot filled with abandoned American cars, a graveyard of stolen and forgotten vehicles. Enrique, waiting on a loading dock to his right, vaulted down the three steps and embraced Cipriano like a long lost brother, holding him tight enough for the Cypriot to smell the cigar smoke that lingered on his clothes. Cipriano felt his own resolve give way. He hid his bitter disappointment deep within himself and offered a smile.

"Over there," Enrique pointed across the avenue, "there she is — just as we planned."

Sylvie lit a match and tossed it into the street, next to the tram tracks that crisscrossed the city like stitching. The last tram was scheduled to arrive at the station at nine. It was past the hour, and the match signaled her father to unlock the entry to the warehouse.

The rest of the operation ran like clockwork. Sylvie and Cipriano slipped through the rear door of the warehouse while Enrique waited, keeping watch just outside. Sylvie carried two torches and the light played softly against the gray concrete of the warehouse floor, illuminating hundreds of small cages built of wood framing and chicken-wire and shoulder-high oak barrels of rum awaiting shipment, the red and gold Bacardi bat stamped on their sides. The numbers lined up sequentially, and as they walked past storage areas with five digits, they realized that their treasure would be deep inside the vast vault. The warehouse felt even more massive inside than it had appeared from the exterior. The owners had maximized the space by squeezing two floors into the space of one. With ceilings barely high enough to stand, Enrique and Sylvie half-crouched, bent at the waist, as they worked their way through the first of the three interconnected buildings.

So many years had passed. Yet, there it was. Number 701, three oblong pine crates bound by barrel strapping that also served as hand-holds for the "coffins." Cipriano whispered for Sylvie to pull the truck over to the loading dock. Then he retraced his steps, found Enrique, and led him to the forklift parked in the corner of the warehouse lower level. They drove the forklift to the three containers, lifted each one in turn, and took them back to the rear entry where Sylvie waited with the truck.

They had underestimated the weight of the cargo. They struggled, heaving and sweating, to slide the crates from the lift onto the rear of the truck. When Sylvie asked if she could help, Enrique told her to get back in the truck just as Cipriano opened his mouth to accept. "She doesn't know what this is," Enrique muttered. "Let's keep it that way."

∎

Two hours later they extinguished the truck's headlights and glided silently behind the protection of the hedgerow between the farmhouse and the road. Enrique slid out of the driver's seat, closing the door behind him.

"Wait," he ordered the other two, shooting an admonishing look at Cipriano. "I'll tell Anna we are here."

Cipriano and Sylvie looked at each other. He had been aware of her arm and leg pressing against him during the jouncing drive from Santiago to Siboney. He had not registered the pressure as anything more than the consequence of the narrow seat. Still, when she half turned to him, putting her arm up over the back of the seat, he found himself aware of how close they sat.

"Will you stay here tonight?" He asked, "I mean before driving the truck back."

"Why do you ask?," Sylvie replied. He thought he felt her move slightly closer to him, her breast lightly touching his left arm.

"I think I would like to see you. More of you. I mean, spend more time with you."

She laughed. The sound warmed his heart. "You men. You think it's just that easy." She tilted her head back and laughed again. "Come to Carnaval," she looked into his eyes. "You'll know me when you see me."

As Cipriano reached for her she ducked under his arm and kissed him softly. "Don't worry. I know how to get back to the city."

She slipped out of the truck and disappeared into the night.

Oliver awoke first. The mid-summer sun, already blazing at seven,
radiated yellow-orange in the humidity of the tropics. Before fitting
the rubber suction membrane of his prosthesis to his leg, he massaged
what remained of his calf muscle. The skin was sewn like a football, the
seam raised and puckered, and felt sandpaper rough. He slipped on his
cord trousers and a green t-shirt that he had washed the night before,
still damp but "appropriately serviceable."

The cup of fresh-made coffee in his hand tasted too bitter. He
much preferred the smooth light taste of Maxwell House. He had
been drinking their coffee at the same place on the South Side of
Chicago for a dozen years, at a joint called *Valois*. Same table, same
over-easy eggs, same cast of characters. Time had frozen there, leaving
him behind. His friends only saw a veteran wounded in some war they
had never heard of. Only the other men in the painting class he took
at the South Side community arts center, with a wonderful guy named
Archie Motley, only they had the smallest understanding of his past.
The Party paid him a small pension, just enough to get by. He lived in
a room on 55th Street, over a check-cashing place. Saturdays were for
movies at the Regal, Mondays for Party Meetings, and Wednesdays for
painting classes. Mezz the mailman knew to deliver his mail at Valois.
He left the envelopes tucked into a plastic napkin holder at a table in
the rear corner, by the window, "rain or shine" as he loved to chuckle.

Valois, that's where the letter I wrote finally reached him, Law told
me. Just a wild hunch, trying to locate him this way. I first addressed
it to Oliver Law, Abraham Lincoln Battalion Veterans, 25 W. 11th St.,
which was the Communist Party's address. No worry, Arthur. Their
newspaper is no match for yours. And I don't think the FBI can

connect me to them, so don't worry about that. The Party forwarded my letter to the address they used for Law's pension check, and Mezz took it over to Valois. I told Law about Cuba, about Anna, and about the possibility of bringing together some of the veterans from Spain "for a good cause."

∎

Oliver walked around the grounds, coffee in hand. Anna had asked him to keep up the recruits' training while Cipriano and Enrique were in Santiago "on business." The men at the farmhouse had eaten well the night before, the feast of Carnival they called it, and remained sound asleep in their hammocks even as the morning heat began its daily onslaught.

Oliver started with the hammock furthest from the farmhouse and worked his way around the outlying woods, waking the men one at a time and telling them to gather on the field at precisely 0800 hours.

They arrived promptly — a good sign — and he lined them up in three groups of five. He spoke to them in English peppered with Spanish.

"You will need to be creative to survive. And that is exactly what we will accomplish now. Does everyone understand my meaning? *Ahora!* Each team will have exactly one hour, sixty precious minutes, to find enough food to consume this evening. *Vámanos!*"

The trainees, as he began calling them, were still out in the field when Anna and Rena appeared.

"Any word from Cipriano and Enrique?" asked Anna, her blue jeans loose and white cotton blouse even looser.

"They arrived late." He looked at Rena, "You sleep okay?"

"That goat we roasted last night. Best food I ever tasted." She looked exhausted, her eyes swollen.

"Where is everyone?" Anna asked. "No one is around."

"I gave them a little exercise, some field work," Oliver scanned the trees for any motion. "They'll be back in a few minutes."

"You what — ?" Anna cut the rest of the sentence, sharing a half-nod with Rena. "Oh. You gave them something to do. Good idea, Ollie. Good idea." Her voice reminded him of one of his elementary school teachers. He wondered what she had intended to say.

"Yes. It was evident to me that we needed to extend their training. Survival being paramount." He liked the sound of his old voice, the commanding one, the one he had left behind at Brunete.

"After they return, find me. I have a great deal to teach them," Anna reached out her hand and hooked it into the crook of Rena's arm.

The trainees appeared a few minutes later. Oliver had them form a circle around him and invited them to show what they had discovered. One at a time, a spokesman from each group held up an example of their bounty.

"The trick is," Oliver explained, "to add something to our store of knowledge, not duplicate it."

One group displayed a Malanga root "for the fufu," another a brace of bananas, then some green pole beans, and last a handful of palm nuts, slippery with oil. Oliver grinned proudly at them. Then hesitated.

"What about the final group. This is no picnic. I expect you to take this seriously."

The leader of the last group turned sideways, forcing himself forward from the mass of men standing around Oliver. "We thought we'd contribute something a bit more valuable."

He fished into a burlap bag slung over his shoulder and with great pride and a shit-eating grin produced a live chicken.

Oliver, Anna, and Rena grinned at each other. Something was working.

Anna crossed her arms.

"How did you acquire this trophy?"

"Simple, comrade," he answered with a wink to the men in his group, "the chicken is a donation from the peasants in the hills. When they discovered that we were there to oppose Batista, that's all the motivation they needed to share."

Anna beamed and stepped forward to speak directly to the trainees. "This is exactly what we discovered for ourselves yesterday, and what you will now never forget."

Oliver and Rena moved closer to each other as Anna spread her arms out before her, talking to the men. She drew them in, flattered them, told them the nation needed them. "The peasants," she told them, "will always help you. They will steal for you, even kill for you. But you must trust them and make them understand that Batista is the enemy."

"Woo, woo, woo." The signal startled everyone. They turned to find Enrique grinning at them, Cipriano a pace behind. They emerged from the back of the farmhouse waving.

"We have good news!" Enrique called out. "Wonderful news!"

The trainees looked up, their faces turned into the sun.

Anna urged them closer. "Tell us, my friend. Tell us."

"We have found the Fountain of Youth," Enrique beamed.

The rest of the recruits stood, stunned. They had no idea what he was talking about, this tough guerrilla leader with a great smile spread across his face.

"You asked us to find some resources?" Enrique motioned for them to come closer. "Come and see what we have brought."

He led the company to the front of the farmhouse where the flat-bed truck sat idling. With a twist he killed the engine, then jumped up on the truck bed. He motioned for Cipriano, Anna, and Rena to join him. When they climbed up he put his fingers to his lips and pointed down at his feet, at the three coffins. Before Anna had a chance to speak, Enrique whispered. "Give me a hand. We'll push these out to the edge. You'll see."

Moments later the three coffins hung over the edge of the truck bed. Enrique draped them with Cuban flags and stood, hands on his hips, next to his colleagues, looking out over the fifty men who had gathered around the back of the truck.

"Comrades!" he called. "Let me introduce the fruits of our labor." With that he bent down and pulled open the first coffin lid. "Come close. I can't lift them up. They weigh a ton."

Anna and Rena gasped with astonishment. Even Oliver, standing on the periphery, allowed himself a smile. The recruits were beside themselves with joy.

The coffins, filled with gold bars, gleamed brighter than the sun.

Enrique and Cipriano drove all the way back to Santiago. Anna followed in the black and white Mercury.

"We'll meet at 2 pm," she glanced down at her small notebook. "Park the truck in an alley behind Plaza de Dolores. It will be safe there." Once they arrived she ordered Cipriano to stay with the truck. Then she looked at Enrique. "You'll come with me."

They followed *Porfirio Valiente* to the intersection with *Calle Aguilera* where the two streets converged on the Plaza — the most charming park in Santiago, Anna winked at Enrique. "The girls there are the most beautiful in the world. Cipriano better be careful," she added before merging into traffic.

She guided the Mercury through the densely crowded streets of old Santiago, east toward the steep hillside that led back down to the waterfront and the harbor.

"Remember this," she felt the tension begin to rise in her chest. "We will come here again soon. We need to know our way around."

Avenida José Antonio Saco carried them past the grand Cathedral of Santiago that dominated the south side of the famed *Parque Céspedes*. The *Hotel Casa Grande,* bathed in white, faced the park. They followed the flow of traffic around the park, Enrique gawking at the hustlers and prostitutes who shared the area from sunup to sundown with a host of flower venders, jugglers, and beggars. At the corner of the square they turned right and crawled slowly down another street.

Adobe houses lined this street. Their terra cotta roofs pitched steeply back from the rough road, barely wide enough for a car. The street itself ran down a steep hill, so each set of doors and windows sat lower than those of the neighboring building. Some of the houses were painted the pale yellow characteristic of Santiago, but others were coated in white and turquoise. It was early afternoon and families gathered at rough-hewn wood tables visible through the door-sized windows. Wrought-iron gates and guards covered these openings. Not a pane of glass in sight.

"There." Anna pointed out a square stucco house, yellow with deep blue trim. She eased the car over the curb onto the stone sidewalk just beyond an open wrought-iron door. "They are expecting us."

A woman in a printed blue dress with white flowers appeared at the door. Her bright red lipstick and dark black hair gave her an uncommon mark of glamour. Almond eyes and a slight cleft in her chin made her look like a flamenco dancer. She smiled and beckoned for them to enter.

"I am Maria Teresa Santamaria," her accent was upper-class. "You may call me Maria. Please sit over here." She pointed to a bench against a wall that faced the front of the room. "May I offer you some coffee?"

You must understand, my old friend, how delicate this information is today. Maria Santamaria remains with Castro. She serves as his most important advisor precisely because she can talk to all of them— Raul and particularly Che. She was the one who introduced me to Sr. Castro and she was the one who saw to it that my messages found their correct destinations. I tell you this, Arthur. No Maria, no Cuban revolution.

Of course, I was mostly in the dark about this depth of drama. How she made all these connections, like a spider spinning multiple webs, remains a mystery to me. But, truth be told, she's one hellofa broad with more moxie than I ever encountered.

Anna motioned Enrique to join her at the bench. Everything seemed so calm. Maria turned into the kitchen for a moment, then reappeared carrying a tray with four cups of espresso, the kind Anna loved. Enrique relaxed and took one of the cups, sipping with his eyes half-closed. Anna had to admit this burly dark haired man with a wild temper cut quite a fine figure. She looked at his hands, his thick fingers, and the break that turned his nose into a crooked hump. He was, she thought, the only Cuban amongst all of them. She wondered what that meant.

"You had an easy ride back to the city." Maria's words a statement not a question. "We were pleased to hear from you." She hesitated. "Both." Her eyes fixed on Anna. "Anna Ekudal. Basque, isn't it?" Again, not a question.

Anna couldn't recall how this woman might know her name. Through contacts in Havana, perhaps.

"I didn't know that the International Battalions accepted volunteers with your background."

"The International Brigades. Everyone makes the same mistake." How could Maria know?.

"Ah, I see. You worked behind the lines? Caring for the wounded?"

"I was a machine gunner. We both were. Met in Madrid, fought together at Brunete." Anna glanced at Enrique. She couldn't figure out the questions. "Why do you ask?"

"We need to find out if you are who you say you are. There are many who seek to infiltrate our ranks." Maria stared at them, then the hardness in her face dissolved. "I think I can see that you are not one of them. Welcome."

"And how do we know you are who you say you are?" Enrique began to twitch, the telltale sign of his mounting anger.

"You can't." Maria smiled. "But I believe you will. Be patient. Please." She rose and touched his hand in a way that Anna found both tender and credible.

"Let us, then, get down to business." Anna pulled her notebook from the pocket of her jeans. "Where are the items we have contracted for? When can we have them?"

Enrique settled back into his seat on the bench. Anna felt him relax and thought to herself that his anger could not disguise how brave he was, and how loyal.

Maria looked back at them.

"Where is the payment? We cannot go another step before that. I was fortunate to obtain the goods on the security of my husband's estate. He must not find out."

Anna raised her eyebrows.

"He is the Cuban owner of American Nickel."

Enrique stood and took Maria's hand. Anna thought he was actually going to kiss it. Instead he bent over and spoke as sweetly as Anna had ever heard him speak, "Patience, my friend. We have what you require. It will all be clear by the end of this day. We hope you will trust us in this," he looked deeply at her. "Didn't we see you the other day? On the beach in Siboney, when we first arrived?"

"You have a remarkable memory. I was only there for minutes. I handed Oliver Law some cash, as I recall."

Enrique held her hand for another second, then turned, beaming, to Anna and laughed. "Let us have a real toast to the Revolution."

Maria went to a small wood cabinet and brought out a decanter of rum and three glasses.

She held her glass high. "It is better to die on your feet."

"Than to live on your knees," Enrique answered as they had agreed back in Havana, at the safe house.

"No pasarán." Anna completed the exchange and they all tossed back the sweet golden liquid.

A late afternoon thunderstorm cracked overhead. Lightning stabbed down from the dark sky, and the room turned a soft-yellow. Anna remembered Cipriano back at the square and hoped he had enough sense to stay dry. Torrents of angry water rushed down the street. Maria walked to the windows and pulled the shutters closed through the channels of rain that splashed over her dress. She wiped her hand over the bodice, as if shooing away a fly. "Everything the movement needs is ready. We can deliver it to you as soon as we receive payment."

"Today?" Anna couldn't quite believe her ears. Only this morning at Siboney had they learned of the gold. Now they could return with… everything.

"I see you are puzzled," Maria lit a kerosene lantern. "Allow me to explain."

The rain outside had lessened, and the sweet smell that followed in its path bathed the room in a soft perfume. Outside the ringing of the tram bell carried the sounds of life back into the house, the neighborhood, even the city. This is the world that I love, Anna thought. But it has been spoiled by the *"gangsterismo"* of Batista and the corruption of capitalism. When we succeed here we will all live in peace on streets like these.

Maria poured them a second glass of rum, then stood before them, her intensity deepening the delicate lines that radiated out from her green eyes.

"Your group, you know, is crucial to the success of the movement. But, we have managed things so there are many groups. You do not know about one another and that is so if one of you is discovered, you cannot give away our plans. That is why I instructed you to leave the other, Cipriano, with the truck. The rest of your team at the farmhouse, they will also know nothing of what I am about to tell you."

Anna nodded in silent assent.

"When we began to plan for a new Cuba we did not know when or how to act. Only that it would be necessary to overthrow Batista and the corrosive dominance of American imperialism. Only this spring did we recognize that the time had come. Batista was planning his own coup, as you well know. And when we learned of it, we started to act. I called on you through that reporter Matthews who met you all in Spain."

Maria stopped and turned to look out the window. "We also sent agents, unaware of one another, to procure arms and material."

Enrique and Anna sipped their rum quietly. It felt like reading a novel, Anna thought. One in which she had become a character.

"There are Cubans all over the world who love their country. In New York and Miami and Mexico City. Some, like you, belonged to the communist or syndicalist parties and trade unions — others, well, they just believe in democracy. We have no fixed ideology, so it doesn't matter to us. We desire only the freedom of Martí."

She hesitated, then offered them white-tipped Marlboros, conjuring two stalks from the cellophane pack with a deft shake of her hand. "Don't say it. A Yankee woman's cigarette. The height of decadence. We all live with our little ironies."

"Our friends arranged credit and began to acquire what we thought we required. And their friends in all these cities, they trusted us, believed in us, and sent arms and ammunition and uniforms to us. They are stored nearby and you may pick your share up later. We had a deadline of July 20th to find the money to pay for everything. We needed a million dollars, a million American dollars."

"You mean, you only had three more days to find the money?" Enrique was incredulous. "What would you have done had we not — ?"

"You know, Major Perez, I don't know what we would have done. That is the truth. We only believed, Raúl and I, that your team would find a way."

"Raúl?" Anna had not heard this name before.

"There are only a few of us who know all our plans. Not even Fidel is aware of everything. This is on purpose. He is a brilliant man, and a great thinker. But he's not a born revolutionary tactician. Perhaps we will find one who is. As I'm sure you've learned, Fidel loves to talk. His brother Raúl and I have been living here in Santiago for the past year. Fidel will return here next week. But we have done the planning. Now, thanks to you, we will have the pieces in place for the next step." Anna wondered what that step might be. But thought better of asking.

"And what is our next step?" Anna asked. Maria pursed her lips and with a slight shake of her head indicated she would say no more, for now.

"Shall we go back to the truck, then?" Anna started to rise, reached her hand out for Enrique and pulled him up. "Our car is outside. Cipriano must be wondering where we are."

"I don't think we need worry. Plenty of pretty girls to look at." Enrique laughed. Like a little boy, Anna thought.

∎

Cipriano had been sitting on a bench in the *Plaza de Dolores* when the storm exploded. He had been there for about an hour, and had never seen such a beautiful place. A towering statue of Cuban patriot Francisco Vicente Aguilera commanded the park — a long triangle of brick walkways, manicured grass and wrought iron benches under shaded trees. When he arrived the park had been filled with black Cubans. He had never seen so many Negroes. Not like Law, whose brown-tan skin made him look almost Moorish. And Enrique, well he was just another Mediterranean-looking guy, and could have easily passed for a Turkish Cypriot. The people in the park had the blackest skin he had ever seen.

The square took on a new life later in the afternoon. At two, as many locals gathered to return to work, new faces appeared. An old pickup truck, brown and without hubcaps, pulled up. Three men and two women jumped out, each carrying a different sized conga drum.

Cipriano marveled as the drum orchestra arranged themselves on the octagonal pavement stones in the center of the park, between two rows of benches.

The drummers leaned over, heads forward, bending their knees slightly to fit the drums at an angle between their legs. The wooden instruments were struck with rough-carved sticks and pulsed with their drummers' beats. The drums provided an astonishing range of sound, from the sharp-pitched strike elicited by the sticks on their sides, to the deep bass thump of bare hands on membraned heads. Cipriano could not believe he was listening to only two instruments. The larger drums played against each other, two distinct voices, stating a theme, then answering. Then the three smaller drums joined in, drummers' hands beating like butterfly wings, their palms slapping the skin and fingers ringing the rims. The complexity of the rhythmic layers made Cipriano shiver. With their eyes closed, faces turned up to the sky, the Conga drum ensemble played with ever heightened intensity until they were all shining sweat.

One of the women had a face from a dream — deep black skin, wide round eyes, and thick sensual lips. Framed by a tangle of braids, each clipped with a white-brown seashell, her face seemed serene and spiritual. She made him think of an icon as she smiled at him. Then she gestured, waving him over. He sat up straight, pointed his finger at his chest, as if to ask, "me?" She laughed out loud with pleasure, her teeth white and shining. Then she nodded, *"venga!"* Then, "come here," in English. She put her hands on her hips and stared right at him.

She wore a multi-colored blouse and tight black pants that ended mid-calf.

"I am playing a rhumba with my friends. We think you must like our music. I like the way you look at me, *señor.*" She held her hands out to him.

He accepted her hand warmly. "What is your name?"

"I am Eurydice. We play here everyday. The people love us. But we play to summon the good will of the *santos*."

Could this be magic, Cipriano wondered. This vision, a daughter of black Africa, sent to him in the guise of a Greek legend.

"I am Greek Cypriot, from Cyprus," he spoke slowly. "I know your name, it is a beautiful one. How did you come by such a name?"

She moved closer to him, held his arm lightly in her fingers. "My mother's family came here from Haiti. As slaves. The plantation named all their slaves after Greek figures. My family kept the names, and now the tradition is our own."

Cipriano felt light headed. He looked down into Eurydice's eyes.

"I see you have found a friend, my friend."

Enrique's voice was filled with humor tinged with sarcasm. Cipriano turned around, startled.

"When did you get here?"

"We need to go."

Cipriano stammered, looking between Eurydice and again Enrique. "I must leave," he bowed slightly to her. "Are you really here everyday?"

"Yes. Come back and you will see."

As he walked away, Enrique's arm tight around his neck, he realized that he had forgotten to tell her his name.

She called out to him as he stepped down into the street. "Don't forget Carnival! In my white head-dress."

Cipriano looked at Enrique, then laughed. "It is Sylvie!"

"Of course. She put up her hair and you are too dumb to recognize her. Sylvie is how she is known to everyone. The other name keeps her out of trouble!"

Anna watched as they walked back to the truck from the shaded park in *Plaza de Dolores*. This city of Santiago, it was like no place she had ever been.

The two men slipped into the front seat of the truck. Enrique gunned the engine, then guided the vehicle into the street and followed Anna to the warehouse where Maria had instructed them to make the exchange. The truck jounced and shook as Enrique played clutch and break pedal against each other, slowing the vehicle, then bringing it to a halt just behind the Mercury.

It took an hour for them to complete their work. "Friends of the Revolution," Maria called the large burly men she had brought to help. "They are my team here."

Anna watched as they unloaded the truck. Muscles straining and arms bare, they carried the coffins as if they were empty and stacked them in the rear of the warehouse.

"Do not worry," Maria read Anna's mind. "They will be gone by evening. Our agents in Baracoa are waiting. The gold will be smelted to repay our purchases, and the rest held in reserve for later. For after."

An hour later one hundred American and British carbines, ten Thompson machine guns, dozens of boxes of ammunition and grenades, and fifty Cuban Army uniforms were loaded in their truck.

"Lucky for us," Maria laughed, "Batista is so cheap that he makes his soldiers buy their own uniforms. They are sold in every clothing shop in Cuba."

She gripped Anna by the arms, then kissed her on both cheeks. "We thank you."

Anna turned to leave, wondering what the days ahead would hold.

"Before you leave the city, pass this address," Maria handed a small map to Anna. "Just drive, don't stop. We will send more instructions soon."

In ten minutes she found *Avenida Moncada* and turned right, glancing in her rear-view mirror to watch the truck negotiate the pedestrians who flooded the street. The constant interruption of the trams, bells sounding notes of caution and alarm, only added to the chaos.

Ahead loomed the massive army barracks at Moncada. They had passed it the first time they drove through Santiago. Then, it had no meaning. Now, it took on a palpable significance. Spread out over a massive four-square block, surrounded by an eight-foot-high stucco wall and guarded by four corner towers, the Moncada Barracks was the symbol of the Batista regime in Santiago. As a target it offered real challenges, but untold rewards.

Washed in the pale yellow paint of the region, its structural beams outlined in white, the complex dominated the east side of Santiago. On the same grounds stood a military hospital, a smaller copy of the barracks.

She drove slowly down the street, the barracks to her right, then past the guard post prohibiting access to the military grounds.

This must be the objective. Surprise, infiltrate, take control of the barracks, subdue the garrison, seize the arsenal and occupy the hospital. But how? And when? She had no doubt they would soon find out.

A glance behind told her that Enrique had managed to follow without incident. She took a deep breath. A long time had passed since she had felt the excitement and then tension that now played in her chest. She had been a young woman then, hard and idealistic. Almost forty now, she looked up at a clear patch of sky and thanked whoever was watching for this second chance. The rest of her life still lay before her, and she intended to put the time to good use.

Like a cat on a summer afternoon, Rena stalked around the house searching for shade. Even the suggestion of a shadow would do. The expedition to Santiago would not be over till evening. There was little to do except wait. Oliver had given the trainees a series of tasks and no one needed her ministrations. She turned the corner of the white farmhouse, thinking that the front veranda might offer her the relief she needed. She unhooked the other strap of her overalls, allowing the bib to fall down to her waist. Too hot, she thought, tucking her white t-shirt.

Oliver was sitting, lost in thought. He must not have heard her approach.

"Penny for your…" She stopped. "Brother."

He looked up. The same man she met in Paris, then again on the battlefield, sixteen years earlier. They had a great deal in common. American Negros with similar educations, they shared the deep belief that true economic equality would end racial inequality. And, of course, they had fought in Spain. That's what had ultimately led both here, after all. But, for all their common history, Rena realized that she had never really known the Oliver Law who the others worshipped, and were willing to follow anywhere.

"You remember what you told me in the hospital? About my leg?"

"I told you that you'd be almost as good as new."

"You were wrong." He smiled wanly, his eyes dull.

"What do you mean?" Rena knew exactly what he meant, but thought it would be better for him to speak the words.

"I'm just not that man anymore. The hero, the leader, the stronger-than-anyone badass. I'm getting by on a phantom reputation and everyone is cognizant of the truth."

"Listen, Mr. Oliver Law. I never saw that guy, that hero. All I knew was the man sitting before me. Someone who is brave beyond limits, who stayed on the path with honor, and who loves the English language." She looked at him directly, trying to read his reaction. "Even when I don't understand — forgive me — comprehend all his words."

He allowed himself to smile and the years vanished. That damn gold tooth, she thought, and the way he carried himself, and his words, always his words.

"Honestly, Rena, your estimation of my prowess is a bit hyperbolic."

It took a couple of beats for her to realize he was teasing her.

"Moth-a-fuck-a," she drew the word out.

They both laughed. Out loud. When she bent down to kiss him, he stood and embraced her. She could smell the tobacco on his breath, feel the brush of his mustache, the warmth of his body. He held her, and she held him, for a time too long to count and too short to remember. Then he put his hands on her shoulders and peered deeply into her eyes.

"Rena. You send me. You really do."

She felt him relax, and read his face. "But not your heart. It's alright, Oliver. I will love you like the others do, and that will be enough for me."

The sun crept around the corner of the house and she could feel the heat at the back of her head. She wanted to cry, but refused.

"Tell me," she found her balance. "Tell me. Why did you pick me for this?"

"Rena, you saved my life. I knew I could trust you. I do trust you. And that is worth everything to me." His eyes had softened.

"Look," she nodded toward the men gathering their equipment in the field, "I think they need more work, don't you Commander?"

For the next three hours Rena watched Oliver put the recruits through their paces, teaching them the tricks of the trade; stealth and ambush, hand-to-hand combat, natural and constructed camouflage, and survival skills. Rena realized that these kids were far from ready. Oliver was great with them, so patient and understanding. Enrique would up the ante, bully them, and force them to become guerillas. But she suspected they didn't have the time to properly train them, and none of these kids had any experience with arms. Opened up a whole new kettle of fish.

∎

When night fell and the stars appeared, scattered across the sky, Rena sought out Oliver. She had resolved to tell him.

"You never thought to ask me why I came here. Did you think it was because of you?"

"Rena. It really never occurred to me to use you that way. It would have been manipulative and dishonest."

She felt him now, really felt him, from across the veranda where they sat, waiting for the others to return from Santiago.

"I have always thought of us as a team, as friends. When Matthews asked for assistance, I thought of us all." He looked sincere.

"Thank you, Oliver. I appreciate that, I really do. I'm proud to be your friend and your comrade." The night awoke around them, the clicking of insects, the rustling of nocturnal animals. "I'm glad you found me."

"We really had no idea of your location. Our only lead was the domicile you reported as your address."

"This is why I wanted to talk to you, Ollie. I was the one being manipulative and I need to apologize. I've lived in New York all these years, since we returned from Spain. Working in an emergency room as a nurse, working for Russian War Relief, and then for the Harlem Community Health Service. I found a great man. Name is Sylvester, but I call him Sly. Plays music, picks up gigs around town. You know how that is. We thought about getting married. But, you know, I never really believed in that stuff." She hesitated, as if she might not continue.

"One day, must have been last September. I was walking home from the subway to our sweet little apartment and I get this feeling, I mean this feeling. Reminded me of walking in Paris that night we met, as if someone was following me."

She would never forget that night. Never.

"Like in that Orson Welles movie, you know, the Third Man. I heard footsteps getting louder. That was scary. No one around, just me and these invisible footsteps. I get to my door, and I'm fishing around for my keys. I should have led him somewhere else, but I was too frightened to think straight. So, I'm standing there, top of the stoop, and this guy in a long coat and a black fedora touches my arm — I about jumped out of my skin. He just asks if I'm Miss Rena Thompson. And then, he pulls an envelope out his pocket and tells me I been served."

"The paper tells me I'm to come downtown in three weeks to answer questions to some Un-American Committee about what I was doing in Spain."

Oliver laughed. "I got the same treatment. About a month after you. Hauled me down to Springfield. Can you dig that? To the State Capital that saw the first race riot. I told them to piss off. I had nothing to lose."

"And that was my problem, Oliver. I had everything to lose — my job and my man. I lost both. The Hospital fired my ass soon as they heard about the subpoena, and Sly moved out, something about being bad for his music business — Motherfucker."

"Amen."

"So you see. Your telegram reached me at the perfect time. I was out of a job, my man took a walk, and I was angry. I'm telling you all this because I don't want you to think I came here because of you. That torch has long since gone out." Rena sat very still, wondering what he was thinking.

"But, then you turned out to be the same man I cared for back then. I mean inside. So, I dared dream a minute. But I'm here because I want to be. Mine is a political choice, Oliver."

"Rena, I'm not sure I've ever met anyone with less mendacity than you. Shows that I made a good choice when I invited you, doesn't it? Thank you, my dear Rena. I'll not underestimate you. Ever."

∎

The squeal of brakes broke the night's silence. Anna stashed the Mercury behind the hedgerow, then walked over to Oliver and Rena.

"Mission accomplished!" she winked conspiratorially. They watched from the shelter of the farmhouse as Cipriano and Enrique backed the truck into the field, summoned the volunteers, and began unloading crate after crate of armaments and uniforms. A bit before midnight the entire contents of the truck had been distributed among the cadre of trainees. With bonfires burning in each corner of the training field, Enrique stood before the men and addressed them.

"Now. Now my beauties we get to work. Sure, you've learned something about how to survive in the jungle. But now there is much more to learn."

The fifty men came to attention, holding their new weapons pointed down toward the soft ground.

"We will be ready for anything. But we will not learn precisely what our objective is for another 48 hours. Remember this, you fight for the future and freedom of Cuba.

"For now, we will only do two things. You will learn to assemble and clean your weapons blindfolded." He paused for effect. "Loaded. With the safety off."

He pointed to a young man standing at the head of a column. "You come stand next to me. *NOW!*"

The trainee stepped forward, shaking, actually trembling. Enrique could not understand the sense in relying on this rag-tag assemblage of kids to topple Batista. A dream, perhaps.

"Hold up your leg." Enrique ordered. "All the way up. Stretch it out there." He pointed toward the trainees standing in four columns. "What do you really see?"

The boy tried to steady himself on one leg, then toppled over. His comrades laughed.

"What the *FUCK* are you all laughing at?" Enrique wasn't sure if he was actually angry. *"EVERYONE* on one leg, now. *EVERYONE!"*

An old trick, but it never failed. Give them something they thought difficult and they would struggle. Show them it was easy, and they'd figure they could do it too.

They all stumbled; some dropped their guns, others fell sideways before catching themselves. He wanted to show them how the sharp needle-pointed rocks, unique to the area, could cut their shoes to ribbons. He laughed as they struggled to gain their footing.

"Alright, you imbeciles. We'll have to find someone to show you how to do this." He turned to the farmhouse. "Hey! Cipriano! Show 'em how a man does it."

Rena read the Cypriot like a book. Standing, lost in his own thoughts, Cipriano found Enrique's soldier routine especially annoying. He startled at Enrique's command. He really hated being pointed out. Ever since childhood when the British teachers in his school mocked his accent.

"I said YOU, Cipriano!" Enrique's voice rose, his lower lip twitched.

Rena watched as Cipriano took one look at Enrique, then turned his back and walked to where Anna had parked the car. She had left the keys in the ignition. In the space of a breath Cipriano started the engine, engaged the clutch, and jumped the car, like a cannon round, out of its hiding spot and onto the road, tires squealing. Enrique stared at him, dumbfounded. And vexed. And then worried.

"He'll be back," Anna placed her hand on his shoulder. "He just needed to get away. You'll think of something to say to him before he returns."

Enrique nodded wordlessly, already lost in memory. The way Anna touched him, the feather of her hand, transported him back to the refugee camp just on the French side of the Spanish border where, thirteen years before, he had turned a corner and found her. Walking calmly, head tilted back, her face toward the sun, as at ease as if she were enjoying an afternoon at the beach.

▮

July 1940, just after the French defeat. He hadn't seen Anna since Madrid. And suddenly there she was, wandering through the camp, weaving her way between torn tents and smoldering cookfires. She wore dark blue pants, a khaki shirt with sleeves rolled above her elbows, and a smile painted red that jumped out against her dark eyes and olive skin.

"*Hola!*" They had greeted each other at the same time, embracing before holding each other at arm's length, unwilling to let go. She exuded the same charisma he remembered from that very first day in Madrid. And, while they had never became lovers, he knew that he loved her. Why else follow her a week later, secretly, to Spain, back into the Pyrenees, climbing high along paths that even donkeys feared, to join her anti-Franco group? Over the next years her comrades had taught him everything about clandestine struggle, about guerrilla tactics, about anything he needed to survive as a partisan.

"Don't think." She had instructed him that first day, high in the hills, their feet freezing in the rushing mountain stream. "Just react." The deep pinewoods, green and lush, seemed impenetrable — a perfect place to hide.

"Should we go down there?" He pointed to a natural clearing, the small space beckoning.

"Shsssssh!" She clasped her hand over his mouth with astonishing speed.

She gestured to their right, just beyond the clearing. A glint of a weapon. Enrique nodded. Schooled, not reprimanded.

"Follow me," she looked back over her shoulder as she bent beneath the bough of a fir, heavy with sandy brown cones, "it will be dark soon." She led him down the banks of the brook, past a hand-hewn stone bridge, and into the mouth of a cave covered by branches.

"You need to learn to read."

"Read?"

"Yes. The landscape. What's there. And, more importantly, what's not. That clearing was meant to distract the eye from the gun hidden just beyond it. The limbs were broken by soldiers — broken too evenly to be done by nature."

Enrique had no idea, that day in 1940, that he would spend the next three years based in that cave, sleeping by day, engaging in stealth operations against Franco by night.

Resistance partisans without a public name and without a history, the Omega Group visited chaos on the mountain towns and garrisons of the Pyrenees. They lived off the land, relied on the loyalty of local peasants and artisans, and learned to improvise in order to survive. Enrique never forgot those lessons. "My university was the underground," he liked to say. They sabotaged trains, stalled delivery vans, corrupted boxes of government mail. When operations slowed, mostly due to terrible weather conditions, the Omega Group contracted with the FTP, the communists of the French Resistance, to smuggle almost anything out of Vichy and funnel it down to the Mediterranean.

In the summer of 1943 they left Spain. Together, Anna and Enrique walked for twenty nights through the valleys of southern France, cutting westward from Perpignan to Bordeaux. The group had decided to disband once Germany had occupied all of France, ending the fiction of Vichy. They thought it was better to leave Franco in peace, however onerous, than to invite Hitler to "relieve" the beleaguered caudillo. The FTP welcomed them with their first mission. Anna they found especially valuable. She spoke French, Spanish, and Basque, and had grown up in Guernica a miner's daughter.

They told Enrique to carry a Sten gun, to make sure no harm befell her. Then they taught him how to break down, clean, and reassemble the weapon blindfolded. Their first assignment was to convey two American pilots shot down the week before safely to the border. The two Americans, tall and thin and handsome, knew nothing about survival on the ground. It was as if they only understood the sky, reveling in the freedom of flight. On land they acted with clumsy irony, mistaking quiet for emptiness, or the cries of birds for enemies lurking in the forest. It took a week of hiking at night, following the mountain streams back up into the jagged rocky outcroppings of the Pyrenees, to reach the Spanish border. They passed the two pilots on to a group of anarchist partisans, bid them *adieu,* and headed back down the mountains. It took another five days for them to return to Bordeaux, to the café where they gathered in the cellar on Wednesday's at midnight. Then, in June of 1944, when they heard of the Normandy Invasion, Anna had told him, "Its over. I'm going home."

And he hadn't seen her since. That summer Enrique worked his way to Paris, and when General Leclerc relieved the city in August of 1944, Enrique had a front row seat. From the turret of the tank "Ebro" he rode though the streets of Paris grinning at the French women who threw flowers at his gun-barrel. He had been at war for eight years. It would be another nine years before Anna telegraphed him.

Cipriano gripped the thick steering wheel. Just one time too many. He couldn't let Enrique do that to him in public. He drove away from the farmhouse without any consciousness of direction or destination, burying his anger in speed.

As he drove his mind flipped slowly though the back pages of his memory. The times Enrique had screamed at him, the times he had forgiven him. The excitement of the gold heist. The sandstorm in Tobruk when he served in the British army in North Africa. Drove a bloody tank then. The tiny Greek-Cypriot shop in London where he swept floors after the war. The owner, a guy named Yiannis Papadakis, had wanted him to marry his daughter. The restaurant in Miami where Anna found him — the Cubans there loved the way he cooked souvlaki, and the waitress, Helena, couldn't get enough of him. The Jamaican whom he did love. Beverly. Round face, apple cheeks. All the women. Anna. Rena. Beverly. And Beverly had refused to marry him.

And that beautiful woman in the *Plaza de Dolores?* Only yesterday. Sylvie, who called herself Eurydice. Of course, how could he forget? He looked up, still gripping the wheel tightly. He had been lost in memory. The narrow streets of Santiago closed in around him. He had lost track of time. How long had he been driving?

Ahead, sitting with its nose sticking out from a side street, was a white four-door Ford. The driver wore a white linen shirt and a straw hat pulled down to his eyes. Cipriano did not register the car as it pulled out and followed him. His eyes wandered, trying to pick up signs that told him where he was.

He didn't mind driving aimlessly. He felt the tension escape his body, felt himself relax as he left the farmhouse behind. Little by little he regained his balance. It occurred to him that he was actually headed to the *Plaza de Dolores.*

The park in the Plaza seemed deserted. He had lost track of time. He pushed himself to remember. Yes. The truck, the arms; it had been late in the day when they returned. Now it was evening. No wonder she wasn't there. They had met in the afternoon.

The park bench still held the heat of the sun and it warmed him as he extended his arms out, resting his open palms on the upper back rung. He stretched his feet and closed his eyes. Reflexively he reached into the front pocket of his trousers and ran a finger around the smooth surface of the purple glass-disk, the traditional evil eye that he carried for good luck. The colors of evening flickered in his closed eyelids — yellows and reds — and the sounds of people strolling past and cars passing by invaded his senses, like a dream.

He smelled her first. Cinnamon and eucalyptus oil. Sitting next to him on that bench. Silently. His eyes remained closed. Then the warm touch of her leg next to his. And then her voice. "Orpheus?"

He opened his eyes slowly and she came into focus. "Eurydice?" He looked into her open round eyes, watched as they darted back and forth, deep black pools of her spirit. Then she laughed, a full-throated lean-back-your-head laugh, and reached her arm around him and rested her fingers on his neck.

"So. Shall I follow you?"

The man in the straw hat slid out of the front seat of his car.

■

Cipriano returned at dawn. Anna, standing in the hallway, watched him try to close the car door, then enter the back of the farmhouse silently. She had to laugh. His attempts at stealth backfired at every turn. The door, ancient, heavy, and hand-made, squealed. His boots, equally heavy and ancient, creaked with every step. Anna couldn't contain herself. She sighed, enjoying, perhaps to much, the way he jerked his head around, first right, then left, trying to detect the slightest dent in the silence.

Finally, she emerged from the shadows. She would never, not in a hundred years, have imagined how visibly upset Cipriano might be. To Anna, his disappearance was due to just one more episode with Enrique, nothing more. But now he acted as if he had been caught doing something naughty. And Cipriano was hardly one to misbehave. A sensitive man, perhaps, one who had seen much action and grown comfortable living underground. But hardly a bad boy. She tracked his motion down the hallway until he was virtually face to face with her. He was coiled so tight that she had to reach out and touch his arm to signal her presence.

"Ten *pesos* for your thoughts."

"Ah. I thought I heard someone," his voice seemed a bit too loud, a bit too forced. "Is anyone up yet?"

"Not unless you include me."

"I meant besides us," he smiled broadly, something he rarely did.

"Look," Anna put her hand on his chest. "Don't worry. Enrique was just being himself. You know he means nothing by it. He loves you like a brother."

"Yes. I understand," Cipriano sounded too agreeable. "I just needed space to think."

The roosters in the distance crowed into the pink streaked early morning as if to frighten away the remnants of night. Anna looked out the window, aware of Cipriano following her gaze.

"Rosy-fingered dawn," he spoke softly, "From *The Odyssey.*"

They stood close to each other for a moment. In the back of the farm the men in the fields remained asleep in their hammocks, near the embers from the night's fires.

"Do you think you'll ever get home?" Anna's question startled him. He blinked widely several times.

Cipriano nodded, stretched, and then raised his head well above hers. She had to look up at him. She always liked the intensity of his eyes.

"One day."

∎

"Woo-woo-woo." Enrique's call filled the center of the encampment. His hands placed to his mouth, he summoned the men. Anna and Cipriano, still at the farmhouse, watched the three teams put on their uniforms, clean and reassemble their weapons behind their backs, and stand at the ready for Enrique's instructions.

Rena and Oliver emerged from the farmhouse together — were they wiping the sleep out of their eyes? Anna told herself to "Change the station." The dial inside her head moved a bit to the left. She waved to them, and they responded by strolling over, chatting warmly. Enrique continued to bark commands, sending his "boys" into a series of exercises designed to enhance their agility. He ordered one of the squads to split in two smaller units, and work with "Commander Law, over there." He shot Oliver a glace that Anna read as "teach them what you can about automatic weapons. But don't hold out too much hope."

They followed Oliver to the shooting range they had built the day before, several bundles of raffia tied together and stacked at the edge of the anarchic jungle that appeared to have encroached at least five meters overnight. Anna could hear Oliver's velvet voice — he never raised it except for emergencies.

"My friends, today we will shoot with live ammunition. Or, almost live." He looked them up and down sternly. "We shall conserve our resources and learn to shoot." With that Oliver strode up and down the three columns of guerrillas handing out single rounds of live ammunition.

Impossible to hear the car's arrival. The simultaneous discharge of firearms created a metallic din punctuated by percussive explosions. The training exercise saw the volunteers scattered to the periphery of the grounds, firing their weapons into the jungle as Enrique and Anna passed among them offering encouragement and corrections. Cipriano and Rena stood, arms folded, in the shade of the farmhouse, watching. Rena, because she wanted nothing to do with weapons, and Cipriano because, as Anna said, he needed some rest.

Anna recognized the robins egg blue Buick Roadmaster first. The car pulled up to the very rear of the house, stopped, and discharged two passengers. One — Maria — Anna recognized from her foray into Santiago the previous day. The other was a man Anna had never seen before.

Maria Santamaria had exchanged her shimmering summer dress for worn fatigues and a loose t-shirt. She wore her hair up, used no makeup, and carried a Colt 45 sidearm. Maria greeted Anna with two kisses, left and right. Then she took a step back.

"This is Raúl."

Anna studied him carefully. His close-cropped hair and skimpy mustache gave him a certain distinctiveness. His round face and narrow eyes made her wonder if he had Chinese ancestry. Short, and lacking the instinct to smile, Raúl conveyed confidence and ruthlessness.

His expressionless look chilled her. Not a man to be trifled with. She laughed at her own naivety; the moment was hardly a trifling one. The revolutionary movement could hardly succeed on sentiment alone either. In fact, she had first heard the name Raúl yesterday, and here he was, in their midst. Raúl dressed in the uniform of an ordinary soldier. A comment on the original non-commissioned status of "Sergeant" Batista, a bit subtle if not ironic. So now, Anna thought, the leaders closest to Fidel himself have arrived.

"I am glad you are here," she spoke. "Shall I gather everyone?"

Again, the look. Cool. His dark eyes darting, seeing everything before responding, Anna thought. He nodded.

He spoke to the assembled men, calling them brothers, inviting them to sit on the grass around him. Standing there in their midst, he turned as he spoke, looking at each of them, praising them for their dedication to the movement, to the Revolution. His short arms, Anna noted, caused his shirt cuffs to bunch up on his wrists, so his sleeves billowed. He looked a bit like a boy in his father's uniform — or his brother's. But he sounded every bit like a man who knew what he wanted and where he was going.

"Why am I here? I am here because I believe the most important thing for free men to do is to protect the freedom of others. And here you are, who believe as I do. Together we will fight for liberty and justice in our land." He looked behind them, toward the mountains that rose steeply upward.

"We fight for them. For the thousands — no, millions — of peasants and workers who are no longer free. The *Sierra Maestra* will be our inspiration and, if need be, our sanctuary."

His voice took an even more serious tone, his gaze dropping down to the men sitting at his feet.

"Tomorrow we will act."

The men stood as one and cheered. They all cried *"Viva Cuba Libre!"* and *"Martí vive!"*

Raúl called Enrique, Anna, Oliver, Cipriano, and Rena next to him. They stood arm in arm, as the men cheered again.

"And we will make history!"

"What is the date?" someone shouted. "I have lost track during my stay in this charming resort."

After the laughter subsided, Raúl replied. "Tomorrow is the 25th of July, my friends. By the next day, July 26, we will have taken our first step toward the liberation of our people and our country."

This time he paused. Looked at his five colleagues. Then at the men.

"We must be vigilant. Our enemy is within and without. Batista, the army, the SIM will do everything to prevent us, to stop us, to kill us. There will be those among us who are not pure of heart. I do not yet know who they are, but they are always there. Beware. We have much to fear."

And for some reason that Anna did not understand he straightened his shoulders, stood just a bit taller, and turned to each of them, held out his hand, and shook theirs. It is as if he's trying to feel our souls, she thought as he grasped her hand firmly in his. His soft skin revealed the hands of a man of words, not labor.

"Tomorrow night we begin. First our leaders," and he nodded to each of them, "will infiltrate the city, disable a critical strategic position, and prepare the way for the rest of you."

Not 'us,' Anna wondered as she cocked and then un-cocked the Tokarev TT-30 strapped to her leg. She grinned as Oliver look askance at her. The eight round magazine was nestled in her other hand.

"We will rendezvous with them early the next morning. The 26th of July, remember that date. Just before dawn. Our objective is to seize the Barracks at Moncada. By the time the sun rises on July 26 we will have subdued the garrison, occupied the armory, taken over the hospital, and launched our revolution."

"Comrade," a tall young man stepped forward. "Tell us, please. Why have we trained for so many day in the jungle if we are going to attack the city?"

Enrique stepped forward. "If you will allow me," he asked

Castro. "Because we wanted to be sure that you could handle any contingency! Yes, of course you now know how to fire your weapons. But, what if you become separated from the group? What if you find yourself in the jungle, up in the mountains? You will thank us for the training then."

Anna could see a shiver work its way through the men. The kernel of doubt Enrique's words had planted could easily become fear. How to balance that?

"For most of you this will be your first time in armed combat. We, all of us," she pointed to the other four, "we all fought in Spain. For liberty, for the Republic. And I will tell you this. Fear and war are intimate partners. You should worry if you feel no fear at all. And, your survival may — no, will — depend on understanding fear, going toward it, and reacting to it. This is what we have taught you here. Go, my friends, go to the fear."

After a long silence that Anna felt unbearably, someone else cried out.

"Where is Fidel?"

"Yes!" Another voice shouted. "Fidel!"

Then another. And then many — "Fidel! Fidel! Fidel!"

PART FIVE

25-26 JULY 1953

CHAPTER ONE
CARNIVAL

Now that Fidel and Raúl are but months away from realizing their goals, Arthur, I think it time to understand the lessons they learned from the failures of Moncada. Law pieced this part of the story together for me. We cannot tell it yet. But, perhaps one day we shall.

I

SANTIAGO, 25 JULY 1953

The car pulled into the square slowly, lights off. It stopped in front of the Cathedral on *Parque Céspedes*. With the streets silent, the tourist stalls along *Calle Heredia* sat empty and the miniature drums and wood carvings wrapped in burlap bags lay slumped in vacant doorways. Down below, toward the port, along the narrow congested streets of the old city, the lights blazed and the music pulsed to the beat of conga drums, trompeta chinas, and timbales.

The driver and four passengers pulled several canvas bags from the trunk, setting them down on the sidewalk. Behind them the Cathedral looked ghostly, its yellow skin bathed in amber from the searchlights set in the square directly across the street. During the day *Parque Céspedes* belonged to the mendicants of Santiago — to the homeless men and women who sold cigar butts, sang melancholy songs, and offered casino tours. At night, the park belonged to the whores and pimps of the city.

During Carnival the square belonged to the city and the night belonged to Carnival. But, not just yet.

They picked up their bags, crossed the street, and climbed up the steps to the portico of the imperious *Hotel Casa Granda* whose white-washed exterior overlooked the park. The veranda provided a sweeping view of the square, and they peered down into the city streets where the sounds of Carnival penetrated the cobalt sky.

"Up here," Anna whispered, realizing that no one would hear them above the din created by the snare drums, wood-trumpets, and congas. Still, they followed her just as they had agreed.

∎

Parque Céspedes remained still. Anna motioned the others back toward the depths of the veranda of the *Hotel Casa Granda.* No one would see them there. She checked her watch. Almost 9 pm. The music from the streets sounded closer, but Anna knew they still had plenty of time to get into position.

"You will need costumes, so I have brought you some," Fidel had spoken softly, scratching the wisps of his beard. "You will insinuate yourselves into the Carnival and raise no alarm, no suspicion." He had stood before them earlier that day, his American-made M1 semi-automatic in one hand. He looked exhausted, Anna thought. No wonder, he had just arrived from Havana, spent the late afternoon huddled with Enrique and his brother Raúl, and then called them together to give them what he termed their "operational directives."

She watched as all but Rena fit themselves into the costumes, pulling the disguises over their uniforms. Rena, whose objective was to help secure the hospital at Moncada, would simply weave her way through the streets dressed like a nurse. Her white uniform with a red-cross armband would provide her only cover.

"Really!" she had exclaimed. "Hide a nurse as a nurse. Are you sure?" She had laughed as they explained this part of the plan to her.

Like the others, she carried a small map of the Carnival's route in her pocket. From *Parque Céspedes*, to the reviewing stand at *Plaza de Morte*, then past the Moncada barracks to *Parque Ferrerio*. By the time the Carnival reached its terminus the armed rebels would be in position, packed into a convoy of cars.

"Like clockwork," Castro had commanded, "It needs to work like clockwork. We have surprise on our side and we must not lose it." He pulled himself to his full height. "And now I will tell you again! This operation absolutely depends on our ability to enter the city undetected," his voice grew more solemn as he looked first at Anna and then at Raúl, "and that depends on your ability to infiltrate the Carnival, to become our vanguard! Your success in neutralizing the guard post will allow us to emerge at dawn, as they all sleep." Then he lowered his gaze and spoke softly, almost a whisper. "Without this we are lost. You are just late-night revelers who have lost their way." He laughed at the irony. "Now it is time to get ready." He stared at Anna for emphasis. "You MUST make sure the guard post is ours."

Oliver, who hated taking off his beret, bent forward to lean on his good leg and reached into the bag, from which he pulled out a huge papier-mâché mask, big enough to cover his torso.

"Be so kind as to encumber me," he showed his teeth in a grimace that became a smile. He leaned so Rena could strap the mask to his head. "Make it good and tight," he instructed, "It would be unfortuitous should it fall off."

"I have no idea what that means," laughed Rena, her fingers tying the two strands of leather that fixed the mask tightly to his face.

Oliver straightened, raised his hands over his head. "Avast, me hearties!" he called and limped over to the balcony, stamping his wooden leg for emphasis. Rena laughed. The others just smiled. Oliver turned to face them. A giant pirate face stretched from the top of his head to his belt. Painted a glowing yellow-green and covered by an eye-patch, it sported one tooth, a minstrel show smile, and a red scarf tied around the forehead. Two small holes in the pirate's headscarf allowed Oliver to actually see from inside. He bowed his head one more time, "If you trifle with me, you'll be walking the plank."

This brought a tear to Anna's eye. It felt like the old Ollie. Not just the playfulness, but the joy.

"Alright. Let's get dressed," she ordered.

Enrique and Cipriano pulled out two *sombreros*, each made from multi-colored raffia. Strands of red, yellow, white, and green covered them from brim to crown. They then put on raffia shirts with long sleeves that ballooned at the wrist. Cipriano wore red, Enrique, black. Finally they added yellow kerchiefs tied around their necks.

"You look like matching harlequins," Anna inclined her head to Rena. "Which one do you like better?"

"I'll never tell," Rena replied as she used her wrist to clean an imaginary spot from her new white nurse's cap. "Wow. Will you take a look at this," she exclaimed pointing at Anna as she pirouetted before them.

"I thought something a bit exotic," Anna announced from behind the gold mask that covered her eyes. The mask matched the feathered turban on her head. A massive cut-glass ruby was fixed at her forehead. Draped across her shoulders, extending in a curve down to her midriff, she wore a shimmering red and gold appliqué tunic studded with turquoise and silver stones.

"May I call you Madam?" Enrique called, trying to conceal his delight.

They stood next to one another for a moment, as if posing for an imaginary photograph. Ghosts from a midnight ball: two harlequins, a nurse, a pirate, and Madam Anna.

■

The sounds of Carnival grew louder. The syncopation of the conga drums pulled the sharp tunes of *trompeta chinas* and *timbales* closer to the square. As the first line neared the Cathedral the twin bells began a deep resonant peal, ringing in the new, covering the dancing mass of people swaying and prancing, one foot forward, then to the side, then the other forward, shoulders leading right and left, hands clapping on the off-beat.

As the first line appeared on the square — a rank of men in white trousers and lime-green linen shirts — the church bells quieted. The six men picked up the beat, hands blurred on tall drums suspended by shoulder belts. As they walked they added layers of beat, their polyrhythms creating a depth of emotional feeling among the dozens of lines and ranks and schools — each from a different neighborhood — who followed them. Onward they pulsed toward the square, flowing though the narrow streets of the *barrio* dancing, driving, their heartbeats seemingly in perfect synchronization.

Anna watched as the first line approached. "Let's wait for several of these groups to pass."

"They are lines," Enrique spoke softly, "crews from every walk of life, each one different."

"Lo siento," Anna replied, straightening the red plume sprouting from her turban. "Wait for several lines to pass. Then join the one with costumes like yours. Just blend in. Later, at dawn, when we approach Moncada, we will meet again to confirm our plans. You each have your own objectives — barracks, hospital, Palace of Justice. I will take care of the guardhouse. *No pasarán!"* She made it sound so simple.

Anna watched as first Enrique, then Cipriano, then Oliver, and finally Rena joined the marchers. Men and women waved from motorized floats, children awash in gold and silver studded shirts and serapes. Platoon after platoon passed with fife and drums, shirtless men banging metal rods against black metal cylinders, young women in blue skirts that whirled in wide uneven circles. An endless parade, dizzying in its display of color and sound, everyone dressed to the nines, taking over the town.

After a half-hour, her senses overwhelmed by the rhythm of the back-beat and the smell of sugar-cane *guarapo*, Anna found the epicenter of Carnival.

As she waited, the square filled with onlookers who intensified the music of the parade. Dozens of teenage kids, some on stilts, dressed in white and black and red, held plastic jugs under an arm and beat a multi-layered tattoo of rhythmic inspiration with one hand.

A new line made its way into the square. Two dozen dancers, moving side to side, marched past the cathedral, then turned directly in front of the hotel. They moved in pairs, dressed in shirts festooned with white chicken feathers sprinkled with glitter that shimmied and shone in the night. The crowd cheered when one of the women, bedecked in a bright pink boa, took a whistle that hung from her neck, puffed her cheeks, and blew until her eyes bulged. The shrill sound silenced the music.

And then they broke into a run, scattering in all directions, white plumage flashing in circles. The dance, spinning out of control, a tableau of frantic motion. A figure clad in red and black materialized.

"Legba!" the dancers cried. "Papa Legba!" The cheer rang out from the crowd.

He stood in the middle of the swirling motion. One pant leg black, the other red, one side of his shirt black, the other red, the front of his three-cornered hat black and the rear red. The King of Carnival.

Anna eased herself to the rear-most ranks of the swaying line. The red-black Legba signaled to the whistle-bearing, white-feathered woman. Kicking high, from hip to heel, arms and fists pumping, Legba led them once around the square, and onto *Aguilera*. Anna followed, walking with a small group of women in gold-trimmed white gowns, each wearing a red plume headdress that matched her own. She looked behind her at the waves of revelers, each more spectacular than the next. Jamaican limbo dancers, sequined cross-dressers, men in tin-foil hats and leopard skin togas, women wearing papier-mâché hats filled with plastic fruit, and the inevitable caricatures of local big shots, including a giant Batista carrying a whip and wearing a black mask. No wonder they tried to stop Carnival in the old days. It was, really was, a riot of freedom, disorder, and social upset. My god, Anna thought, Carnival was the embodiment of revolution. No wonder they had chosen it for cover.

White feathers, he kept saying to himself. White feathers. Everyone here is dressed in white. And how will she know me? I must be the only Cypriot dressed for Carnival who's never been to mass.

Then she appeared, right before his eyes. At the head of a line of young women dressed in green silk skirts that kissed the pavement and tight yellow tops that clung to every curve. And, yes! All in white from the feathered cap that spilled down over her eyes to the one-piece suit that extended from a scooped neck-line to her ankles. She swayed back and forth, holding her hands above her head, snapping her fingers.

"Perhaps, *señora*, you recall inviting me to find you this sweet night?"

She didn't look at him. Instead she took his hand and led him to the periphery of the Carnival parade as it worked its way along *Aguilera*. He felt a momentary pang of guilt. Anna had issued strict orders to remain in the flow of Carnival. Here he was taking chances. Well, why not. A beautiful woman could hardly be considered a mistake.

They walked several blocks, until the cacophony of the parade had faded.

"Sylvie," he took her hand.

"Tonight I am Eurydice."

∎

26/7 0200
Anna knew the route would follow *Aguilera* from *Céspedes*

past *Plaza de Dolores* and then to *Plaza de Marte*. And there, at the midpoint of the celebration, each line and float and band and crew would pass in review. The closer they wound their way toward the *Plaza de Marte* the more dense the crowds became. The police had blocked the side streets with wooded barriers, and local merchants had cobbled together a *barrio* of ramshackle food stands and homemade carts filled to overflowing with husk-roasted corn, chunks of grilled pork, fried *churros*, beer, and best of all *aguardiente*, the local schnapps. Clear and bitingly strong, the liqueur was sold by the shot in newspaper rolled into a cone. By the time Anna's line had reached *Plaza de Dolores* the pavement was lined with alcohol-saturated newsprint.

She remembered that they had parked their truck near this place only the day before, where Cipriano had waited for them. It occurred to her that his disappearance might have led him back. The clamor of a trio of dancers broke her thoughts. Each dancer had dressed head to toe in wild and fluffy feathers — one dressed all in red, the other yellow, and the next green. Even their heads were encased in feathers, leaving only their eyes and noses outside the cocoon of their costumes. The three pranced and jumped, running in circles and calling out words that had no meaning. Their energy was infectious and the revelers around them soon joined their gyrations.

Hundreds of local dignitaries filled one side of the reviewing stands around the Plaza. Their seats, reserved by a billowing yellow ribbon, came without charge. The other bench spaces were made available to the public — for a price. By two o'clock that morning the grandstands bulged with onlookers, many well past drunk, others still on their feet. Anna reached out for a pork and shrimp sandwich, coated with oil, on bread still fresh from the oven. She devoured it quickly and then bought a bottle of *Hatuey*, the beer of Santiago "Since 1927." She watched as each group wheeled to face the grandstand

and raised cups of *guarapo,* sugarcane juice, in salute. Legba pranced as each line presented itself to the judges, smoking a long and thick cigar and stomping his feet, a bottle of rum held high triumphantly in the night.

The crush of revelers slowed the celebration to a halt, each new line collapsing into the backs of those in front. Anna could barely see over their heads. She mounted one of the grandstands, high enough to gain a view. Sure enough, Rena and Oliver, his pirate mask only a bit askew, had found each other. They waited, watching the ceremony at the grandstand, quite still. Anna wondered if he were exhausted from the walk. She knew he would never admit if he was.

Then she found Enrique, shouldering himself through a tightly packed knot of young women in gold-lamé gowns and silver masks held aloft on a single stick. He seemed to be moving toward something. But it wasn't until she saw Cipriano that she understood. They must have separated. As Enrique approached his old friend, Cipriano reached out to pull the hand of a woman, dressed in white feathers, toward him.

She was the most stunning woman Anna had ever seen — with a beautiful round face and braided hair held together with cowry shells. Cipriano had indeed found a woman this night.

∎

26/7 0500

Anna had instructed them to wait just beyond the *Plaza de Marte* at the intersection of *Calle Hernán Cortés* and *Avenida Victoriano de Garzón.* A smoky dawn, with just a hint of pink, revealed a city hung over. Men and women in costume slept in doorways, on park benches, even in the street, with their heads resting on the curb. The wrought-iron outer doors of the turquoise and yellow two-story houses that lined *Aguilera* reminded Anna of Havana — a kind of crumbling colonial glory, neglected, in need of repair.

A more elegant building curved gracefully around the corner where they were to meet. On its upper floor Anna could see a series of connected balconies framed in light-blue, a vision of elegant wrought-iron and white plaster. At street level, the symmetrical row of plate glass windows mimicked the kind of ritzy upper-class shop that she knew existed in Barcelona. The windows, like the building, wrapped themselves around the corner, and displayed the most recent fashions — floor-length pale green and rose silk gowns, elegantly bejeweled, beneath sculpted black hats. The kind of clothing Anna imagined no one would ever wear in Santiago. As she looked at her dim reflection in the window, and saw the white cloak and red headdress on her petite frame, she could only laugh.

∎

7/26 0530

Oliver leaned into Rena, feeling her warmth next to him in the early morning air. Time to ditch this mask, he said to himself. His hair touched with gray, his gold tooth still flashing, and his beret back in place, he felt like a vintage version of himself. Not exactly the guy on two legs who could tell the "man" to go fuck himself, but not exactly a has-been either. He had to admit it felt more satisfying to play a real role at the center of action. Hell, that's why he had responded to Matthews in the first place, and that's why he had found Anna. These last months had been revelatory. He liked the word, "revelatory." He still had a life to lead. It had been an adjustment to relinquish real leadership to her, but he could accommodate the necessity considering the circumstances.

He turned to Rena. Their connection was so real. He honored

the role she had played in saving his life. And wondered why he had neglected to acknowledge it overtly. Maybe it had been ill-considered to have thought of her as a sister. But the deeper truth was that his leg functioned as an impediment. He reached out to touch her hand.

"What time did they say we were to rendezvous?"

"About now." Her hand felt soft. He didn't dare look into her face.

"Remember the test in Paris?" he responded, craning his neck to look back down the avenue, scanning the route they had just taken.

"Are you waiting for the others?"

"You didn't take the hint, did you?" he continued.

"Why Mister Law, what made you think I was that slow?"

"There were so many pretenders back then. We had to make sure."

"So if I didn't agree to fuck you then I'd be reliable." Hardly a question.

He had never fully accommodated himself to her salty language. His word, "salty."

"Something like that," he finally responded, after discarding three other retorts.

"Maybe it's not too late," she replied, then hesitated and added, "for us."

At that moment the others — Anna, Enrique and Cipriano — materialized. Rena and Oliver startled — they had crept up on them silently.

"You two were so engaged," Anna seemed to be smiling, but Oliver couldn't quite tell. "You didn't hear us. And, the stealth king over there," she pointed to Enrique, "makes enough noise for a division."

I

MONCADA, 26 JULY 1953

Dawn. The city was sleeping and Moncada was only blocks away. They had accomplished the first part of the mission: to infiltrate the target without raising alarm. Now everything would be "like clockwork," Anna remembered Fidel's words, "like clockwork."

They stuffed the remnants of their costumes, a motley array of rags, into the soft bag that Enrique carried. Deftly they pulled on their green field shirts, the number 26/7 stenciled inside the front flap pocket. Anna insisted on red for the numerals to help with identification later.

"If not, we'll just be shooting ourselves," she had been patient in the face of some opposition to apparent aesthetic vanity. "We all have the same damn uniforms otherwise." The Castro brothers knew she was right and readily agreed to the decoration. "It's not less democratic to be smart," she had smiled.

The uniforms, still smelling of mothballs, covered them from the waist up. "No pants, wear your trousers as you will," Anna instructed as Oliver hitched his ancient rope belt, pulling it tightly. He somehow seemed smaller than the man she remembered. With the sun, a ball of deep orange, hovering over the city, the five linked arms briefly, kissed each other on both cheeks, and walked towards the intersection of *Trinidad* and *Paseo De Marte*.

Anna checked her steel Omega field watch, the one with the black dial that she had worn in Spain. They had engraved *"Viva la República"* on the back and gave it to her just after the battle of

Madrid. She wondered if Castro had the same sentimental streak as General Kléber. Toughest human being she had ever met, but, he cried at the drop of a hat, or rather, at the drop of a ceremony. Anna used her right hand, two fingers pressed together, to point twice to the left and then twice to the right, dividing the team in half, motioning Rena and Oliver across the street while she and the boys remained half-concealed in the shadows.

She glanced up at the second-story veranda of the building across the street, just where Oliver and Rena were walking. Arm in arm, just two soldier revelers making their way slowly back to the barracks. The light blue frame of the stucco house had faded and the wrought iron gates that guarded the sidewalk-to-ceiling windows had rusted to an orange-brown. She wondered if, in the fullness of the summer heat, anyone had slept up there, on the balcony above. She wondered if she would sleep that night. And where.

Lying in the street, leaning up against the concrete curb, a half empty bottle of Bacardi was also sleeping off the night. Anna bent down to pick it up and tucked it under her arm. Then she motioned her two companions to her side, slid her bottle-arm around Cipriano's waist and her left hand on to Enrique's elbow, and nodded. Her head barely came to Cipriano's shoulder, but was even with Enrique's own broad and furrowed brow. Five minutes, and not a second more had passed, but the sun had already cleared the rooftops, and she could feel a coating of sweat form at the base of her throat. The brigade would be there in a few minutes. It was time for them to take their stations. She took a deep breath and smiled inwardly at herself. A forty-year-old female guerrilla revolutionary. What in the world had she been thinking?

■

The caravan rolled slowly, silently, down the narrow *Avenida Moncada*. Anna and the two men stood, still arm in arm, on the corner of *Trinidad* and *Paseo de Martí*. Castro loved the choice of rendezvous. Martí, he had reminded them for the tenth time the previous day, Martí was the real father of Cuban independence. He, Castro, merely the amanuensis. When Cipriano whispered "what the fuck is that?" Oliver had nudged him in the ribs and answered "assistant." No accident that Castro planned the attack for this very day. The Centennial of Martí, the end of Carnival, and as he had told them the day before, "If we shit in our pants tomorrow and the government finds out what we are up to, all we need to say is that we are the vanguard of the communist revolution and The Sergeant will play the Cold War fool and arrest us all." No one needed to ask who he meant by The Sergeant. "But we will not fail." Anna remembered how his face had grown florid, "we will be the spark that sets the fire of revolution burning through the country. The *campesinos* will rise up and greet us as liberators. The workers will barricade the streets and tell the communists to go fuck themselves." He picked up his rifle, aimed through the scope, and pulled the trigger. Then he paused and looked over at his brother. "Right Raúl? Isn't that what will happen to your young communist cousins."

His younger brother, just returned from an international meeting of the World Youth Congress in Vienna, smiled slyly to himself. "And then they will publish pictures of us with ants in our mouths."

Fidel took the warning in stride. "Lest innocent blood be shed," he cried, raising his rifle over his head with his right arm. "Our brothers will rise up with us and they will turn this pebble in Batista's shoe into a grenade."

They believed they had planned the final stage carefully. The first three cars would assemble their teams as they made their way toward the three objectives. A gray 1949 Pontiac would drive directly into the Moncada Courtyard, to guard post number three. Castro, seated next to the driver of this lead car, was to pick up Anna, Cipriano, and Enrique just before entering the grounds of the barracks. A green four-door '51 Plymouth driven by Raúl would find Oliver on its way to the *Palacio de Justicia*, and the blue 1950 Dodge, with three armed volunteers, was to scoop up Rena, who waited along *Trinidad*, and take her to the hospital. The mass of the volunteers were to follow behind the lead cars and wait for the bursts of gunfire that would signal them to storm the barracks.

The operation rested on their ability to maintain its secrecy. They counted on the combined effects of Carnival's celebration and the early morning stupor to disguise their intent. As she stood there, the pale yellow structure of Moncada rising to her left, Anna felt the moment was theirs.

∎

The Pontiac drove slowly down *Avenida Moncada*. The driver saw Anna, Cipriano, and Enrique but continued to roll slowly toward them without coming to a full stop. Several other automobiles, but not the full complement of volunteers Anna expected, followed closely behind — out of place, she thought. Too soon. She shrugged inwardly. Nothing to do about that. The front and rear doors on the passenger side of the Pontiac swung open, like gates on a barn, leaving the seats and middle pillar in full view. Anna ducked down, slung her rifle over her shoulder, and started to stagger drunkenly toward guard post number three, her objective.

Anna motioned for Cipriano and Enrique to climb into the rear seat and listened as they cocked their Thompson automatic pistols; the distinctive metallic click from each followed by the sound of the first bullet chambering. Then she noticed him. Castro. Craning his head over the roof of the car. He grinned at her.

He looked full of youth and hope. His bearded face and dark eyes were sinister, but his long elegant nose made him seem so — aristocratic. Passion also burned in that face — she remembered it from the student demonstrations in Havana. The excitement and the glow of sweat transformed his skin from olive to chiaroscuro.

The guard post appeared deserted. Just as they planned. Anna tripped, caught herself with one hand, glanced behind her. Ten meters from the post she caught Castro's eye; her signal that all was ready. Castro stood on the running board of the car, holding on to the rain-channel with his right hand and brandishing his semi-automatic rifle with the other, holding it high. Like a cowboy, Anna mused. Like a cowboy.

Still, something felt amiss. She squinted, as if the type were too small to read. But what she saw was like looking at a doctored photograph. The omission only perceptible by its vacuum, not by its identity. She had already turned onto *Trinidad*, a tight right, and now stood almost directly across from the guard post — still silent and empty. The convoy idled softly behind Castro's car.

The street narrowed as it entered the courtyard of the barracks. To her right spread the vast expanse of the green parade grounds, surrounded by a concrete wall whose turrets mimicked the actual structure of the Moncada Barracks to her left. The street ran along the full length of the building, at least 100 meters. Once inside, there would be little chance for escape.

That was the missing piece! There was no way for them to leave — the street was too narrow and the cars behind her blocked any hope of turning around. They had become prisoners of their own planning. She wondered if Enrique had read the courtyard the same way. It was what she had taught him to do in the Pyrenees, wasn't it? How to read.

No going back now. She squatted down, her head lower than the sliding window on the street side of the guard post. The door, half a meter beyond the window, stood ajar. She crept toward it, her right shoulder brushing the side of the kiosk, automatic pistol drawn. No noise. She held her breath, listening. Ten, twenty, thirty seconds. Barrel first she peered into the door. Nothing. Not even the sound of someone deep and fast asleep. Anna smiled. She twisted slightly to her left and waved at the car behind her.

Anna watched the car slowly roll past her, its rear wheels now even with the kiosk door, nosing its way into the barracks entry road.

Moments later the car's suspension relaxed as Enrique and Cipriano swung the door open and tumbled out onto the pavement, pistols at their shoulders. They spun onto their sides and in a single motion gained their footing. The driver gunned the engine in neutral, and the roar of the engine burst into her ears. Castro, his jaw set, crouched next to the car, his rifle aimed up the steps that led from street level to the wood entry doors of the barracks.

▌

Oliver swiveled himself into the green Plymouth. He swung his leg awkwardly, using his right hand as a fulcrum, then reached out and slammed the front door shut. He could hear the clatter of small arms fire coming from the barracks entrance as the driver spun the wheel of the car and turned right onto a wide entry drive that ran parallel to Trinidad. Ahead he could see their objective, the brand new *Palacio de Justicia,* its massive grey concrete frame a contradiction of its name. Three stories high, its oversized windows shown a dull, opaque green, like visors shielding the eye of justice. It reminded Oliver of images of Soviet architecture, of those impenetrable venues of Kafkaesque mystery.

The three men in the rear seat of the car suddenly ducked down. "Get out of sight," one of them hissed at Oliver. The car stalled, and the engine coughed then sputtered. Oliver craned his neck to see the disposition of the two other cars in his column. Raúl was in one, but he wasn't sure which one. Outside, on the pavement between the three cars and the *Palacio*, the rising sun cast long morning shadows. The dark patterns of the automobiles stretched like elongated footprints. There was not a soul to be seen.

"Vámonos," he called to his companions. "Let's go. Now." He kicked open the door of the car, grabbed the Garand automatic weapon that he had chosen the day before. It felt right, balanced, in his hand. The wood of the stock, worn smooth, was soft in his palm. The same carbine he carried that day in Spain. He blinked in the light and raised his left hand to shield his eyes. "Here," he called to the squad that gathered around him. "Follow me." That felt good. He realized that there was no fear in his mouth, no tinge of bile. Only the adrenalin pumping into his brain. They had planned to divide into two small attack groups. Raúl would lead his squad around the rear of the building and up to the roof, and Oliver would secure the ground floor and control entry.

The six men crouched down, holding their guns, their eyes darting from the street to the "objective" and back again. Oliver could feel their fear. None of them had ever been in battle before. He knew. Green, he said to himself, but not yellow. He tensed his muscles, willing them to conform to his thoughts, ordering their compliance. That was how he had taught himself to survive, to drive a straight-line right through the terror. He checked that his squad had followed him up the steps and over the pavement of the building's stone apron. Turning his back on the entry, he waited for his squad to catch up before he shouldered his weapon and turned to enter through the glass and steel front doors of the *Palacio*.

The glass felt cool against the palm of his hand. He pushed and the door swung open easily. He checked again, hoping to balance the excitement of the moment with caution. He raised his eyebrows in a gesture of disbelief, then motioned his squad to the other entry doors.

Three stories high, thirty meters wide and deep with a cavernous interior courtyard, the building worked like an echo chamber. Oliver could hear the others' breath against the soft echoes of their footsteps. The chamber's marble floors and soft indirect light made Oliver feel he had entered a mausoleum. They stopped and stood a moment, weapons ready, silent. The moment turned into a minute that stretched into the silence like a shadow.

∎

The five men surrounded Rena, their faces so close she could smell the rum on their breath, see the stubble on their chins. Two of them grabbed her by the upper arms and lifted her up. Three others followed as they ran up the steps of the hospital, taking them two at a time. Her own heart thumping, Rena gave no thought to physical struggle, focusing only on calming herself. She took two deep breaths even as they continued to carry her up the stairs. This was not how they had planned it.

The only other woman in the camp at Siboney that last day, Maria, with the almond eyes and black hair held high on her head with sliver combs, had taken her aside. I will meet you at the hospital, she told Rena. I'll have a white uniform. I can change and go right upstairs into the wards. The guards will never know who we are. Then she had fixed her gaze on Rena and asked if she could use "this." She held up a small automatic handgun, popped the clip out into her palm, and presented the gun. "I'll give you the clip tomorrow."

The men all carried pistols, a few armed with carbines. Their black boots thumped against the green floors of the hospital reception area. The echoes rattled against the stucco walls. Finally they set Rena down. Her shoes skid on the floor for moment before she regained her balance.

"You can't go in there," cried out a voice from the shelter of a nun's habit. "It is strictly forbidden."

How many times had she heard that? "You can't go in there." As a young nurse at Harlem Hospital when she knocked on the door of the chief of staff. Or, when they told her in Spain that she wasn't needed as an operating room nurse. Same old shit, she thought. Same old shit.

Rena motioned for her escorts to stay put, as if dismissing them like an officer. She tugged at her old nurse's cape and approached the desk. Pointing to the Red Cross on her armband, she pointed with her other hand to the stairs that led to the upper wards. The nun stood, smiled benignly, and beckoned Rena to follow her. Only when they had left the reception area, the men in Rena's unit standing guard at the main door, arms ready, only then did the nun turn to Rena. She bent down and pulled something out from beneath the hem of her habit.

It felt heavy and solid in Rena's hand. The nun smiled again and motioned with her eyebrows. "Follow me," she whispered as Rena slapped the clip into her revolver.

Rena looked at her carefully and replied, "Yes, Maria. At your service."

∎

Something was wrong. Anna knew it in her bones. It was too quiet. Fidel, followed by a dozen others including Cipriano and Enrique, bounded up the steps of the barracks, and now stood outside the doorway on the upper level. Just as they planned, wasn't it? Take the garrison by surprise, everyone would be asleep — fast asleep, thanks to Carnival. The scene all froze for a moment in Anna's mind. Fidel at the doorway, the others behind him on the steps, the sun bright, showering the tableau with golden heat, and Anna at the foot of the steps, the guard post deserted behind her. She watched as Fidel raised his right arm, his carbine tucked into his shoulder, and cried out. "Here. This is where we attack."

The broad staircase, rimmed by wood banisters, rose about six meters from the ground level to the entry area above. Fidel's men lined up behind him, crouching in pairs on the stairs, guns pointed up at the dark windows on either side of the double-hung deep brown wood doorway. Above the entry level the walls of the barracks rose another ten meters to the turret-protected roof.

Anna remained in the street, her back to the car, her carbine aimed over the heads of the men on the stairs in front of her. Behind her, to the left of the intersection of *Trinidad* and *Moncada* the guard kiosk, turrets on top, windows on its curving walls, sat round and squat. Just minutes earlier the interior seemed black and vacant. That's what their intelligence had told them. No one would be in the sentry post that early in the morning, leaving the way clear for the attack.

Anna lowered her carbine for a moment to check if Cipriano and Enrique had joined the attack group on the steps. It took a moment for her to identify Enrique, his IB gold combat pin glinting in the sunlight. She sighed. He couldn't go to war without it. As she searched for Cipriano, her eyes scanning up the steps, she felt a fragment of motion, like a wave in the hot summer air.

A machine gun opened fire, a series of concussions splitting the air, taking her completely by surprise. Anna jumped, not fully registering what had begun. Noise, screams. Bullets exploded, sending cordite into the air and raking the men on the stairs with tracers. It took a split second to realize that the gunfire came not from the main barracks itself, but rather from the sentry post behind her.

The men on the steps spun around to face the machine gun. Two collapsed immediately, falling face first onto the steps. They did not return fire. The others knelt and took aim at the yellow guard tower, now spitting bullets that splintered the concrete all around them, sending fragments of stone whirring into the air. Even as the shooting began another series of automatic weapons opened fire — from above, from the door and windows of the barracks itself. Fidel and his men, Anna realized, were trapped, caught in a cross-fire that that would chew them up in minutes.

She watched as dozens of Cuban regular army troops, clad in American-made khaki uniforms, charged down the steps. They each carried new automatic carbines, shooting as they ran. Anna turned and propped her arms up on the roof of the car and sprayed the window of the sentry post, aiming at the dark window, hoping to silence the machine gun. An arm dangled over the sill, blood dripping down the wrist, and the gun stopped.

Turning back to the barracks, she saw only mayhem. Dead or wounded volunteers lay on the pavement between the car and the staircase, arms and legs akimbo, black silhouettes stenciled on the ground. Several men, surrounded by Batista's troops, stood in the shadow of the upper landing. Two minutes, Anna thought. Two minutes and it's over.

Anna looked down *Trinidad*, toward the cars that they had used to enter the barracks. Fidel and Enrique ran toward the last car, the lime green Plymouth. She ran after them as the car spun its tires, lurched a half-turn in reverse, then careened around the corner. With Enrique at the wheel, the car slowed for an instant on *Avenida Moncada* and picked up three others fleeing the carnage. Then it sped away. Anna watched from the silenced sentry post, the bullet holes from her own fusillade a random pattern of entry wounds in the yellow stucco wall. The car disappeared and Anna, after a moment's hesitation, turned and ran.

∎

PALACIO DE JUSTICIA

Oliver could hear the silence of the vast inner vault of the building. Raúl must be on the roof. Oliver had been assigned the task of sealing off the entrance and occupying the building. Once they had the Palacio secured they planned to bring in any government officials they could find to stand immediate trial.

The revolution would begin with gunfire and end with justice, Fidel had announced in Siboney. When Cubans awoke after the Moncada attack, he predicted, they would take up arms and carry the movement to Havana. The small corps of volunteers would be but the match to ignite the "tinder of Batista's corruption." When the popular army of peasants and students arrived in Havana, Batista would flee. The revolution would proclaim liberty in Havana and justice in Santiago. "This is why you must take the *Palacio*." Fidel had looked right at Oliver. "This is why you are here, a grand hero of Brunete. This is why we sent for you."

Oliver had staggered under the weight of this responsibility. The fires had burned low in Siboney as the men gathered in small groups, dreaming aloud of Cuban liberation. Oliver and Anna found themselves sitting apart from the rest of the encampment. He had stretched his "new" leg out before him, placed his palms on the grass, and leaned into Anna's back.

They sat like that as the evening lengthened into night. Occasionally he leaned his head back and rested it on her shoulder.

She told him in soft whispers that she still cared for him. He felt his heart jump. It had been so long. And tomorrow? He replied that he knew. What about Rena, she had asked. She's not you.

He couldn't recall now, as he watched the doors of the *Palacio* for any military presence, when he had fallen asleep. But she had been lying next to him, her hand in his, the next morning. She pinged his gold tooth with her right forefinger and told him to wake, that it was time to get into gear. He looked into her eyes and told her it was the nicest awakening he'd ever experienced.

He startled at a footfall, then chastised himself for daydreaming. He motioned to the men in his squad. Well-to-do teenagers searching for adventure, filled with idealism. Hardly soldiers. He waved them to the stairs, flicking his wrist as if to say, "get up there and see what's going on." He punched his hands, palms down at the marble floor. I'll wait here.

Alone, he paced the length and the width of the lobby. Took in the office directory, white letters under glass. Opened the outer door and stuck his head into the morning air. His watch read 0745 and outside it was as quiet as inside. He stepped back from the building, put his hand over his eyes as if to see more clearly, and looked up at the roof. Still nothing. The men must be up there by now. They should have joined Raúl's force and announced that they had taken the building. Still, only silence.

■

MONCADA HOSPITAL

Just as they reached the landing, the automatic weapons opened fire with a roar of a dozen fighter planes. The sound buried them.

Rena turned to go back down. Maria grabbed her arm. "This way." She pulled the two of them up to the second floor. The barrage below did not let up. The steady staccato told Rena only that the soldiers who had accompanied her were still alive.

The two women entered the general ward, reserved for women neither in labor nor at death's doorstep. Rena could see the range of maladies — broken noses covered by dingy gray bandages, arms and legs encased in plaster dangling from straps over the beds, feverish moans and irregular whoops of laughter. It was like any other ward she had ever worked at. Except for the fear. The women who could, sat propped up in their ancient white metal beds, eyes wide-open, hands twisting, their hair wild.

Maria pulled the habit up over her head. Maria, momentarily naked, reached into a nearby closet to find a nurses uniform, one-piece, that buttoned up the front. Maria kicked her discarded habit under the nearest bed. Moments later the two began their morning rounds. Only then did it occur to Rena that the staff of the hospital was nowhere to be seen.

Maria motioned her to the back of the room and whispered. "I think they are coming up."

"What must we do?" Rena startled, feeling fear.

"You start there," Maria pointed to the end of one line of beds, "and I'll begin here."

Government soldiers pushed through the ward, guns swiveling back and forth like divining rods, intent on ferreting out any revolutionary rebels hiding under the beds. Ignoring their presence, the two nurses calmly worked their way down the rows. The soldiers' shiny black boots squeaked against the red-streaked green linoleum as they swept the room. Rena hunched over an elderly woman, holding her fragile and waxy wrist to take her pulse, carefully studying the layout of the ward, scanning the doorways for an easy exit.

She held the chart close to her face, tracing the pencil scratches with her finger, her senses heightened as one of the soldiers walked past. The odor of garlic followed him, and she could see the marks that pocked the back of his neck. The only difference between him and the boys in her group? Luck. And social class. The patient at her feet looked up at her with pleading eyes. They were red-rimmed and flecked with telltale signs of jaundice. "Help me," the woman called. Rena noted that the last entry dated from 48 hours earlier. And then, out of nowhere, the smell. The acrid stench of urine. These patients had been left unattended. She wondered, even as she signaled to Maria, why?

They had planned to occupy the hospital to treat their own wounded. This, Rena remembered, had been Oliver's idea. The Cubans couldn't imagine any losses. Oliver's experience told him otherwise. "It will be imperative to secure a place for treatment and triage," he had announced. His way of speaking was, Rena knew, how he kept his distance from many things, his past and even those around him. His version of *usted* rather than *tú*. The Cubans had merely shrugged. Rena knew it was a form of respect that they had not actually objected. And she also knew that it was what kept her from him — his wall of language and manners. And, yes, of frailty in the face of great bravery and command. She had seen him at his weakest and most vulnerable and he couldn't completely regain his lionhearted stature in her eyes. She knew this troubled him.

"What shall we do now?" Maria stood close to Rena, her dark eyes intense and worried.

"Let's find you some new shoes," Rena replied, looking down at the black oxfords that Maria still wore, a remnant of her previous identity.

∎

Enrique sent the Plymouth screaming into a three-point turn. A moment later he spun the steering wheel with his left hand and slammed the gear-shift back into first with his right. The streamlined lime green sedan hesitated for an instant and then rocketed from the Moncada inner courtyard and out into the morning traffic that had turned Santiago into a driving nightmare.

"What the fuck!" Fidel called out from the rear seat. "What the fuck went wrong? They were waiting for us!"

Enrique rode the brakes of the car down the tumble of cobblestone hills toward the Siboney highway. The three fighters bouncing in the back seat had already ripped off their uniforms and put their ancient rifles down on the floorboard. Kids from the city, Enrique thought, out for a holiday, a lark. What did they know about armed struggle and revolution? He caught their image in the rear-view mirror. Light-skinned middle-class students, hardly the vanguard of the proletariat. Reminded him of himself twenty years earlier. Naive and full of idealism, but without the mature political consciousness of his generation. Ortodoxo, Communist — didn't matter to Enrique. They were only labels for authority, for followers. He felt at home only with the syndicalists, the union workers who didn't give a fig for ideology and hated taking orders from Commissars.

"Stop here," Fidel pointed, and Enrique steered the car onto the curb along *Paséo de Martí*, barely a hundred meters from where they paraded only hours earlier. And Cipriano? Where did he go?

Fidel exited the car awkwardly, his long arms flapping and legs wobbly. He emptied his wallet into his palm, then tore his driver's license and his lawyer's bar identification card into dozens of tiny pieces. After jamming them into a trash bin, he collapsed into the back seat of the car, breathing hard, his face round and florid.

"We've been betrayed..." he whispered, then reached up and touched Enrique on the shoulder. "Let's get to Siboney and see what we can do."

■

Anna watched the car pull away. She glanced at the pastel citadel. Government soldiers ran every which way, waving their carbines, poking them into the mouths of the wounded who lay prostrate and bleeding on the pavement. Men staggered to their feet, some bloody and others simply dazed, only to be surrounded by more soldiers who herded them onto the parade ground on the other side of Trinidad. They looked dismal, these young men, still dressed in the uniforms they had donned for the attack. We had the surprise. And they were waiting for us!

She hurried past the sentry post, turned up the next street and walked calmly toward *Palacio de Justicia*. The automatic pistol beneath her clothes rubbed against her side, but she strolled as if she hadn't a care in the world, head back, watching the morning sun as it climbed into the cloudless blue sky. She thought of the morning in Barcelona when they had walked down the Diagonal, the last remnant of the International Brigades. She never dreamed then that she would feel that solitary ever again. Ollie walked with her that day, stride for stride, disguising his pain with talk. She loved him for that.

The magisterial façade of the *Palacio* towered above her, casting the street into an eerie noiseless cityscape. She was less than a kilometer from the mayhem at Moncada. She looked up at the roof, hoping to identify the fighters who they had trained to secure the area. Only a few snipers had accompanied Raúl for this assignment. She remembered the sharp debate at Siboney, with Oliver insisting that the tactical advantage of posting sharp-shooters on the roof outweighed the strategic liability of spreading the attack force into several segments. Pure Oliver, all the military jargon dressed up in elegance. Not everyone had agreed with his vision, but all had seemed willing to go along with it.

What they hadn't realized was that while the roof of the *Palacio* looked down at the barracks, the structure of Moncada itself blocked the angle of vision. Anna could see this now, looking up at the roof with the actual barracks behind her. There was no way that men up there could peer into the area between Moncada and the parade grounds. No wonder it remained silent. They must have left as soon as they realized they had lost their sightlines.

The rays of the morning sun glinted sharply off the entry door, flashing white into her eyes. Through the narrow slits of her vision she made out the shape of a dark figure standing on the steps of the Palacio. He had his own hand over his eyes, shielding them from the sun behind her. No mistaking Ollie.

■

Cipriano had arrived two minutes late. He dashed after the first wave, running up the stairs of the citadel, and stormed into the foyer — to be greeted by a platoon of army regulars.

They disarmed him and paraded him up the stairs, hands held high. As more gunfire erupted in the courtyard below, Cipriano leaned to his left to call out over his shoulder, as if to an advancing friend. His captors turned their heads both ways, toward the gunfire and in the direction of Cipriano's voice. An instant was all he needed to throw himself headlong into the window and out onto the street in a hail of broken glass.

Cipriano hit the ground running. The crunch of shards grinding against his boots as he bent low and sprinted down *Trinidad* toward the sentry post.

The government soldiers who cornered him only minutes earlier stood at the broken window and fired round after round. But he zig-zagged, just as they had trained him in Spain. Hell, if they aimed as well as they guarded he had nothing to fear anyway. Might even welcome a nick, say on his arm, just to show the others that he had been in on the attack.

At the corner of Trinidad and Moncada he sagged, leaning over to rest his hands on his upper thighs, gasping. Behind him hulks of the convoy cars were riddled by bullet holes, their windows shattered, tires flat, abandoned helter-skelter across the blazing road. Reminded him of the aftermath of a British attack on a Cypriot independence movement safe house that his communist cell had secreted in a stone courtyard in Nicosia in 1936. Betrayal all around. No one had been truly innocent. It sang in his mind like a morning call to prayer, a mantra. No one is truly innocent.

∎

The memory of her musky cinnamon scent caught him by surprise. He hadn't expected her to be so incredibly passionate. Like a dream. Eurydice. She had reached out for his hand as they danced down the street together, the conga drums beating layers of rhythms, the snares snapping in the warm night air. A vision in white, with promises in her hand of more to come, as her forefinger touched his palm, her nail an instrument of excitement. He felt the current and looked into her amazing eyes, the cobalt blue shining back at him from the smooth café au lait skin of her face. Her beauty numbed him, lured him, enticed him and he followed her as she led him away from the parade. *"Shusssh,"* she had whispered. "It isn't far."

∎

As he hurried down Moncada and then east on *Avenida Victoriano de Garzón,* Cipriano wondered how to find the others, how to get back to Siboney. He slowed to a normal walk, then ducked into a side alley, squeezing himself between worn stucco walls. A mongrel pup dozing in the shade raised his head, then, seeing no new source of food, returned his nose to its place atop his paws. Cipriano stripped off his uniform and tossed it into an open window at the rear of the alley. Fishing into his pocket he found a package of Pall Mall's, struck a match, and sauntered back out onto the street, the cigarette dangling from his lips. Like Jean Gabin, he smiled, smoothing his hair with a swipe of his palms. Three half-ton Ford trucks rambled past him, their open flatbeds jammed with soldiers. He waved as they passed him. "Dumb fucks," he muttered as several waved back. Must have thought he was just another Carnival left-over.

▮

MONCADA HOSPITAL

The soldiers ignored them. Rena sighed in relief when she realized that they were simply looking for rebels. Two men walked up each aisle in the ward, the barrels of their carbines swinging back and forth, sweeping the space before them. Occasionally they stopped, squatted down, poked their guns under a bed, then stood again. They worked their way up and down the ward, yawning, motioning to each other with hand signals, stopping to scratch their elbows or backsides.

Rena bent over a woman with no teeth and a few wisps of white hair. Her chart displayed no indication of any illness, and there were no medications listed. The old woman looked at her with vacant eyes and Rena realized that she had simply been stored at the hospital. There was no cure for her advanced dementia. She patted the woman's hand, then ran her palm across her waxy brow, showing the soldiers how intent she was in providing care. Out of the corner of her eye she could see Maria doing the same thing three beds down.

The soldier closest to her, a young man with a scant mustache and crooked teeth, turned suddenly. Rena froze, her breath in her throat, and stared even more intently at the dazed figure on the bed. The soldier swung his gun across his body, pointed it to the floor, and grinned from ear to ear. She could see tiny scars on his chin where he had nicked himself shaving, and dozens of pockmarks on his cheeks. He came closer, his head centimeters away from hers. Rena shivered.

"Please, can you look at something for me, *Señorita?*" The fear eased its clamping hold on her insides, and she felt herself relax. After all, she actually was a nurse.

"Tell me what ails you," she asked, keeping Maria within her sight, hoping that she would remain calm. "I'll see what I can do."

He was only a boy. A boy soldier. And, something like the enemy. He rolled up the sleeve of his left arm, pushing the material over his biceps. The blood had already clotted into brown-red ooze, the size of an American Silver Eagle dollar. She could see where the bullet had entered but there was no exit wound. Rena could only imagine the pain. She probed his arm as gently as possible with the tips of her fingers.

"Mierda," he moaned, tears in his eyes. Hardly her job, she thought to herself. She could send him on his way, tell him that she had no training for treating battlefield wounds. And, if she did treat him, would she give herself away? A trained military nurse in a ward for the elderly.

"You need surgery," she told the boy. "I can't do this here."

"But it hurts terribly," he looked as worried as he did pained. "And they won't let me leave the detail, especially after what just happened."

Another fold in the dilemma: should she ask what happened? Or ignore him altogether.

■

SANTIAGO

A blast from a factory steam whistle crackled the mirror of Cipriano's memory. The street filled with workers on their way to the morning shift at the rum distillery. They walked slowly, their heads bound in brightly colored kerchiefs, their feet wedged into straw sandals. Ahead, a green and yellow city tram rumbled down the street, past *El Baturro Café*, a pink and blue lunchroom and bar already packed to overflowing, its upside down Martíni glass logo no less incongruent than its surroundings.

How out of place he felt, in his rumpled khaki trousers and worn white cotton shirt. Someone would surely turn him in, and fear gripped him unlike any he had ever experienced. He pushed away a fragment of memory. It still haunted him, but he refused to allow it to eddy the waters of his consciousness now. He knew the hubris of his Cypriot past would never disappear.

A brightly painted veranda, orange concrete surrounded by a meter-high wrought iron fence and gate, beckoned. More likely the young woman standing there, arms at her waist, caught his eye. She wore a white cotton dress with a blue scarf wrapped around her deep black face. Her skin shone, the moisture of the morning humidity coating her like dew. She smiled.

Cipriano nodded. When she looked down demurely he slipped open the gate and took a step into the sweet shade of the veranda. Silently she turned and entered the apartment that opened out onto the porch. He followed, wondering if they were alone.

"You are late," her eyes looked deeply into his. "I've been waiting for several hours."

"I got here as soon as I could," he played for time.

"We had the room ready for dawn. Just after Carnival. I made the bed so you could rest first."

"That was very considerate." Cipriano saw the uniform of a Cuban army officer hanging on a peg. "Perhaps, since I am so late, I can just wash up and be on my way."

He wondered if this was to have been a safe house set up without his knowledge. Made no sense, not with the uniform.

"What time does your husband get home?" He saw the Sergeant's strips on the sleeve of the khaki uniform.

She looked at him, her eyes dancing with amusement. "My husband?"

Then she covered her mouth with a hand as delicate as a bird and swayed, sending her skirt into motion, her bare feet gliding over the wood floor.

"Oh." She glanced at the shirt, her eyes wide and winked. "He has been asleep since the end of Carnival." She grinned at Cipriano. "He was the five o'clock appointment. You were to have been the six."

Cipriano forced himself to hide his surprise. So, one of the government soldiers at Moncada had scheduled a rendezvous. He was inside, in the room.

The door opened and a huge man appeared. Red suspenders hung from his waist, his undershirt askew on his hairy chest, and the stubble on his face begged for a razor. Barely noticing Cipriano, he reached out for the woman and embraced her, his arms around her back, pulling her close, burying his head in her neck. He held her for a moment, the straightened his arms and looked down at her face.

"It is on the dresser," he announced, patting her rump. "This was just what I needed, Nena." He looked over at Cipriano, "You won't be disappointed brother. It's just what you hope for, perfect before going back on duty." He kissed his thumb and forefingers.

Cipriano smiled back, gave a jaunty salute, and walked toward the doorway of the bedroom. He turned and called over his shoulder to the woman. "Don't be too long, baby. Time is money."

The rumpled bed took up most of the floor space and the only illumination came from the light streaming in from the window that looked out to the back alley. Cipriano listened as the soldier and the woman said their goodbyes. On the tiny dresser he picked up a soiled business card that sat atop pile of crumbled pesos.

TIA NENA CLUB
ATENDIDO POR
LINDAS MUCHACHAS
TELF 6969

Below the writing was an embossed image of a reclining woman dressed in only high-heels and leopard skin panties, her bare back exposed as she twisted to look back over her shoulder, smiling.

"Jintera," Cipriano muttered to himself as he stuffed the money and the card into his pocket, opened the bordello window silently, and dropped down onto the cobblestones below.

■

MONCADA HOSPITAL

Rena helped the soldier up from the bed, swinging his legs over the side then reaching under his elbows to allow him to stand. He screwed his face up in pain, tears in his eyes. He had been lying in the hospital bed clad only in his underclothes. She wondered how long he had been there as she tried not to notice the tears and snags that ran across the back of his filthy shirt.

She maneuvered him down the aisle, careful not to catch her cape on the rough iron bed-stands. The boy could barely support himself, and she allowed him to lean into her as they navigated the ward.

"Where are you taking me?" he objected. She could feel his body shaking. And wondered if she had made a bad, no dangerous, decision.

"Shush! You asked for help. I'm going to clean your wound so you won't get infected."

He started to speak. Rena clasped her hand over his mouth and hissed.

"Please be quiet. Now!"

She walked him toward the end of the ward where she expected to find a supply room, standard for any hospital. The boy sagged in compliance and she pushed open the door of a small bandaging room filled with several white metal stools whose round seats spun with the touch of a finger. Behind the stools a wall of grimy wood cabinets loomed over a black marble countertop.

"Sit."

The solider bowed his head as Rena picked through the supplies, finding gauze, tape, antiseptic. Her back to the doorway of the tiny supply room, Rena stared intently at the boy as she considered what to do. The wound on his arm oozed under congealed blood. There was no anesthetic, not even a bottle of ether. Rena straightened up, put her arms on her hips, and took a deep breath. She could help ease his pain and do nothing about his injury or she could probe the wound and hope to extract the bullet. It would hurt like hell.

"What is your name?" she asked, peering at his face.

"Manuel," he replied softly, eyes widening. "They call me Manny."

"Well Manny, are you brave and strong?"

"Like a bull!"

Rena reached behind her and found a heavy glass bottle of alcohol on the counter, the cork jammed tightly into its mouth. She grabbed it.

"Be quiet now," she whispered softly. The way his eyes wavered back and forth, searching for something to reassure him, took hold of her memory. She saw Oliver lying in that wretched field hospital, his leg dripping from the maggot-infested dressing, his eyes streaked with red veins. He had been so brave.

She felt hard metal against her head, then a harsh voice.

"Mother of a whore. What do you think you are doing?"

The soldier pushed the gun barrel into the back of her head, forcing her chin down onto her chest.

"Get out and go back to your bed," he ordered the boy.

"And you. You do not work here. I know all the girls. And you are not one of them." He smelled of sweat and bacon grease and his voice was raspy.

Rena spun around on her stool to face the man. As she turned, she reached behind her cloak and pulled the revolver out from her waistband.

A shot exploded in her face. She could feel the burn of the bullet as it grazed beneath her right ear. The revolving stool brought her face to face with the raspy soldier, whose eyes bulged as he sank to the floor. The back of his head had disappeared. She looked down at her right hand. The pistol was still cool. She had not fired her weapon.

Not two meters away, Maria stood framed in the light of the doorway. Her pistol leveled at the spot where the soldier had been standing.

"I never said I was a real nurse," Maria's lips barely moved. "Let's go."

∎

SANTIAGO

She didn't dare offer her arm. Oliver would be too proud to lean on her. Instead she slowed her pace imperceptibly — or she imagined. The gunfire from the barracks had died down and the street before them was empty of any movement. How to get back to Siboney?

"We need a car." She looked up at his face and found a placidity that took her by surprise. His eyelids half closed, he smiled back.

"Maybe not." He paused. "We have lost our tactical advantage. If I'm right, the whole affair is ruined, and our comrades have scattered. *Sauve qui peut,* and all that."

"What does that have to do with needing a car?" She regretted the tiny whine to her voice. "I mean, if we lost our advantage, shouldn't we be getting out of here?"

Oliver grinned. It made her feel safe, that grin, like he had wrapped his arms around her. He looked down at her, put his arm across her shoulder and drew her to him.

"I mean only that we need not return to Siboney."

"But that is the back-up plan," she reminded him, "it's what we all agreed." She allowed her head to rest against him as they continued to walk away from the Moncada vicinity, back into the heart of the city.

"I'll bet they are all on the lam, the ones who are not dead or captured," he looked at her again, intently, his dark eyes dull. "We have no idea how many have survived. The ones who have, including your Fidel, will head for the hills. Of that I'm certain."

"My Fidel?"

"Ok. Our Fidel. Maybe it should be Matthew's Fidel. He's the one who found me first."

"And then you found me."

"I was planning on it anyway." He grinned again and she felt his pleasure.

"Enough of this pillow talk. What shall we do?"

Oliver reached into the back pocket of his cord trousers and produced a wrinkled envelope. "Here," he handed it to Anna. "I've been holding on to this for just the right occasion."

"Oh, Ollie!" her voice sang in mock ecstasy, "You shouldn't have."

"Not to worry, my dearest. I have not." The envelope fluttered in his hand and she could see that it had been addressed to him and bore an American stamp.

How odd, Anna thought to herself. He's acting courtly. Not just polite. Something more. In the tilt of his head, the way his smile curled, even the softness of his voice behind that sarcasm. It thrilled her.

What was she doing, acting like a schoolgirl? She shook her head. Half the police of the city must be on the lookout for them. Anna wrapped her arm around Oliver's and leaned her head into his jacket. Together they looked out over the city.

She took the envelope and held it up to the light.

"You might assess opening it," he flicked the corner of the envelope with his right forefinger. "I can't stand the suspense."

The two train tickets slid easily out of the envelope. One way, Santiago to Havana, on the express, first class.

"I had sent them to Maria the day before the coup. Just in case. Maria told me I was all wet. Well, not in so many words. 'You can't always freelance,' she wrote back. Still I paid her no mind. They will deserve the swank, I reminded her, if this all goes down the clapper. Actually, I telexed, 'If this opera doesn't have a third act.'"

The name of the railway company stamped in raised letters, *Ferrocarriles Consolidados de Cuba*, told them that the tickets were, in fact, real. No small hedge against counterfeits, Anna knew. Some even produced by government officials with Batista's winking denials of corruption.

Even before she could ask who, Oliver took her hands in his and looked down into her eyes.

■

SIBONEY

Enrique glided the car behind the earthen shield, the hedgerow they had constructed between the farmhouse and the road. The red-brick walk led him to the open doorway, a dark entry that revealed no other inhabitants.

Enrique waited in the car as Fidel strode in, his carbine at eye level, and shouted, "Where is everyone?"

Fidel took his time, checking each room, even though the farmhouse was clearly empty. They had left no one behind, and Enrique was the first to return.

What had gone wrong? The plan to infiltrate Carnival and use the revelry as a springboard to the early morning attack seemed clever enough. True, he had told Fidel that this motley team of university dropouts and middle-class white-collar workers were hardly the stuff of revolution. But, as he had also pointed out, the advantage of surprise would outweigh their lack of experience. The more he thought about it the angrier he felt, the old assault on himself from within that he had been fighting since childhood. One teacher had told his parents that he had a problem with anger and that they should stop giving him anything with sugar. His father, a cane cutter with calloused hands and shoulders as wide as a truck, had a simpler solution. He said he would beat him if he didn't behave in school.

Enrique had run away from home soon after. First to work, then into the syndicalist union, and finally to Spain. He smiled inwardly, for that was where he had met the crazy Cipriano, his oldest friend. Where the fuck was that Cypriot communist now?

Fidel opened the door of the car and spoke directly.

"Up into the hills. Now. It is our only chance of survival."

■

The Plymouth labored under the strain. Not built for a jungle path. Enrique glanced over at Fidel who leaned out the open window, right arm bent at the elbow, carbine tucked into his right shoulder.

"It's not getting any easier," he announced.

"Keep going. Deeper. I know this place. We'll be so far in that they'll never find us."

Yeah. I know. Your father's land. That he squatted on and leveraged into a plantation principality. Just another poor Spanish peasant come to Cuba to fight the Yankees in 1898. Now his son wants to kill the golden calf that allowed his father to become a lord. What a fucking story.

"If you think so." Enrique looked up the path, just two narrow trails, axel wide, and saw only the jungle as it reached out with deep green darkness.

"Keep driving," Fidel repeated the order from the passenger seat.

The jungle canopy opened suddenly and light splashed out into a small clearing. Enrique feathered the brakes to slow the car, then allowed it to idle. The tracks divided. One path bent slightly down and to the right, the other up and to the left. Impossible to see where they might eventually lead.

"Which way, do you think?" Better to defer for the moment.

"Right."

"I can't see where it goes."

"Do not be concerned, Enrique. I know this country like the back of my hand. Don't forget, I was raised here."

Not likely, thought Enrique. Not likely. He lifted his foot off the clutch and gave the car just a bit of gas, rolling it forward in first, creeping down the dark passage that Fidel had chosen.

"For the name of God!" Castro screamed, "Look out where

you're going!"

A black man towered over them. Through the windshield he looked larger than life, his muscles rippling, the distortion of the glass obscuring his features. In one hand he held an ancient rifle, probably a single-shot American model left over from the War. He held up the other hand like a traffic policeman.

He came around to the driver's side, stuck his head in the window.

"You can follow me." He turned and walked down the path, turning once to motion them forward.

∎

MONCADA HOSPITAL

Maria took Rena by the hand and led her out of the bandaging room and into the stairwell. They walked as quietly as possible, kicking off their shoes and balancing on the balls of their feet. The gunmetal gray stairway, grimy from years of traffic, stained from decades of trysts, and covered with stains of stolen cigarette breaks, could have been anywhere. Harlem or Birmingham or Havana. Made no difference — they all looked and smelled the same.

This way, Maria motioned with her eyes, pushing a door open. They had climbed the final two flights and now found themselves on the fourth floor with nowhere else to go. Maria pushed the door inward and gasped. The condition of this ward made the other look like the Ritz. Men and women, old and young, sat in chairs, stood on their bare feet, or lay curled in their beds. Some wore grimy hospital gowns, others just crumpled and filthy clothing — underwear, assorted uniforms from the gas and electric companies. There were two tram operators, a police officer, even an old man in a white SIM *guayabera*. In the corner two women, hair tangled like rats' nests, hunkered over a table covered with chess pieces that occupied every square and overflowed onto the border. A few others looked on, shouting encouragement. The ward seemed strangely silent beyond the urgings of the spectators at the chessboard. It was barely half filled, and many of the beds lay empty. No one looked at either Maria or Rena, and no one uttered any sound of welcome or alarm.

"What is this?" Rena asked softly.

"It is something I've only heard rumors about," Maria's face seemed to shrivel as she shook her head. "The *desaparecidas*."

Franco had done the same thing, Rena thought. Used the secret police to scoop up anyone suspected of disloyalty and tossed them into mental hospitals, cancer wards, even shipped them off to leper colonies. The detritus of the Cuban police state, the imagined enemies of Batista, discarded and forgotten, transformed into nothingness.

Voices behind them announced the approach of two government soldiers. They came from beyond the dented white metal doors that led to the ward.

Carbines loaded and cocked, the soldiers waited for an order to begin their sweep. The sounds of their voices, muffled by the doors, startled Rena and forced her to register the chaos spread out before her.

She pointed to a bed in the far corner of the ward, one that looked as if no one had slept in it for a month. As Maria made her way across the room, nodding her assent, Rena slid between two giggling women who were plucking each other's eyebrows. She put her fingers to her lips and slipped into the nearest bed. Glancing across the room she saw Maria with the sheets pulled up to her chin staring blankly at the ceiling. Rena turned onto her side, tucked her knees up to her chest, and closed her eyes.

The light flickered red and yellow streaks beneath her eyelids. Rena slowed her breath, trying to induce a meditative state — an exercise that her tiny black supervisor Bunny had taught in nursing school. "Always breath slow as you dream," she had instructed. "Slow as you dream." Rena held the phrase in her heart as the soldiers sauntered around the ward, indifferent to the state of the human beings around them.

A powerfully-built man entered, two civilians trailing in his wake. He wore the uniform of a general, down to his splendid cavalry trousers neatly tucked into an obscenely shiny pair of black riding boots. One of the two civilians carried a notepad, the other a square news photographer's camera, its flash-bulb reflector glinting in the slanted light that cast the room in ironic cheer. Rena peeked through her closed eyelids as she used her breath to remain relaxed.

"You see, gentleman," the General addressed the two men, "everyone is happy here." He glanced at the two men, whose heads were hunched into their shoulders as they scribbled furiously on the small steno pads they cradled like bibles.

"I want, el Presidente wants, we all want you to understand how caring and humane we are." He waved his arm, the medals on his chest clinking with the motion, as if to sweep their vision across the macabre scene before them. "You see how happy they are here, do you not?"

He clapped his hands and the door swung open to reveal two young soldiers who prodded a line of a dozen men into the ward. The men, all in their 20s, walked with their hands clasped before them, then knelt as ordered in mute silence in the center of the room. The life had left their eyes. Men whose defeat was as much moral as physical.

They were a dozen of the trainees who had left Siboney the night before to launch the attack. They looked the same age as Rena had been in the Civil War. Had she actually been as young and innocent in Spain as they were now? Impossible. But, she did not recognize these men from her group. They belonged to the force that Fidel and

Enrique led at the barracks. Only then did Rena feel dread creep cold into her veins. The operation had failed. There was no mistake. Rena shivered as the General instructed the press.

He paced before the kneeling prisoners, stiff and formal and gloating, then motioned with his head at the guards. With gun muzzles at the back of their necks the young men bowed their heads as the soldiers tied their hands behind their backs.

"You may stop shaking," the General sounded so gentle or a moment, then shouted, *"Now!"*

He waved his hand another time and more civilians entered, six or eight men and women, dressed in the ordinary garb of a summer day. The women had bright scarves covering their hair and wore cotton blouses with elastic necklines that scooped from one shoulder to the next. The men, in *huaraches* and *guayaberas*, all had dark black hair combed smoothly over wide brows.

"Ladies and gentlemen of the jury," the General stood straight and peered down at the men kneeling before him. The newcomers bunched closely, standing now behind the kneeling captives. "I will present you with the evidence of treason collected against the men before you. Please pay careful attention." Rena wanted nothing more than to cover her ears. She dared not move a muscle.

The general handed several photographs to the "jury," and offered his commentary as each examined the evidence before passing it along.

"A nun's eye! What do you think this is worth, good citizens of Cuba? One of these men plucked it out with the point of his knife, like taking out the pit of an olive. You can observe that the blood still runs from the socket." He paused for the impact of the horrific photograph to take effect. Rena wondered how they developed the picture in just a matter of hours.

"And here. I will read a secret document that we have just

discovered. It will tell you just how nefarious these rebels have been, how unscrupulous their leaders are."

He pulled a sheaf of papers out from the dispatch case tucked under his arm. Rifling though them, he stopped, put the document back, and picked out another.

"They had no idea that a secret source informed us of the latest movements and goals of the coup they planned. I was with one of their advisers last night. He believed their affair to be a romantic one. I was amazed that he spoke such good Spanish. I soon found out that he had been, as he called it, "educated" in Spain. They planned to attack the barracks at Moncada this morning at six, when they believed the troops would be exhausted from the excesses of Carnival."

The General spoke sternly to the men kneeling before them. "You see, *amigos*, we knew what you had planned. You were betrayed before you even began."

Then he turned to the "jury." He spoke more slowly, deliberately. "Here is the evidence, then, that I share with you today. A photograph showing the abject brutality of these rebels and an unimpeachable source informing us of their plans before the attack. Of course there is more. Much more. And we will make it available to the press and the public after all the treasonous rebels are rounded up."

Such rubbish, Rena thought. He's got no evidence. He's bluffing. They were only ten meters from where she lay curled between the sheets of the hospital bed. Her body ached and she fought the urge to stretch her arms overhead and to breath deeply. She feared for the men kneeling before the general and she feared for herself. And Maria! What would they do with her?

The General's voice boomed. "I can see from your faces that you agree with the government. These men are guilty of treason. The question remains of what shall be done with them."

Rena strained to see something, anything, through the curtain of her eyelashes.

"We are not a cruel government. Our leader wishes only to enjoy the love of his people." He stopped, heightening the drama of the moment, speaking to the journalists now. "We have brought our most respected correspondents here to show them how mercy and justice may prevail. Even in the face of incontrovertible evidence — of both brutality and of conspiracy — we do not wish to inflict more pain upon our people."

Rena could hear the captives inhale. A sob broke the stillness of the room. And then a cry, *"Viva La Revolución."*

The shout stunned the prisoners, the jury, the journalists into mute silence. Someone tried to stand, Rena could hear his knees and then his shoes scraping for purchase. Then the General spoke.

"Take this man and tie him to the chair. Yes, right there. Blindfold him. We intend mercy, but we will not tolerate sedition. What say you, members of the jury? I recommend, and justice demands, immediate resolution!"

They bound and gagged the young man who refused to be silent. Rena thought she remembered him from Siboney, an architecture student who talked about building for "the masses" by adopting the style of the Bauhaus to the tropics. He was a tall, thin fellow with a pencil mustache and a shock of wild black hair.

"You will release the safeties of your weapons," the General instructed his two armed guards. "Tomorrow there will only be ants in the mouth of this vermin. His death will serve as a lesson to all. Then, I will send his tongue to your Castro."

The other prisoners began to sob and Rena felt her fists clench, her nails digging into the soft flesh of her palms. Just boys, she thought, just boys.

She heard the solid metallic click of the bullets being chambered. Impossible. Here in a hospital? In a mental ward?

"On my order," the General commanded. The stink of human excrement invaded the room. The boy had shit himself and Rena could hear the so-called jury turn away, their shoes scuffling against the linoleum floor.

"Ready, aim," and then the General laughed. The peals of a maniac, high and sharp.

"Do you think we are really barbarians?" He spoke though his laughter. "*Presidente* Batista shows mercy to all his people. Even a traitor like this."

The boy, still tied to the chair, sobbed.

"Take them away. We will round up the others and take them all back to Havana."

His boots echoed sharply in the fetid air as he turned and walked out the door.

■

SIBONEY

Cipriano had walked through the brush, parallel to the road, for six hours. The sun settled over the *Sierra Maestra* range, bathing his path in pink and gold. An omen, he thought. Perhaps telling him to keep moving. They had agreed to meet at the farmhouse, hadn't they? Cipriano's fingers found the purple disc, the evil eye his father had given to him years ago. It once belonged to his grandfather, an Orthodox priest named Kiriakos. A genial, elderly man with a voluptuous white beard and deep blue eyes. Family legend told of his bravery in the face of Ottoman authority and his political allegiance to Cypriot independence. "Do not tell anyone that a priest carried the evil eye," his father had instructed. "It is your patrimony. It will bring you good fortune."

Superstition. But, if there were ever a time for magic... Darkness crept into the brush like a thief. It stole the light and covered the world with a cloak. Something from Homer, no doubt. But, then again, Cuba and Cyprus had much in common — the sea, the light, the danger.

By his own calculations he ought to arrive at the farmhouse within the hour. Perhaps five kilometers further. Not more. He heard nothing coming along the road. With a deep breath he started walking. He calculated that he would emerge just north of the rendezvous.

The sputtering and backfiring of an automobile engine startled him. Peering out toward the road he tried to focus his vision. Then, as the engine caught, Cipriano made out the red glow of the two rear lights. They moved slowly away from him, up one of the trails that led into the hills. He stood there, hands on hips, watching. Stifling an impulse to run after the car even to cry out, he stood still, tracking the lights as they grew smaller in the distance.

■

MONCADA

The boy's sobs echoed through the ward. Two men in the corner playing checkers looked around, then turned back to their game, and a woman with bright red hair knelt in prayer, shaking as she called for Ogun to release her from "this hell." It looked like a movie, Rena thought, where everything froze for a moment and then motion returned where it left off. The word "normal" came to her mind and she laughed in derisive dismissal. There was nothing normal here.

Maria walked across the ward, her face a mask of horror.

"What do we do now?" The question sat between her teeth, her hospital gown a map of wrinkles.

"We can't stay here," Rena knew that the soldiers were everywhere. "We had planned to get back to Siboney in case we failed in the attack."

"Let's go then."

"After dark."

∎

An hour later, Maria led Rena through a maze of back lanes and alleys, over cobblestone streets and into cul-de-sacs that opened into secretive squares, so protected by stucco buildings and palms that only the people in the district knew they even exist.

They walked sideways down a steep set of concrete stairs that took them into the neighborhood overlooking the harbor. Maria turned and slid sideways between two stucco houses. Rena followed her into the courtyard that opened before them.

"We rest here for a few minutes," Maria sat, wiping her brow.

Rena leaned back against the pale blue wall of the windowless house behind her. She raised her right leg, bent her knee, and placed her foot against the wall behind her for support. The Pall Mall bit into her throat and she allowed the smoke to escape slowly from her lips and sighed.

∎

The truck lurched and bucked, the choke didn't work, and Rena found the clutch didn't grab easily either. The floor-mounted gearshift pressed into her right palm as she leaned forward to peer through the moisture that had collected on the windshield. Rena pulled her cloak around her shoulders. She wondered how long it would take them to reach the farmhouse.

The night descended suddenly, without warning. One moment twilight, the next, midnight. She flipped on the headlights, but Maria told her to run on dim and to drive even more slowly. Hard to see and navigate, thought Rena. I need to be careful. She slowed to maintain her traction as she crept along the road that connected Santiago with Siboney.

They were upon the donkey cart even before Rena realized that something blocked their way. She brought the truck to a jolting halt. She leaned her head out the window, trying to peer around the barely visible cart, boy and donkey. She noticed the motion next to her as she concentrated on keeping the truck on course. The boy driving the cart must have felt sorry for her, because he veered the donkey off to the right, straddling the side of the road and allowing her to pass.

It was only then that Rena realized that Maria had vanished.

■

SIERRA MAESTRA

The headlights of the Plymouth played softly against the worn path that extended into the night, the white-yellow glow revealing the jagged underbrush only just before the wheels of the car crushed it flat. Ahead, the black man guided the car as it crept up the side of the mountain.

"My childhood playground," Fidel announced. "All my boyhood adventures took place in these hills."

"So, then, where is this man taking us?"

"Could be anywhere. They have lived up here so long, these squatters, that only they really know where to go and how to get there."

"Can we trust him?"

"I thought he'd take us up to the *Gran Petra* bridge — it crosses the *Carpintero* river somewhere up here. Now I'm not sure."

"But can we trust him?"

The man ahead trudged along, never altering his pace, even as the

263

mountain grew ever steeper. Night enveloped their car, softening the headlamps.

"I think we should turn off the lights completely," Fidel leaned forward in the front seat, resting his elbows on his knees.

Enrique could read the exhaustion on his face. Almost a full twenty-four hours since they had left the farmhouse for Santiago. And now... it felt like Spain all over again. Defeat collapsing the great hopes for the day, night falling darker and darker.

Their guide wiggled his flashlight for them to follow. He was only five meters ahead of them, but without any other illumination it felt like penetrating into some unearthly realm.

"I should kill myself." Fidel's voice was hardly a whisper. "All is lost."

Enrique whipped his left hand around and pulled the gun from Fidel's hand.

"Not tonight. Not while I am here." He heard his own voice, hard and fearless. It sounded different inside his head. This adventure, that's what he called it to himself, this adventure had all the markings of a tragedy. What had someone said about history and those who forgot being doomed to repeat it? No, it wasn't that they had followed in the same idealistic path that took them to Spain. It was that they had remained blind to how much in the world had failed to change politically. Same bullshit, same rivalries, same — he paused for an instant, aware that Fidel had sunk back into his seat — same betrayals.

Their guide held up his hand and Enrique lifted his feet off both pedals as he steered halfway onto the fringe of the jungle.

"We will wait for daybreak," the guide announced. He took out a large knife and hacked two leafy branches from the limb of a kapok tree. He spread them at his feet, a bed of leaf and seed and smiled. "Special place. The tree of the Virgin Maria, we call it *Ikoro*. No harm will befall you here. It will protect us."

Fidel motioned for Enrique to leave the car. "I have much to think about," he flashed a pencil, "and to write about."

"I don't mind staying in the car," Enrique turned to see Fidel with his knees propped up against the passenger's side seat-back.

"You don't need to worry about me. I know we have lost. Now I must prepare my defense."

"I'm not ready to give up," Enrique replied, feeling the anger rise inside him.

"Nor am I. They can't kill ideas!" Fidel took a deep breath, his eyes darting left, then right. "But I need to think about what might happen if they find us."

"If or when, who knows," Enrique struggled with his own sense of realism. "Who knows anything?"

"Of this I am sure," replied the voice in the back of the car. "History will absolve us. I am sure."

∎

Enrique woke to the mournful cries of dawn. The *"toco, toco, toco"* call of the resplendent green, red, and blue trogon opened his eyes to the jungle around him. The black man who had led them the night before was nowhere to be found, and Fidel lay sprawled across the back-seat of the car, snoring.

The song of the wild bird directed Enrique's eyes deep into the interior of the jungle. He rose and followed the sounds, first of the bird and then of something that he could not yet identify. Careful not to disturb Fidel, Enrique snapped the clip out of his automatic pistol, stuffed it into his pocket, and wedged his weapon into the belt of his fatigues. He made his way through the underbrush, looking up at the swaying royal palms to mentally mark his path. He had learned to use nature as his guide as a boy, in *Camegüey*, in a tiny village called

Santa Cruz del Sur, beyond the other side of these mountains. That was where his father and uncles had taught him to survive by both his wits and instincts, and instructed him on the virtues of democratic syndicalism. He was still certain about the former — it allowed him to teach Fidel's baby guerrillas as best he could. The latter, however, seemed suddenly out of date and he didn't know why. Perhaps Cipriano was right. He shrugged and continued walking. The early morning sun that filtered down from the canopy splashed his path with white and gold.

The clearing startled him. The jungle canopy cover gave way to a scene that belonged on a tourist postcard. A dozen *bohíos* were arranged in a circle around what looked to be a common fire pit, their thatched roofs fresh with morning dew. A group of African-Cuban farmers stood in a circle around the pit, their black skin shining beneath the red and gold tapestry of their serapes. Each smoked a rough-rolled cigarillo as they roasted a wild pig over the fire.

"It's the squatters' village, the Maroons." Fidel appeared behind Enrique. "I heard about them long ago, but this is the first time I have seen their village."

The man who had guided them through the jungle motioned for them to enter his *bohío.* The interior smelled like charcoal mixed with fertilizer. Enrique blinked in the almost opaque darkness and only slowly began to make out the outlines of human figures sitting on the dirt floor, their backs against the inner wall's rough-hewn wood planks. There were at least a dozen women and children, most clad in the loose pantaloons or nubby muslin dresses of rural peasants. One of the women held two nursing infants swaddled in bleached rice sacks.

"My family," announced the man. "I am Tino," he paused. "And I know who you are." He looked at Fidel.

"My father told me about your village once," Fidel squatted down on his haunches, holding his carbine in one hand for balance. "He called it a hamlet of slavery."

"Yes. Exactly. Where we sit was once the property of the Juragua Iron Company."

Enrique shifted his weight as the two men talked.

"And my family are descendants of the slaves who worked here."

"I don't follow," Enrique spoke softly. "When they abolished slavery in Cuba there were no iron mines."

"Ah, Señor. I can tell from your accent that you are a well-educated man." Tino looked directly into Enrique's eyes. "Don't protest. I do not hold it against you."

Fidel laughed, his face assuming an ironic smile.

Tino continued. "We are all that remains of Haitian slaves who were brought here after Toussaint's revolution. Their French masters never freed them and forced them to work in the mines hidden in the valleys of this range. Twenty years ago, the owners left and forgot about us."

Enrique walked into the clearing. The smoke from the cooking fire sent a cloud of gray ash up into the open sky. Women and boys tended the fire, turning spits of roasting pork slowly in the shimmering heat. He stretched his arms high over his head and thought that he could stay in this peaceful place. For how long? And Cipriano, what had become of him? Likely another woman had led him astray. Or, perhaps, something less simple. One never knew.

A rooster strutted regally around the fire, then raised his cock's comb high and crowed. Not loud enough to startle Enrique, only to make him think about the kind of life one might lead in a quiet place like this undiscovered village. Behind him he could hear Tino and Fidel talking softly about the amount of daylight left to them. He did the calculations himself, perhaps seven hours till dusk. Until then they needed to remain hidden. Government troops would, by now, have discovered the Siboney farmhouse. It was only a matter of time. He thought to find pencil and paper and make a map of their escape route. It might prove useful later.

He walked back to the car and opened the front door.

"How good to see you, my old friend," Cipriano's voice spoke from behind a pistol. His eyes narrowed and seemed to turn from blue to brown.

CHAPTER THREE
AFTER

I

SANTA CLARA, CUBA 27 JULY 1953

Anna liked how Ollie smelled. Even after an all-night train ride across the backbone of Cuba. Even after 24 hours in the same clothes. Even after 15 years. The intoxicating combination of tobacco and the anise scent he thought he hid from her was so redolent. She closed her eyes as the train swayed through the hint of early morning, chugging its way just ahead of the sun. She felt the engineer apply the breaks and the train slow to a halt. But still she kept her eyes closed, her head leaning against the soft cotton of Ollie's sleeve. It was a moment that she didn't want to lose.

"Santa Clara." The conductor had pulled open the door to the compartment just enough to call in the name of the station. He slid it shut behind him, checked his watch, and swayed down the corridor to the next compartment. Anna felt Oliver shift his weight from one side to the next, adjusting the pressure on his leg, trying to find a comfortable position. She knew that this was virtually impossible. Twenty minutes and he would cramp. His palm pressed into the velvet seat in the space between them as he lifted his body ever so slightly and then let it settle back down.

The door again. This time with a sudden bang that snapped their eyes wide open. In place of the conductor were two soldiers, rifles slung casually over their shoulders. Their dusty uniforms had wrinkled in the heat and a sheen of dry sweat coated their brows.

No politeness. Just a bark. "You must leave the train now." The door slammed closed. The corridor had already filled with passengers struggling with baggage — wicker food baskets, wood orange crates, brown and white speckled suitcases bound by worn leather belts, and canvas duffle bags with stenciled names and military unit designations. Anna relaxed. At least they weren't simply looking for them. Or were they? Roust everyone and see who turned up? Old fascist trick. Intimidate and search.

They elbowed their way through the crowded railcar, Anna holding Oliver's hand, prattling away in her inimitable Basque-inflected Spanish. "Just keep looking down" she whispered under her breath to him in English. "They will think you are a Moor."

"Excuse me, sir. Pardon, Miss. Please. Do go ahead."

Oliver grasped the rail that descended to the track-bed, his "real" leg poised on the top step. The car slowed to a crawl, and the station platform stopped its motion. *Hombre, how about getting down?"* someone behind Anna called briskly, "don't have all day!"

Anna stiffened. She didn't want Ollie exposed, didn't want him embarrassed. She turned to the crowd behind them.

"Seems we are early," she said. "Perhaps we all need to take a breath and let the train come to a full stop."

Somehow her calm took the starch out of the men and women lined up back into the corridor.

"Its okay," she spoke quietly, "we can get off when the conductor lowers the stairs."

Anna sighed. Last thing they needed was to alert the SIM undoubtedly lurking along the platform. They had come so far. Two government soldiers stood at the base of the stairs that unfolded down from the carriage. They held sheaves of paper with photographs of men, like images from a school newspaper. As passengers descended, the soldiers narrowed their eyes, trying to identify them, hoping to earn an extra day's pay. Quickly she ducked under Oliver's arm and squeezed between him and the metal railing, coming up a step below and in front of him. She turned on her toes, leaning her face up to his, and kissed him passionately. It was both intoxicatingly intimate and completely contrived.

"Move along now, Señorita. You'll have time for that later," the guard laughed as he waved them onto the platform.

Oliver held her hand tightly. He leaned into her, a grin spreading across his face. "I never knew," his voice cracked with humor and relief.

"After all these years," she winked, "I figured you had some notion."

They followed the crowd along the platform to the tunnel that took them under the tracks and up onto an adjacent makeshift platform. Anna couldn't believe her eyes — they now faced another train, an iron Leviathan of three cars coupled onto a massive locomotive belching smoke and fire. The cars looked windowless, and, Anna realized, their armored-clad skin had been painted the gray-white-mustard colors of military camouflage. Atop the three cars tank muzzles menaced the sky, their mechanical turrets swiveling back and forth, back and forth. Batista's famous armored train, she thought to herself. Never seen, always the subject of legend. Oliver had told her that it was refitted from the Red Army train that Trotsky had once commanded, built by the Škoda Works in Czechoslovakia for Beneš when he was Prime Minister. In Cuba, Batista could command the breadth of the island, appearing out of nowhere to stun his opponents, to scoop them up and deposit them in prison without leaving a trace. It was even said that the American gangster, Meyer Lansky, had a special room fitted for him on the train — appropriate because Lansky had financed the deal in the first place.

All smiles and pencil mustaches, two SIM operatives materialized and started funneling the passengers toward a second train that had pulled along the station's siding. They shepherded the passengers across the tracks, two at a time, ordering them to "keep your eyes forward." Too late. The armored train was now behind them, smoke belching from its pistons as if from a rent in the surface of the earth. "This way. You don't want to miss the connection."

Anna could not help but shudder. She had already seen too many transports. Oliver reached his hand to steady her elbow, as if he could read her memory. It offered small comfort in the space where she now found herself, between danger and nightmare. "Just look ahead," he spoke as softly as possible between his teeth. "Don't react. Follow my lead."

Hard to believe that only 24 hours ago they had tried to assault the armory at Moncada. Now here they were in Santa Clara walking across the beds of gravel that lined the railway tracks halfway to Havana. Oliver held her steady, as if his own leg had shed its weakness. They picked their way across the ladders of iron rails and ties beneath their feet. Ten meters ahead the new train sat silently, waiting, its red siding the color of blood.

"This is where you change," the soldiers ordered as they marched the passengers across the tracks. "The train departs in ten minutes." Anna hunched her shoulders, hefting the weight of her valise as she approached the train.

"Take a gander at that," Oliver motioned, tipping his head back as he spoke. The red train, actually a half-dozen cars without an engine, stood still, silent. Its rooftop electrical bridge-work, diamond shaped, ran beneath the twin cables that Anna could now see tautly stretched above the train tracks. "Looks like a bloody trolley." Oliver enjoyed the Britishisms he had picked up over the years. And, thought Anna, it did look like a group of streetcars. But, with a difference.

Each car had the name HERSHEY stamped in gold block letters on its side. They looked no different from the electric trams in Barcelona, buses on steel wheels with wraparound windows and seats facing forward and back. Hershey owned one of the largest sugar plantations in Cuba and needed their own train to get the big shots and the sugar back and forth to Havana. Fidel's words rang in her ears: We will rid the island of both Batista and of American exploitation. That's what had taken them to Santiago. And now look what would bring them back home.

Funny, it felt the same as it always had. Cipriano doing something estupido, really fucked up, and Enrique standing outside himself, the ire rising in his gut, his jaw quivering. He looked his friend in the eye and started to laugh.

"You dumb motherfucker," he waved his hand behind him, sweeping his arm across the dense trees that separated Cipriano from the village. "You hold a gun on me?"

He could see the sweat on Cipriano's brow, the exhaustion in his eyes, the webs of tiny red capillaries covered by rheumy film.

"You hold a gun on me," he repeated. Then he grinned from ear to ear and turned. As he walked toward the clearing, toward the squatter village, he muttered "baseball."

Two paces, then three. Enrique heard Cipriano exhale. He imagined him lowering the pistol and setting the safety. Enrique kept walking away from his friend.

The air fluttered in his ears. Reminded him of a day in Spain, a day when the *Condor Legion* had flown low overhead, tossing hand grenades on a column of refugees. He felt the pressure in his eardrums, as if some cosmic disturbance had penetrated into the wilderness.

The sound, like a hummingbird's wings, beat more resolutely. The chopping cadence from the sky grew more accented, drawing closer with each passing moment. Enrique turned to face Cipriano. The sounds from above were now a whirring thrump, thrump, thrump. The unmistakable signature of a helicopter rotor, forcing the air down where he stood.

Enrique locked eyes with Cipriano. He stared as the Cypriot crumpled slowly, his body collapsing, head, then waist, then knees folding in turn as he fell, fell, fell to the ground.

The US built Sioux helicopter tilted to its side, as if in salute, and spun away from the clearing, its rotor churning like a pinwheel.

Cipriano lay at Enrique's feet, his eyes staring straight up, his face a sneering smile, his mouth agape. Even as Enrique bent down to examine the wounds he knew that his comrade was already gone. The side of his head was shattered, his right-eye a bloody pulp, shot at close range. Hardly the work of a helicopter sniper, and there had been no one perched on the chopper's skids. It took a long moment to process this dissonance. The noise, the helicopter, the execution of his friend.

Enrique reached down to take the revolver from Cipriano's hand. The safety remained on, the barrel cold. A man clad in the white-shirted uniform of the SIM emerged from the shadows, a stubby Walther P38 pistol in his hand, a leer marking his lips. Enrique hadn't seen a Walther since 1938, when an SS Colonel had shot himself in the head rather than face summary execution in the field.

Kneeling over Cipriano, Enrique weighed his choices. He then stood to face the SIM man, leaving Cipriano's discarded gun on the ground.

"How did you know?" he asked, even as he knew part of the answer. The helicopter had tracked Cipriano and radioed the coordinates. Simple. Keep talking, he told himself, give Fidel a chance to slip away.

His thoughts cascaded down on one another in layered confusion. Who else was with the SIM agent? What did they really know? How did they know anything? And, more troubling, where did Cipriano fit in all this?

As if to answer Enrique's unspoken thoughts the SIM agent pushed his wrap-around sunglasses up over his forehead, and turned to look back behind himself.

"The others are not far behind me," the calm in his voice was chilling.

But, to Enrique's eye, the agent looked to be a solo operative. "You have left the clip in the pistol, *señor*, but the safety is off," he growled. "Only men working in teams take the luxury of leaving their safety's on."

Better odds. He tried to listen for any hint of Fidel's getaway.

The agent shrugged. His face, a mixture of cruelty and calm, twitched. Enrique knew the telltale sign. There was no one else, not for the moment. Keep talking. Don't let the bastard think you are really going to do something.

"I see you have the advantage," Enrique hoped he sounded sincere. "I am yours."

The SIM agent's forehead glistened and his broad nose flared.

"Since you are so able," Enrique lowered his voice, "could you perhaps do me the honor — "

"There is no honor in your communist shit-pile of a so-called movement." He lowered his eyes for an instant, just a flick. "So, you will tell them to give themselves up."

Enrique was now certain the agent was on his own. Checking his watch, anxious for the others to show up. No time like the present. How to best distract him?

"Please, *señor*, I will do as you request. Just tell me how you found out?"

The agent's weakness, his sense of self-importance, gained the upper hand — as Enrique had expected. His ego could not bear to keep his information secret. Reaching his right hand into the pocket of his tan twill trousers he found an object.

"We all have our weaknesses, do we not," he sounded triumphant as he tossed the purple evil eye disc at Cipriano's chest, where it sat casting its cobalt look back up at the sky.

"The girl in white, she works for us. She fucks who we tell her."

Shocked. But not surprised. Enrique had spent his whole life surviving because he understood the weaknesses of others. Fuck! He swore as much at himself as at Cipriano, still lying at his feet. He found himself laughing. And then laughing uncontrollably. The irony of the universe had just visited its justice on him. Where the fuck was the honor!

Behind him a rustle — hardly a disturbance. Just enough that the SIM agent heard it as well. Enrique watched the man's grip tighten on his pistol, and then saw how his eyes tracked something in motion behind Enrique's left shoulder. The noise froze him for an instant as he calculated his options. Astonishing how fast we actually think, he mused, as he dove to his left and imagined that Fidel would somehow understand that this was about the purity of the movement; that the communist lying dead on the ground had been the traitor, and that Enrique's own sacrifice would show the way to the future. If he had to die, let it be for a syndicalist Cuba, he thought as a bullet shattered his jaw, exploding into his brain.

EPILOGUE

LA GUERRE EST FINIE

Anna walked across the kitchen and switched on the radio.

"What time does it commence?" Oliver spoke softly from the adjacent room where he sat on the shabby gray settee, reading a copy of The New York Times that Anna had found in the lobby of the *Hotel Nacional* earlier that morning. The gray light barely illuminated the area where Anna stood, rust stains scarring the worn porcelain sink to her right.

"Within the hour," Anna answered, brushing a lock of graying hair from her forehead. "Shall I bring you a beer?"

"I'll find one when I'm in need of refreshment."

His voice sounded pleasant enough. Same Ollie, same words, always words. But Anna knew he resented her attempts to serve him, as if her kindness deepened his wounds.

Six weeks ago it really had seemed possible that he might forgive her well-being. The last leg of their train ride to Havana had gone off without incident. Yes, the country had been on some kind of emergency military alert. Soldiers, police, and SIM were everywhere, all armed. And rumors were rife — they heard everything, from Batista's suicide to the mass execution of Castro and his closest collaborators. One nationalist newspaper even suggested that a "core of battle-hardened guerrillas trained in Spain" had formed the backbone of the coup.

But instead of being trapped by the ever-lurking secret police, they had grabbed a cab at Havana's train station and gone directly back to Anna's apartment. "This is where it all began," Anna had thought when they pushed open the faded green wood door, Oliver breathing heavily after the three flights of stairs.

The apartment had smelled the same as it had — coffee and cinnamon, a combination of bitter and sweet, and just a touch of tobacco.

As he set down the suitcase and switched on the lights, Anna had taken Oliver in her arms.

"I'm scared," she admitted. "I don't know what we should do."

His eyes had twinkled, the old Ollie, and he had caressed her cheek with the soft palm of his hand.

She leaned her face back from his, finding the gold tooth, like a lighthouse beam. "Won't they come looking for us here?"

"There's an old southern saying," he slid his hands to her shoulders, "about the best place to hide being in plain view."

Anna felt his gaze bathe her, soothe her. It told her that this was a different form of home. And the feeling had remained to this moment, despite her sense that her attentiveness sometimes rankled.

"What time did you say?" he called again. Anna heard him rustle the newspaper as he folded it the way he did, first in half length-wise, then in half-again vertically, the perfect position for the crossword.

"Within the hour. Didn't you hear me?" Then walking from the kitchen, she said to him teasingly, "Ollie, it's Thursday and you've been at that crossword for long enough, aren't you finished yet?" She enjoyed tweaking his vanity, his self-proclaimed prowess at solving the challenging end-of-week puzzles in no time.

She turned up the volume but could only hear the murmur of voices in the courtroom, nothing more, nothing distinct, over the hiss of the Philco. She listened every morning to the "Government Propaganda News," which Ollie called "Batista's Follies." Which, as he said, would be "preempted" for a different form of drama that day.

She reached out her hand for a small plate on the marble windowsill. *"Cara mio,"* she whispered in faux seduction, "would you care for something to eat?"

Anna knew the answer. Ollie loved the anchovy and pepper *pintxos* that she still prepared. The tapas from her Basque childhood provided more than nutrition. She rolled open the top of the tin, using a long knitting needle for leverage, and then licked the oil off her fingers.

They didn't need the commentator to tell them that the defendant, Fidel Castro, would appear that day dressed in his lawyers' robe. Since his capture at the beginning of August, Castro had made it clear that he would turn this trial into an indictment of the Batista regime. The proceedings, which Oliver likened to the Soviet Purge trials of Zinoviev and Kamenev, had dragged on for more than three weeks. Now only Castro remained out of the sixty-five indicted revolutionaries. The day before, the tribunal had ordered the mysterious Maria to appear. She agreed to confess, but only to her role in the hospital. She told the judges that she had "seen nothing" and, along with another unnamed woman, had worked only as a nurse during the events at Moncada. When Oliver heard her testimony, he jumped. Anna knew the other nurse was Rena.

And now Castro. Anna imagined him standing, adjusting his robe, clearing his throat, gesturing. He talked for three hours. Same voice that she remembered from the University Square barely six months earlier. Hard to believe that they had actually tried to overthrow the regime. He recalled the tyranny of Batista, the lessons he learned as a child, the heritage of Martí, and the valiant spirit of the Cuban people. And he spoke of his month on the run in the Sierra Maestra mountains, and of the treachery of the secret police.

Oliver stomped into the kitchen. He turned down the dial. "And what of our comrades in arms, of Cipriano and Enrique? Is there to be nothing said about their exemplary bravery?"

He rarely raised his voice. Anna could not remember the last time she had seen him outraged. Rumors had reached them weeks earlier that their two friends had been found in a clearing in the hills, each shot in the head. "Political executions" was the standard explanation broadcast over the rumor wire that connected those who had managed to avoid capture.

She reached for the radio dial and cranked the volume back up.

"Here's the windup," Ollie announced. "Hear his voice rising. The great climax."

"Windup?"

"Baseball term."

"I see," but she didn't exactly.

Castro's voice reached even higher, reminding Anna of the moment last spring when he had jumped on the table. She now understood Ollie's comment — Fidel was getting ready to deliver his final rhetorical flourish.

"And — " Castro's voice climbed, "and history will absolve us!"

She turned off the radio and allowed the kitchen to rediscover silence. Oliver sat back against the wall, his bad leg stretched out, and put his hands behind his head. He smiled at Anna, his tooth a glint of gold. A sentence from Marx came into her head, and she couldn't recall where she first learned it. In the mines, perhaps, or at the militia training. Who knew? "All that's solid melts into air," she said quietly to herself as she turned to gaze out the window louvers.

Her eyes found an envelope dangling from the window, behind the kitchen table.

"Welcome back," the block print letters read. Maria had taped it onto the louvers of the window that allowed light and air from the street below. The shadows played along the linoleum floor, like ripples reflected down on the sandy bottom of the sea.

Through the louvers Anna spotted Rena standing on the other side of the street, smoking, her boot pressed against the wall behind her, nurses' cloak tight against the cold. Out of the corner of her eye, Anna caught a movement, the flicker of a shadow. Two SIM armed with automatic submachine guns fixed their gaze first on Rena and then up toward the window.

Anna shivered and snapped the louvers closed.

New York native Peter Rutkoff has been teaching at Kenyon College in Central Ohio since 1971. From 1999-2001 he held the National Endowment for the Humanities Distinguished teaching chair at Kenyon, and from 2009-12 he was the Robert Oden Distinguished Professor of American Studies. With William B. Scott of the Kenyon history department, Peter developed the *North By South* course that served as the senior seminar in American Studies.

With several colleagues, Peter helped develop the American Studies program, first in 1990 as an interdisciplinary program, and since 2002 as an interdisciplinary major. His current scholarly interests include African-American cultural studies and African-American migrations, the subject of his new book with Professor Scott, *Fly Away: The Great African-American Migrations*. He is also the author of several books of fiction, including the novel *Irish Eyes* (2012).

Peter Rutkoff has also served as the executive director of the Kenyon Academic Partnership (KAP), which links the college with a network of thirty secondary schools in Ohio. Students in KAP take dual-credit courses for high-school graduation and Kenyon transcript credit.

CPSIA information can be obtained
at www.ICGtesting.com
Printed in the USA
FFHW011418251019
55688754-61555FF

9 781880 977491